ACCLAIM FOR *FORGET ME NOT*

"The gifted Melton does an excellent job building emotion, danger, and tension in her transfixing novel."
—*Romantic Times BOOKclub Magazine*

"Riveting . . . a compellingly eventful romance with realistic emotions."
—*Booklist* (starred review)

"Fascinating . . . an enjoyable tale."
—*Affaire de Coeur*

"An intriguing romantic suspense . . . Readers will take great delight."
—*Midwest Book Review*

"Refreshing . . . fine writing, likable characters, and realistic emotions."
—*Publishers Weekly*

"Entertaining . . . moving and passionate . . . with plenty of action and suspense . . . *Forget Me Not* is a winner; don't miss it."
—RomRevToday.com

"A thrilling romance."
—TheBestReviews.com

"Amazing . . . fantastic . . . a riveting plot, engaging characters, and unforgettable love story . . . not to be missed."
—NewandUsedBooks.com

Also by Marliss Melton

Forget Me Not

IN THE DARK

Marliss Melton

NEW YORK   BOSTON

Copyright © 2005 by Marliss Melton
Excerpt from *Time To Run* copyright © 2005 by Marliss Melton.
All rights reserved. No part of this book may be reproduced in any form or by any electronic or mechanical means, including information storage and retrieval systems, without permission in writing from the publisher, except by a reviewer who may quote brief passages in a review.

Warner Forever is a registered trademark of Warner Books.

Cover art and design by Dale Fiorillo
Book design by Stratford Publishing Services

Warner Books

Time Warner Book Group
1271 Avenue of the Americas
New York, NY 10020
Visit our Web site at www.twbookmark.com

Printed in the United States of America

First Paperback Printing: June 2005

10 9 8 7 6 5 4 3

Acknowledgments

Special thanks to my multitalented father, an aviator and a former lawyer for the United States Air Force, whose expertise was badly needed and much appreciated.

Thanks to Tom McMurray, who helped with aspects of military law.

And special thanks to my editor, Devi Pillai, who gave me extra time and wonderful suggestions.

IN THE
DARK

Prologue

The high-pitched whine of a mosquito roused Hannah from a drug-induced sleep. She lurched to a sitting position, heart pounding in expectation of imminent danger, her body drenched in sweat. She found herself alone, disoriented, in a room that came slowly into focus.

Where am I?

The only sound besides the mosquito and the heavy thudding of her heart was that of rain pouring down outside the barred window. She'd regained consciousness once before, long enough to sense the rolling movements of a boat beneath her. But that feeling was gone. She was back on dry land.

Weak with hunger and thirst, Hannah swung her feet to the floor. The drugs that fouled her system caused the walls to shift closer, the floor to jump up, hitting her bare soles. She held still, waiting for the unpleasant effect to pass.

She sat in a gloomy cell with four stone walls, a door, and a window. The cot she sat on hung suspended from chains pegged into the wall behind her. A crude toilet stood nearby, giving off a terrible stench.

Why am I here? What happened?

Hannah pressed fingers to her clammy forehead, trying to think past the nausea that roiled up suddenly. Memories rushed back:

As seen through the rearview mirror of her Mustang, the brown van with its gleaming grille bore down on her.

A woman with flaming red hair leaned out the passenger window with a rifle. *Pow!* The suppressed shot hit Hannah's rear tire. She clutched the steering wheel, fighting to keep the car under control.

Her effort to convey information to the authorities was being thwarted. Furious, Hannah jammed on the brakes in reprisal, sending the van plowing into the back end of her car. *Crash!*

The vehicle was still moving when she thrust open the driver's door and scrambled out. If she didn't get away, these people would kill her, just as they'd killed her colleague. She ran straight into the arms of a huge man with pale eyes, who'd apparently moved faster than she had. He seized her in a vice-like grip, pressing a wet cloth over her face. Hannah held her breath, but the fumes of chloroform scalded her nostrils as she struggled to break free. From the corner of her eye, she saw the woman bend toward her flat tire with a special kit in hand. Within seconds the woman had inflated and patched the tire. She got into Hannah's car and drove away. The man wrestled Hannah into the back of his van. She knew he was going to kill her for knowing too much.

Only she wasn't dead . . . not yet, anyway.

Instead of killing her, he'd stabbed her with a needle and put her on a boat that rocked endlessly on a storm-tossed sea.

With her knees quaking uncertainly, Hannah stood up. She had to hold her head with both hands to keep the room from shifting. Spying two bowls by the base of the door, she shuffled toward them.

One was water; the other rice. She sank to her knees, slurping the water into her parched mouth. The rice she ate more carefully, praying it wasn't laced with more of the same drugs that had kept her unconscious for how long?

Days now.

As she chewed and swallowed, she assessed the door before her. Made of stainless steel and bolted into the wall, it resembled something found in a Swiss bank, except for the sliding panel through which her food had likely come. A peek through the panel revealed an empty, whitewashed hallway on the other side.

With the bowls empty, Hannah came to her feet to determine where she was. She crossed to the window and looked outside. Rain spattered what appeared to be a flagstone courtyard two stories below. Vegetation held the courtyard in a grip of bougainvillea. Vines grew everywhere, crisscrossing the ancient courtyard, strangling what was once a fountain. Two Hispanic-looking men wearing battle-dress uniform stood in the shadow of a doorway. They both carried rifles. Hannah was locked up in a fortress of sorts, an obviously old one.

Beyond the wall, sheets of rain swept a tourmaline-green body of water, wide and deep and shaped like a horseshoe. She could be anywhere in the Caribbean, or even on the Pacific coast near the equator, given the peculiar shade of the water and the palm trees edging the sandy shore. On the opposite side of the bay, glitzy hotels betrayed the existence of a tourist trade. They taunted her with the promise of freedom, so close and yet so far away.

Despite the stifling humidity, Hannah shivered. If three years of studying satellite imagery and topographical maps couldn't help determine where she was, then no one else was going to find her, even if they managed to piece together the bizarre events that had brought her here.

She might as well have fallen off the edge of the earth.

Chapter One

"We're not going to stand for this," Luther reassured his subordinates.

The four-man SEAL squad sat on the veranda at the Shifting Sands Club, back-dropped by a darkening sky and the pitching waves of the Atlantic. Laughter and the tinkle of chinaware leaked through the panes of the restaurant. The storm sparking lightning out at sea had driven all but the SEALs indoors. There was just enough light coming out of the restaurant behind them that Luther could see each one seated around the stone-top patio table.

Chief Westy McCaffrey had grown a full beard in preparation for his assignment in Malaysia. Teddy "Bear" Brewbaker was a black junior petty officer, as broad as he was tall. Vinny "The Godfather" De Innocentis, just nineteen years old, looked amazingly like a young Al Pacino.

Luther Lindstrom was the OIC, officer in charge, of the squad. As an all-American, upper-middle-class over-achiever from Houston, Luther would have sworn up until today that Uncle Sam could do no wrong, but the findings of the Naval Criminal Investigation Service had him reeling with disillusionment.

"It's a fucking cover-up," Westy pronounced, taking a swig of his beer.

It had to be. A week ago Admiral Johansen had assured them that Commander Lovitt would face charges for the fiasco aboard the USS *Nor'Easter,* yet somehow the NCIS had walked away from their investigation blaming the wrong man.

Their platoon leader, Lieutenant Gabe Renault—aka Jaguar—was going to be charged for the crimes Commander Lovitt was responsible for.

"The Navy wants to avoid a scandal," Luther agreed.

"How're we going to prove that Commander Lovitt wanted to kill Jaguar?" Teddy railed. "Think about it. Everyone's dead." He held up a beefy hand and started ticking people off his fingers. "The DIA officer who was snooping around a month ago died in a car crash. The second one, who was supposed to get us the notebook, disappeared. Then the executive officer went and shot himself in the head. Who else is there?"

No one, Luther thought. Lovitt had done a fine job of covering up his trail, except for Jaguar who hadn't been so easy to kill. But Jaguar had memory problems from post-traumatic stress disorder or PTSD.

"Well, fuck, we can't just sit here!" Vinny exclaimed, thumping the tabletop.

Luther squeezed the tense muscles in his neck. He had no intention of letting Jaguar take the rap for the debacle Lovitt had caused, but short of offering their own testimony, which the NCIS had obviously ignored, how could they prove to the upper brass that Lovitt was responsible?

"Sir."

Luther looked up. It was Sebastian León, materializing out of the dark and catching all four men by surprise. The master chief of SEAL Team Twelve had a knack for showing up when he was most needed. Luther hoped that was the case right now.

With a quick salute, Sebastian dropped onto the bench next to Vinny. "I have news," he said. His habitually impassive expression made it impossible to tell if the news was good or bad. "The FBI believes they've found Hannah Geary," he imparted in his subtly accented English. "They want our help to get her out."

The men exchanged swift glances.

"Out of where? She's still alive?" Vinny asked in astonishment.

"Alive," Sebastian corroborated. "They wouldn't tell me where."

Luther had worked with the FBI before. "Who's heading up the investigation?" he inquired, wondering if the request was accidental or intentional.

"One of their top men. Special Agent Valentino."

Luther's eyebrows went up. Valentino had made himself a legend by breaking up enormous drug cartels and arresting two untouchables from the Italian Mafia. Why would he be involved in the disappearance of a single female?

"I'll go," Westy volunteered, always restless. "I have two weeks before my next assignment."

"I'm with you, Chief," Luther said. "I want to put a bug in the FBI's ear, if there isn't one already."

"Here's the contact information, sir." Sebastian handed him a folded piece of paper.

"Hey, if we could get Geary's testimony, then maybe we'd have a shot at clearing Jaguar," Vinny deduced.

Luther was counting on it. A strategy began to take shape in his head. He gave himself a second to think it through. "Okay, guys, here's what we're going to do. Westy and I are going to find Geary and bring her back here so she can testify for us. Master Chief, you and Vinny need to break into the XO's apartment and see if you can find any proof that Miller didn't kill himself."

"I'd rather go alone, sir," Master Chief said softly. SEALs always worked in pairs or small groups, never alone. Luther regarded him questioningly.

"We could all face charges if Jaguar is convicted," Sebastian explained. "No one needs to cross the line right now."

That was true, and since Sebastian had achieved the highest rank for an enlisted man, it would take an act of Congress to part him from his pension benefits. "You're right," said Luther, turning his attention to Teddy. "Teddy, you and Vinny keep things up and running at Spec Ops while Westy and I are wheels up."

"Yes, sir," they mumbled, clearly disappointed to be denied time out of the office.

A bolt of lightning lit the men's resolute faces. Thunder rumbled overhead, and a fleck of rain struck Luther's cheek. "We'll all check in at the end of each day. Jaguar's first hearing is on Friday. Make sure you show up at zero eight hundred at the Trial Services Building in dress whites. Any questions?"

The men looked at each other. "No, sir."

"Let's call it a night." With a plan in place, Luther couldn't wait to get the ball rolling. He stood up, towering over his companions.

As the only officer present, he felt a certain sense of obligation to his teammates, as well as to Jaguar, who was immediately senior to him as platoon leader. "Jaguar's not going to take the rap for this, guys," he reassured them, sweeping them with a steady look. "I'll pick you up at zero four hundred hours, Chief," he added to Westy before turning away.

"Good night, sir," the men called.

Luther jogged down the steps that took him to the parking lot. The rain started falling in earnest as he jumped into his Ford F150. With windshield wipers slapping a fervent tempo, he drove to his ranch-style rental in a suburban neighborhood. No upscale mansion for Luther, not anymore. He'd given up his privileged lifestyle when he quit the NFL.

Pulling into the driveway of his home, he noted the darkened windows with a grimace. No one was waiting for him, but—hey—that was fine. Since he'd asked Veronica to leave, he could actually hold his head up again. Better to live alone than be made a fool of. He wouldn't make that mistake twice.

He dashed for the door, averting his gaze from the nearly empty living area as he snapped on the lights. His ex-fiancée had taken all the furniture when she left, except a hunter-green sofa that weighed too much to move.

Kicking off his sneakers, he stripped off his damp T-shirt. It was a crying shame that Jaguar was in custody, but in a way Luther was grateful. He could channel his energies into proving Lovitt's perfidy and Jaguar's innocence. It sure beat prowling around his empty house wondering what part of his marriage plan had gone awry.

Ronnie had been pretty, educated, raised in a two-parent home. How could he have known that their physical attraction would fizzle, that she'd make him look like an idiot by seeing other men? His determination to live a wholesome, simple life was undermined by Ronnie's complexity.

If he ever got engaged again, he'd make damn sure his bride was smart but uncomplicated; a sensible woman with practical plans and domestic dreams.

He just hated it when a well-laid plan went awry.

FBI Headquarters,
Washington, D.C.
17 September ~ 10:42 EST

Special Agent Rafael Valentino looked nothing like the hard-nosed FBI agent Luther had pictured in his mind. He wore a silver-gray Armani suit over a black turtleneck. His ebony hair, shot with threads of silver, was combed back from a strong Italian forehead, making him look more like the famous NBA coach, Pat Riley, than a veteran of the NYPD, which he was, according to the plaque on the wall behind his polished desk.

"Have a seat, gentlemen," Valentino offered, his quiet baritone betraying no hint of his Italian heritage nor the inner-city dialect he'd surely spoken while growing up in New York City.

Luther and Westy eased into elegant leather armchairs

as Valentino sorted gravely through the piles on his desk. The man had to be pushing forty, but aside from the silver in his hair, he looked fit and formidable. "I have a statement that your master chief gave to the military police at Quantico, back when Miss Geary's vehicle was found there," he said quietly. He opened a file and skimmed through it. "Apparently Miss Geary was on her way to Quantico with information that implicated your commander in stealing weapons?"

"That's correct," said Luther.

Valentino leaned against the high back of his throne-like chair. Through dark, inscrutable eyes, he regarded first Luther and then Westy. Luther had the distinct impression that the man was measuring their character. "I'm going to tell you something that stays within these walls," he divulged.

Luther held his breath.

"We are aware that your commander has been stealing weapons."

Relief welled up in Luther only to come crashing down at Valentino's next words.

"For the time being we need to leave him alone. We want the man he works for, an entity who calls himself the Individual."

Say what? Luther swung an astonished look at Westy, whose blue eyes were blazing.

"The Individual funnels weapons to various political groups worldwide," Valentino added. Unlike most Italians, he spoke without using his hands. "Stolen weapons are cropping up in Nigeria, Haiti, and Yemen, in the hands of unpredictable factions. I'm sure you can appreciate how dangerous that is."

"Absolutely," Luther said. To think that Lovitt was involved in an operation like that! Wouldn't it be great if they could prove it? "I suppose you have proof of Lovitt's involvement?" he asked, wondering what it would take to get his hands on it.

Valentino just looked at him. "We have an intercepted e-mail that we've traced to Lovitt's IP address. It makes reference to certain cargo being ready for shipment. But for the time being the evidence remains with me."

"Who's the Individual?" Westy demanded. Typically forthright, he hated batting words around.

"I'm sorry," Valentino answered, his expression neutral. "We've reached a critical point in our investigation. I can't afford a leak." He reached for a second pile of documents and pulled it before him. "I will tell you that the Individual knows Miss Geary, which may be the reason she is still alive."

But . . . Luther looked at Westy. They'd assumed it was Lovitt who'd made the woman disappear.

"One of the Individual's buyers is a Cuban, a potential revolutionary named Pinzón. According to our intelligence, Pinzón is guarding an American woman in his compound, which is in Santiago."

Luther's eyebrows rose. "Santiago . . . Cuba?"

"That's right."

"How did Geary get from Quantico to Cuba?" he asked, utterly confounded.

"She never made it to Quantico. It took us a while to realize that," the agent admitted, "especially when the guards at Quantico remembered waving in a red-haired woman in a green Mustang. Once we considered that woman wasn't Miss Geary, we had more options to consider."

He cracked another file and read out loud, "'At two twenty-three P.M., August 29, state police received calls from motorists reporting a high-speed chase along Interstate 95, south of D.C. Subsequent calls notified police of an accident involving a minivan and a Mustang, with at least one injury.'" He looked up. "Our guess is that Miss Geary was grabbed at that point and put into the second vehicle. Her car, which showed up at Quantico, had a patched rear tire and showed signs of a recent collision.

"Our leads dried up until Occoquan police came forward with video footage of a man bearing a woman of Geary's description aboard a stolen yacht. The man was Misalov Obradovitch." He withdrew two photographs from the file and slid them across the desk for Luther's and Westy's inspection.

Westy scowled down at the man's photo. "He looks familiar."

"He should," said Valentino. "Obradovitch is a Serbian assassin. He and his wife have been among our Most Wanted for years. Wearing a wig, the woman bears enough resemblance to Miss Geary to have used her ID at Quantico. We believe she left the car there to mislead us."

Luther memorized the features of the stone-faced criminals. *Hannah Geary must have been scared out of her mind,* he considered, sparing her a thought.

"Getting back to the yacht, I was able to track its progress using commercial satellite imagery and marine radio communications. All indications point to Santiago as its final destination."

"Why not send your own people in if you know where she is?" Luther asked. There had to be a reason Valentino had asked for them specifically.

"Because I've been here before," he admitted, placing an elegant-looking hand over the file he'd just closed. "The Individual isn't new to us; we've been aware of his activities for years, and the last time I got this close, he disappeared. If he senses that I'm closing in, he'll clean up house before I can find the proof I need to shut him down. I require you to camouflage my investigation," the agent summarized.

Luther considered him for a long, thoughtful moment. "Agreed," he said, at last, "but we need something in return. If this woman, Geary, is alive and well, we'd like to borrow her." He summarized Jaguar's legal situation while explaining that Geary could potentially relieve him of his charges.

Thoughts ebbed and flowed in Valentino's dark-as-night eyes. "You're asking me to put her welfare into your hands," he pointed out. "The Individual might well target her again."

"Understood," said Luther. "I think we're capable of watching her, sir." He flicked a look at Westy, who nodded.

Valentino scrutinized them through his eyelashes. "Very well," he finally agreed. "If you can extract Geary from her current situation, then she may remain with you until my investigation is complete. But I insist that you check in with me often and keep me apprised of her situation."

"We will," Luther agreed. "Where do we start?"

Valentino conjured a map that he handed over to the SEALs to peruse. Luther recognized the shoreline of the eastern portion of Cuba and the familiar outline of Guantanamo Bay, where he'd spent extensive time participating in live-fire exercises. Near the city of Santiago at the mouth of the bay was a structure that resembled a fort. Valentino had circled it in red.

"Let's go over this together," he invited smoothly.

Chapter Two

Hannah lurched from the clutches of a too familiar dream. She sat up on her cot, bathed in a clammy sweat, her heart still racing. If she closed her eyes, she would fall right back into the nightmare.

In some ways the crash that had killed her parents three years ago seemed like yesterday. At the same time, those had been the three longest years of her life. With shaky fingers, she brushed the hair from her sticky face and looked around.

The thumbnail moon at her window revealed that it was late. Over the muted roar of waves outside, Hannah heard a noise that pushed the unpleasant dream into the recesses of her mind and brought her more widely awake.

There were footsteps in the hallway. She drew a breath and held it, listening as the steps grew louder. Much to her surprise, the interloper stopped outside her door.

Someone meant to pay her a visit.

She lay back quietly, pretending to be asleep.

Anticipation knocked against her eardrums as the bolt grated to one side. Her door yawned open, and there stood a slight man in uniform, silhouetted by the light in the hall.

Hannah recognized him as the leader of the soldiers that drilled in the courtyard. She'd overheard him addressed as General Pinzón. He wore a pistol in the holster at his waist and shoes so highly polished that they glinted in the darkness, but he stood half a head shorter than she did.

He didn't stand a chance.

Easing the door shut behind him, the general approached her cot. The purpose for his visit became clear as he fumbled with the zipper of his pants.

Slime bag.

His knee hit the edge of her bed. He leaned over, groping.

Wait.

Now! She seized him in a headlock, gouging his eyes to blind him. As he reared back, she thrust her feet into his abdomen, giving him no time to snatch up his weapon. He hit the opposite wall with a thud, sinking toward the floor.

Hannah flew at him. Before switching to the DIA, she'd been trained at CIA camp how to disable the enemy with the least amount of force. But in the dark, and with adrenaline coursing her bloodstream, the blow that was supposed to hit the side of his neck landed dead center.

Crack. The cartilage in his throat snapped. His mouth gaped open. He grabbed his neck, trying in vain to gasp for air. Hannah snatched up his gun before he thought to shoot her with it.

She backed away, watching in horror as he opened and closed his mouth, looking like a fish out of water. The gun in her hand felt cold and heavy. At last, his movements grew more feeble and he stilled. The only sound in the room was her shallow breathing.

I killed him, she thought. *I actually just killed a man without even meaning to!*

The instinct for self-preservation roused her from paralysis. She lurched for the door. No time to consider her actions now. Easing into the empty hallway, she closed the door behind her, and slid the bolt home, sealing the general inside.

And then she ran.

Down a hall that split immediately in two different directions. After darting into several confusing alcoves, Hannah located the stairs. To her dismay, there were guards below her. If she shot them, it would cause a ruckus. She spared a moment to check her ammunition. The clip was empty, anyway. The gun was useless.

She hurled it down the stairwell, prompting an immediate stir. With a shout, the guards stormed the second level, but Hannah had tucked herself into an alcove and they ran by. She dashed down the steps behind them, her bare feet making no sound at all.

The buzz of insects masked her dash to the outdoor kitchens, noisy with the clanging of pots and running water. She scraped her elbow on the sandstone wall as she edged along the kitchen's periphery.

Not so fast.

There were more guards here, three of them, lighting cigarettes by the vine-choked fountain. Could she count on her filthy shirt to keep her hidden in the dark?

She paused to catch her breath. It was then that a cry came from a second-story window—*her* window, she determined, glancing up.

"El general está muerto!" a voice cried out—*the general is dead!*

And, look, the woman is missing.

Now the whole place would light up like the D.C. Mall at Christmas. This was nothing like the stealthy escape she'd envisioned.

As the soldiers tossed down their cigarettes, seizing their rifles, Hannah sprinted toward a crumbled portion of the wall. Nearing a motion-detecting spotlight, she dropped to her belly and elbow-crawled through the vegetation.

Once safely past, she sprang up again, legs wobbling beneath her. The sound she dreaded reached her ears.

"Allí está!" The two remaining guards had spotted her. *"Alto! Manos arriba!"*

She lengthened her stride, thighs quivering in protest to her sudden exertion. Bullets peppered the wall in her wake, inspiring her to run faster. She arrived at the crossover point within seconds, leaping up to grasp the top of the wall. To her horror, stone crumbled beneath her fingers and she fell back to her feet.

The guards were running toward her, thankfully out of ammunition. She jumped again, grasping a sturdy vine. Her bare toes scrabbled for leverage, but it was useless. Her arms were weak with terror.

With a sob of defeat, Hannah stilled. They were going to capture her and likely execute her for killing their leader.

Thoop. Thoop.

Those unexpected sounds had her peering over her shoulder. She found her pursuers flat on their backs, dead.

In amazement, she whipped her head in the opposite direction. Someone outside the compound was aiding her escape!

Suddenly a hand came out of the palm fronds, then an entire arm and a powerful shoulder. She made out her rescuer by the whites of his eyes and realized he was lying on the wall just feet away. "Take my hand," he commanded brusquely.

She groped for it, tears of joy burning her eyes.

He was American! His grip was firm and sure. He shook the leaves off his body as he hauled her up beside him. Sitting next to him she could scarcely make him out. He was dressed in black from head to toe, his face painted.

"Hannah Geary?" he clipped. She got the impression he was annoyed.

"Yes, who are—"

But he didn't let her finish. He swung her down on the opposite side, into a pair of waiting arms. Then he jumped to the sand beside her and scooped her up into a fireman hold. Hannah squawked in protest, finding herself suddenly well above the ground.

"Quiet!" said the commando.

"I can walk on my own!"

"Can you see in the dark?" He was moving fast, and she had to appreciate that fact because the estate was seething with commotion now: shouting, another burst of gunfire.

She couldn't see in the dark, but apparently he could. He clambered down the bluff at lightning speed, heading toward the water. The noise behind them swelled as the shouting continued. A beam of light shot out over the water. Perhaps once a beacon for ships, it was now being used to hunt her down.

But she wasn't afraid. The man beneath her moved with the sinuous confidence of a super athlete. She already knew he carried a weapon, and as he jogged along the surf, he covered ground *fast*.

The land beneath them curved like a sickle. At last he stopped, tipping her into ankle-deep water. The other man pushed a rigid inflatable boat across the sand into the water and the big man helped Hannah climb on board.

As he fired up the motor, Hannah clung to the center seat. The second man took his place at the prow, and they were off, slamming into the waves, away from the light that strafed the shore.

Up and over the crests they flew, soaring and falling. Hannah had no idea the water in the bay was so rough. She would have drowned trying to swim across it.

The noises on the shoreline faded. Eventually the only sound was the humming of the RIB's motor. Eventually, her rescuer cut the engine and they slid across the swells to a standstill.

They listened. All was quiet.

Her rescuer flipped a switch on a transmitter, spouting naval code-speak to request a pickup.

"Roger. It'll take us twenty minutes to get there. Sit tight. Out."

Hannah pried her stiff fingers from the side of the boat. "Th-thank you," she said, shuddering with cold.

He scooted closer. "Are you hurt?" He ran large but gentle hands over her wet skin.

"I think I'm okay," she said, teeth chattering as adrenaline gave way to icy-cold shock.

"Westy, toss me a blanket," the commando requested, and his partner tossed him a rolled object that he shook open and draped across her shoulders. Hannah gathered the crinkly material closer, feeling instantly warmed.

"So what was going on back there?" the big man asked. His annoyance was unmistakable this time.

"Er . . . I was trying to get away?"

He kept quiet for a moment. "Another three hours and we'd have had you out without a soul seeing us," he revealed.

Oops. "Sorry. I didn't know anyone was coming for me. Who are you exactly?"

"Navy SEALs. I'm Lieutenant Lindstrom." He stuck out a hand. "Call me Luther. My helmsman there is Chief McCaffrey. Everyone calls him Westy."

Luther Lindstrom's hand was wonderfully big and warm. Hannah commanded herself to let go but couldn't. She glanced at Westy, whose face was also painted black. The man had a beard of all things. "From Team Twelve?" she guessed.

"Yes," the lieutenant confirmed, tugging his hand free. "You were delivering a notebook to us when you disappeared."

He shouldn't have reminded her. Hannah put her forehead to her knees and squeezed her legs so her shaking would subside. Memories of the last two weeks panned through her mind like a terrifying slide show.

She'd been trained to cope with hardship in a mock captivity back at CIA camp, but that had been a cakewalk compared to the last two weeks. Now that she was safe, the enormity of her experience pegged her in the chest. She made a sound in her throat that sounded embarrassingly like a sob.

Lieutenant Lindstrom put a hand on her back. "Hey,

you're okay now. I've got you right here. You're absolutely safe." His dense thigh brushed hers.

She could feel the heat of his hand burning through her filthy blouse. To her shame, she threw herself at him and hung on tight. A man this solid had to be real. She wasn't dreaming.

After a second's surprise, the lieutenant pulled her closer, his arms like bands of steel. His diving suit did nothing to conceal the awesome proportions of his physique: broad chest, trim waist, thighs hewn out of rock. For the first time in her life, Hannah knew what it was like to feel petite.

Her shuddering slowly subsided. "I'm okay," she said, forcing herself to withdraw.

But he held her fast. She sighed and went limp. Her isolation these last two weeks had left her hungering for human contact. She closed her eyes, lulled by the steady beat of his heart.

"Patrol's coming," Westy said.

Without releasing her, the lieutenant hailed the approaching craft with a special signaling device. The larger vessel loomed alongside them, its motor almost silent. He helped her climb a ladder that was lowered to them.

There were no lights on board the bigger boat. In the darkness and all the way to Guantanamo Bay Naval Installation, Hannah clung to the SEAL, one part of her appalled by her need for reassurance, the other certain that he understood.

✦ ✦ ✦

U.S. Naval Station Guantanamo Bay
19 September ~ 09:16 DST

Luther quit knocking at Hannah's door and put his ear to it to listen. Maybe she wasn't in there.

They'd secured rooms at the bachelor quarters in Guantanamo at well past four in the morning. Given the woman's exhaustion, she could easily sleep another ten hours. But since their flight back to CONUS—Continental U.S.—was leaving in just two hours, they needed to prepare for departure now.

The silence in the room convinced him she was already up. He hastened to the lobby, more than a little concerned. Through the double glass doors at the rear of the building he caught sight of her, seated by the outdoor pool across the table from Westy.

The scene looked like something out of a swimsuit calendar, with the pool and the multicolored umbrella back-dropped by the Caribbean Sea. Sitting under the umbrella, Hannah could have passed for the model in the calendar, only instead of a swimsuit, she was wearing a peach sundress and sandals Westy must've bought her in the gift shop.

Last night she'd resembled a drowned rat in stained clothing. Luther'd held her for the better part of an hour, one part of him conscious of the fact that she felt like a hundred percent woman, even though she was filthy. She'd clutched him in a purely feminine way that had made him feel good about the mission, despite the fact that it hadn't gone as smoothly as it could have.

Upon their arrival at Guantanamo, he'd seen her in the

glare of artificial light. He'd found her tall and lanky with matted hair and a face filthy with dirt and dried blood. She'd looked so exhausted he'd thought he would have to bathe her and tuck her into bed, only she'd shut her door politely in his face, making that unnecessary.

Clearly she'd found the wherewithal to scrub up, and—to use an expression that made his mother wince for its grammatical inaccuracy—she cleaned up pretty damn good.

With curiosity goading him, Luther pushed through the doors for a better look.

Her hair, freshly washed, was cherry-red. Cut sassy-short, it left the length of her neck exposed. She turned her head in his direction, and he had to concentrate to keep from tripping over his own feet.

Green eyes gazed out of a face that struck him as translucent, despite the dusting of freckles. She had winging eyebrows, a trim but strong nose, and a mouth that was wide and pink, even without lipstick.

Awareness leaped out and grabbed him by the throat, followed immediately by a surge of annoyance. He didn't want to be attracted to Hannah Geary, who was certainly the antithesis of the uncomplicated female he was looking for. But here he was, stuck with her, at least until Jaguar's charges were dropped.

Ever the enlisted officer, Westy surged to his feet. "Morning, sir!" he said, sounding in awfully good spirits.

Then again, the freckles on Hannah's nose would put any man in a positive frame of mind.

"Good morning." Luther's gaze slid helplessly in her direction. "Hello."

"Hi." She eyed him with open interest, as if trying to

reconcile him with the camouflaged being he was last night.

"Mind if I join you?" he asked Westy, who had yet to sit.

"I'll get us all drinks." And with that, Westy was gone, leaving Luther alone at the table with a woman he'd held in his arms, having no idea how incredibly hot she was. He took the seat beside her, determined to resist her appeal.

"So how do you feel?" he asked, spying a cut on her neck and several nicks on her bare arms.

"I'm okay," she said. Her voice was pleasantly husky. "My hands took the brunt of it."

"Let me see?"

She held her palms up for his inspection.

A reluctant thrill chased over him as he assessed the abrasions on her soft-looking palms and long, slender fingers. "Can you make a fist?" he asked.

She curled her hands obediently. "I'll be fine." Her eyes came up, and he was struck with the feeling that she could see way down inside of him.

His mind went blank for an awkwardly long moment. "That was a brave attempt on your part to escape," he said. "Sorry if I sounded edgy about it."

"I understand," she said with a quick smile. "You didn't want to kill anyone."

Maybe she *could* see inside him. "It was unsettling to watch them shoot at you when I wasn't in position to help out," he explained.

"I imagine it was. I'm sorry it came to that."

"That's okay." It wasn't really. But given a choice between them dying and her dying, he'd sure as hell done the right thing.

Westy reappeared just then to distribute three tall glasses of crimson-colored juice. "Papaya, pineapple, and orange," he explained at Luther's curious glance. "Did you need me for something, sir?"

"In a minute, Chief. Sit down and enjoy your drink. We need to talk first."

As Westy sat, Hannah eyed Luther expectantly.

"Miss Geary—"

"Hannah."

"Hannah." He cleared his throat. "The FBI sent us to Santiago to recover you." He fingered the condensation on the outside of his glass. "The main reason we're involved is that we need the information you were trying to get to us in the first place. Without it, Lieutenant Renault is in a heap of trouble."

Her eyebrows dipped with worry. "The last time I talked to your master chief, Lieutenant Renault was headed to a meeting with Commander Lovitt. I had a really bad feeling about it."

Luther acknowledged her concern. "Lovitt took him out on the patrol craft, promising to return him to active duty." Jaguar had been—and still was—on disability leave due to his PTSD. "But that was just a ploy. Obviously Jaguar saw something that Lovitt doesn't want him to remember. Your call probably saved his life."

Her eyes flared. "He tried to kill him!" she exclaimed.

"We flew out on a helo while Jaguar held three of Lovitt's men at bay. We got there just in time, but you're never going to believe the outcome. Lovitt convinced the

NCIS that Jaguar went ballistic on him, shot him in the arm, and then went after the crew."

"You're kidding!" she breathed with horror. "What about your testimony?"

"Supposedly we made up a story to protect our platoon leader. The NCIS didn't believe any of us."

"That's outrageous!"

"We think so," Luther said, heartened by her support. "Now Jaguar needs all the help he can get to counter the charges he's facing."

"What are the charges?"

"Destruction of military property and two counts of murder. There were three sailors on the PC that day. Obviously, they were working for Lovitt, who says that Jaguar shot and killed them. He didn't; we saw two injured men jump overboard to avoid being taken. Jaguar took the third man out when he tried to blow up the boat with an antitank round. The NCIS agreed that was self-defense. Hell, he saved us all."

"You have my testimony," Hannah promised with poise.

"There's more," Luther warned her. "Commander Lovitt isn't just stealing weapons for his own purposes. Apparently, he works for someone called the Individual."

She shook her head. "Who's that?"

"The FBI's not telling, though Special Agent Valentino thinks it's someone that you know."

Her brow reflected puzzlement. "Why would he think that? I don't know anyone called the Individual."

Luther could see she was telling the truth. "We don't know what's going on exactly," he admitted. "Special Agent Valentino is pretty closemouthed about his investigation, but he did admit that the Individual influences various factions by supplying them with stolen weapons."

"Another Ollie North," Westy illustrated. "His motives are obviously political."

"The weapons he distributes come from Lovitt, who stole them in the first place."

Hannah touched two fingers to her chin and frowned. "I'm confused," she admitted. "Was it Lovitt who abducted me or the Individual?"

"Probably the Individual," Luther answered. "Your abductors were Misalov Obradovitch and his wife, both Serbian assassins," he added gently. "I don't think Lovitt has those kinds of contacts."

Beneath her freckles, Hannah paled. "They weren't exactly friendly," she agreed.

To Luther, she seemed incredibly brave. "Valentino's been after the Individual for years, now," he added. "This time he wants to camouflage his investigation, which is why he sent us in to get you out."

Thoughts flickered in Hannah's green-as-grass eyes. She sat forward and in a husky voice confided, "I don't know if this means anything, but my father was in the CIA. So was I, for that matter, but that was several years ago."

Luther shared an astonished look with Westy. "You were CIA?"

"I was training to be a case officer," she explained, her eyes growing shadowed. "But then my parents died in a plane crash, and I promised my godfather I would work for the DIA for a while. He didn't want to lose me, too," she added with a sad smile.

Christ. "I'm sorry," Luther said, sensing bottomless grief beneath her admission. "Who was your father?"

"Alfred Geary. He was nominated to be the next director right before his plane went down. My mother was with him."

Luther remembered hearing of the tragedy on the news about three years back. He floundered for consoling words. "That must have been rough," he offered lamely. "Both of them at once."

She glanced down at her scraped-up palms.

"So you're saying your father knew a lot of people," Luther guessed. "And maybe one of them is the Individual?"

"Maybe," she said with a shake of her head. "But why was I abducted and shipped off to Cuba, of all places?"

"For protection?" Luther hazarded.

She raised her eyebrows at him. "I was starved and isolated. The general intended to rape me. I wouldn't exactly call that safe."

That gave him pause. "Valentino says General Pinzón is a revolutionary. The Individual's supplying him weapons for a coup."

"There won't be any coup," she said quietly. "The general's dead. I killed him."

His mind stumbled over the unexpected confession. But then he recalled hearing an agitated cry last night about something being dead. "What happened?" he asked, thinking that she had nerves of steel to sit there and talk about it calmly.

Her arms stole across her chest. "He came into my cell and all I could think about was getting through the door." She shrugged, and for a split second he glimpsed the terror she'd been feeling. "I miscalculated my aim and force."

Luther glanced at Westy, who was staring at Hannah with his mouth open. "Remind me not to piss her off, sir," he said with feeling.

Luther could feel his neck growing stiff. "I'm sure you did what you had to do," he comforted. Remembering the way she'd clung to him last night, he knew she wasn't as impervious to the trauma as she appeared to be. No doubt about it, Hannah was a complex woman. "Let's talk about the notebook," he suggested. "Do you know what happened to it?"

"It was hidden in my car when that couple caught up to me."

"Do you think it's still in your car now?"

"Wherever my car is."

"It's at Quantico. Tanya Obradovitch used your ID and drove into the base to throw the authorities off track."

She threw her hands up. "How could the Individual have known where I was headed?" she wondered aloud.

"Maybe your phone was bugged," Luther suggested. "Maybe Lovitt alerted him. Where in your car did you hide the notebook?" he persisted.

"In a cubby under the console. It's not the only copy, though. There's another available at my office."

Hot damn! Luther felt his tension subside. If all went well, they'd soon have the evidence they needed to shred Lovitt's reputation to pieces.

He smiled at her approvingly. "Now we're getting somewhere," he said. "Here's the plan. Valentino's content to let us keep you for a while, but we need to change the way you look. I know it's a hassle, but like I said, you're Jaguar's best witness."

"It's not a hassle," Hannah reassured him, her green eyes narrowing. "Nothing would please me more than to send your commander to jail. He killed my colleague, remember?"

Ernest Forrester, the first DIA officer. That was one more person close to Hannah that had died. "I remember," he said. "You're sure Lovitt killed him?"

"You tell me. Going by the notebook he left behind, Ernie was one step away from exposing your commander. He died in a hit-and-run. No one ever came forward."

"Okay. So let's find the notebook," Luther said, including Westy in his remark. "You all set, Chief?"

Westy shot to his feet. "Yes, sir."

"Head on over to the MAC terminal, would you? See if Valentino has cleared us to get Miss Geary on board."

"Done." Westy shot him a salute and disappeared.

Hannah's quick smile made Luther's innards cartwheel. She was gorgeous, brave, and brilliant in a way that rocked his equilibrium. Her courage amazed him. But Hannah was as different from the uncomplicated woman he intended to marry as the CIA was from the DIA. For that reason, he'd be stupid to let his attraction run the show. Hannah was a teammate on a common mission. Anything more was simply impractical.

Chapter Three

Peering out of the P-3C Orion ASW patrol craft, Luther tried to pinpoint the plane's progress by the contour of the coast. From an altitude of fourteen thousand feet, the seaboard had been sharply defined in contrast to the shimmering expanse of the Atlantic Ocean. But then they came upon a low front, and for the last hour there was nothing under them but clouds.

Hannah had fallen asleep in the seat next to his. As the flight progressed, she listed in his direction until she fell against his shoulder. He eased both their seats back, lowering the arm between them to make her more comfortable. The woman had to be exhausted.

She snuggled closer, pulling his arm between her warm breasts. He steeled himself against the pleasure of her touch, but it was impossible not to notice that her breasts were real, unlike Veronica's enhanced mammaries—and her hair smelled like strawberries.

Thank God Westy was soundly asleep in the seat across the aisle or he'd be snickering under his breath at Luther's expense.

The plane dropped without warning, and Hannah lurched awake, throwing her arms around the back of the chair in front of her. "No!"

Her cry wakened Westy, who reached uselessly for his weapon, which was down in the belly of the plane.

"Easy, easy," Luther soothed, taking in Hannah's wild-eyed disorientation. "That was just an air pocket."

She drew a shaky breath. "Sorry," she apologized. Seeing her seat tipped back and the arm lowered, she cast him a suspicious glare before bringing both back into position with hands that shook. Then she sat there, head pressed against the headrest, hands clasped tightly in her lap.

Luther returned his own seat to normal. She'd seemed fine upon boarding the plane—a little antsy, maybe, but not privately panic-stricken. And then he realized—oh, damn—she had to be thinking of her parents' deaths. How could she not think about it every time she got on a plane?

He knew from counseling younger SEALs that the only way around fear was to talk through it. "How old were you when they died?" he asked.

Hannah took a deep breath. "Twenty-three," she said tonelessly. "It happened three years ago, this fall."

He considered what it would be like to lose his parents. At twenty-three he'd been fresh out of college playing professional football, getting wrapped up in all the wrong vices. If not for his parents, he wouldn't have rallied from the incident that changed his life. "Do you have any siblings?" he continued.

"I have a little brother. He was eighteen, then."

Jesus. "You must have both been devastated."

"It changed a lot of things," she conceded.

He waited for her to explain.

"I was just about to get my first assignment overseas." She looked at him with regret in her eyes. "I wanted to be a case officer like my father—you know, travel abroad, make contacts, ferret out information that would help protect our country. But when my parents died, my god-father convinced me to switch to a less dangerous career. At least until Kevin was out of college."

"He's got—what—a year to go?" Luther guessed.

"Actually, he's working on a dissertation for his PhD. He finished undergraduate school when he was nineteen. He's pretty smart," she added.

"No kidding. That's impressive as hell."

"I'm proud of him. But he's all brain and no common sense. He forgets to eat sometimes, which is why I agreed to switch to the DIA, at least till Kevin completes his studies." She gave him a sudden, startled look. "What if Kevin's not safe? The Individual must know him, too." Her concern was palpable.

"We'll ask Valentino," Luther reassured her. "I'm sure he's thought of that."

She faced forward, concerned but mollified.

"So, do you still want to be a case officer?" he inquired. It unsettled him to think of her cavorting about in foreign countries, meeting up with strangers for the sake of national security, but she seemed to have the nerves for it.

"Absolutely. It's all I've thought of for three long years." She clutched the arms of the chair as the plane started its descent.

If she wanted to travel, she'd better get over her fear of flying, Luther thought. "I have sisters myself," he volunteered, keeping her distracted. "Their names are Liberty and Justice."

That got her attention. "You've got to be kidding."

"I'm not. My parents thought Justice was going to be a boy. By the time she was born, they were so attached to the name that they kept it. My sisters are older than I am. They used to dress me up like a girl; put bows in my hair and stuff. This is purely classified information," he added, giving her a stern look. "Don't tell the guys." He flicked a look at Westy, whose eyes were shut—not that that meant anything.

Hannah gave a husky chuckle that assured him he was doing the right thing. "What about the name Luther?" she asked. "Where did that come from?"

"That was my grandfather's name. He died in a sub in World War Two."

Her smile faded. "So that's why you joined the Navy," she guessed with accuracy.

"That's why."

"It all comes down to family," she reflected, glancing out the window where the familiar structures of the nation's capital—the Washington Monument and the Lincoln Memorial—shone white in contrast to the charcoal sky. "Wow, we're almost home," she said, her tone brimming with relief.

"You live around here?"

"Alexandria. You can probably see my town house from the other side of the plane," she said, eyes bright with emotion as she peered across the cabin.

"You're glad to be back," he guessed.

"I didn't think I'd make it," she admitted thickly.

The plane continued to descend. Luther talked about

his first visit to D.C. with his family when he was only seven. He'd gotten lost in the National Air and Space Museum. "They found me in the flight simulator," he added, drawing a wondering smile from her. "I spent all my money mastering the simulation drill."

"Why didn't you become a pilot?"

"I am a pilot. Even SEALs need aviators," he explained. "They sent me to aviation school. It was a dream come true."

"Lucky you," she said, "getting to realize your dreams."

"You will, too," he answered, responding to the wistfulness in her tone. "You said Kevin's writing his dissertation, right? He's almost done."

"Yeah, but I still have to convince Uncle Caleb to let me go. He tends to coddle us," she sighed.

"What does he do over at DIA?"

"He's the director," she surprised him by responding.

She turned a wary gaze out the window, hands tight on the arms of her chair, as their plane descended into Andrews Air Force Base. Not until it came to a shuddering stop did she relax, unfurling her fingers. She smoothed them on her lap. "Thanks for talking me down," she said without looking at him.

"You're welcome." He felt a peculiar kinship with her then, like he'd known her for a long time.

He wished he felt nothing for her at all.

"Stay behind me," Luther instructed Hannah as they left the MAC terminal en route to the long-term parking lot.

Westy placed his body between her and the terminal building, hand resting casually on the butt of the SIG

Sauer P226 that he'd revealed at the customs checkpoint. Seagulls wheeled overhead, warning of impending foul weather. A warm breeze molded their clothes to their bodies as they hurried toward the cars.

I'm home! Hannah marveled, lifting her nose to the brackish scent of the Potomac River, intermingled with the smell of car exhaust, vague ethnic scents, and maturing oaks.

"Pick it up," Luther urged, and she lengthened her stride, reminding herself that she wasn't safe.

As they approached a big blue pickup with a quad cab, Luther pulled her off to one side while Westy proceeded forward, dropping to scan the underbelly of the vehicle. Hannah's scalp prickled. Surely the Individual wasn't one step ahead of them.

He wasn't. Westy gave the all-clear, and five minutes later they were on the highway, headed south. Hannah heaved a sigh of relief and settled deeper into the leather seat, which she shared with the luggage. The skies opened up, dumping rainwater over their vehicle as they merged into interstate traffic. Luther kept a deft hand on the steering wheel, flicked open his cell phone, and hit a button.

"It's against the law here to drive and talk at the same time," Hannah informed him.

He handed the cell phone over the back of the seat. "I'm not talking to Valentino. You are."

Hannah took the phone just as a smooth voice sounded in her ear. "Valentino."

"This is Hannah Geary," she said, a little discomfited to be speaking with a man she didn't know, who probably knew a lot about her.

"Miss Geary." Valentino sounded surprised. "How're

you feeling? Lindstrom painted a pretty harrowing picture of your extraction."

"I'm fine," she said. "I'd like to know what's going on, though. Why did the Individual target me?"

The silence that followed made her feel like she'd spoken out of turn. "He and your father worked in similar circles," he admitted.

"Who is he?" she pressed.

"I'm sorry, I can't tell you that. Perhaps you have some idea."

"Me? Until today I'd never heard of him."

"Did General Pinzón happen to mention who supplies his weapons?"

"I never actually had a conversation with the general," Hannah answered, feeling her throat grow tight. She would have to tell Valentino that she'd killed Pinzón. "Is my brother in danger?" she asked, switching topics abruptly.

"We have two agents shadowing Kevin's every move. There's no reason to believe he's a target."

Hannah's grip on the phone tightened. "They'd better keep a close watch on him," she warned with a protective shudder.

"I'll pass that along," he reassured her. "How are you holding up?"

"Fine."

"I apologize for leaving you with the SEALs. I owe them a favor, and this helps to screen my investigation."

"No, that's what I want," she assured him.

"Good. I have to leave the country for a couple days, but between their training and yours, I'm sure you'll be safe."

So he knew she'd once been CIA. "I have to tell you

that I killed the general," she blurted, before she lost the nerve. It wasn't easy to say the words out loud. She was conscious of Luther's sympathetic regard through the rearview mirror.

Valentino was shocked into silence.

"In self-defense," she added, breaking into a clammy sweat.

"I'm sure it was necessary," said the agent, recovering. A thoughtful silence preceded his next statement. "We should expect an act of reprisal," he warned, on a note that made her shiver. "Take every precaution to conceal yourself. Don't contact anyone you know, not even your brother. I'll have my agents relay that you're safe."

"Thank you."

"I need to talk to him," said Luther over his shoulder. He'd driven the truck off the highway, bouncing them into the nearest parking lot.

"Yee-haw," Westy exclaimed.

Hannah relinquished the phone. As Luther spoke to Valentino, she reassessed him. Could she trust these men with her life?

Appearing at the poolside, Luther had looked nothing like the black phantom that he'd been last night. In civilian clothing he resembled something off the cover of *Sports Illustrated*—six and a half feet of solid muscle. She'd been drawn to him instantly, and not just because he was good-looking, with dark hair and deep blue eyes. Nor was it the blue button-down shirt, jeans, and casual shoes that in conjunction with his military haircut made him look honest, clean-cut, and squared away. It was the integrity in his eyes that made her like and trust him instantly.

She liked Westy, too, though his auburn beard made

him look more like a biker than a SEAL. Despite his tough exterior, Westy'd shown consideration in buying her the peach sundress she wore. He made the ideal NCO, answering Luther's orders without question, putting himself at risk by searching the truck.

Her instincts told her she was absolutely safe with these men, despite Valentino's disturbing prediction of reprisal. Between their training and hers, they ought to be able to keep one step ahead of the Individual.

"I'd like to search Hannah's car."

Luther's request recaptured her attention. He glanced over his shoulder as he relayed Valentino's reply. "He says they searched your car thoroughly and found nothing."

Hannah cringed as she considered what a thorough search entailed. The car had been a gift from Uncle Caleb. "We ought to look anyway," she advised.

"Permission to search the vehicle again, sir," Luther requested. "Yes, sir. She says she also has a copy at the office." He listened and looked back at her again. "Valentino says an undercover agent searched your office. They found the copy in the shredder."

Hannah pulled a look of disappointment. She'd run that copy through the shredder herself just in case her office was searched. But no one could have found the information she'd taken great pains to conceal, only Valentino didn't need to know that. Keeping an ace in the hole was one of the basic tenets of the CIA.

"I suppose that's it, sir," Luther concluded. Then, "Roger. Out." He put the phone away while backing them out of the parking lot. "We need to change your appearance first thing," he said, stepping on the gas.

"I don't have any money," Hannah realized. "I had to

leave my purse in the car." Oh, what a headache. Someone was probably maxing out her credit cards and she was helpless to stop them.

"It's not a problem," Luther said.

Westy glanced over his shoulder and gave her a long look of surprise. "You don't know who he is, do you?" he inquired with a peculiar smile.

"What do you mean?" Hannah demanded. "Luther?"

"Can it, Chief."

With a shrug, Westy turned front. He crossed his arms over his chest and set his jaw.

Hannah looked back and forth between the two men. She was certain she had missed something, but she'd be damned if she'd humble herself by asking. Apparently Luther was something more than a SEAL and an aviator. She'd keep her ears peeled until she discovered what.

Neither man spoke again until they pulled into the multilevel parking garage at Tyson's Corner, one of Virginia's most prestigious indoor malls. Luther found a parking space close to a main entrance. He gave brief instructions to Westy, then escorted Hannah inside.

The mall was practically empty on this weekday afternoon, with teenagers just beginning to drift in, their school day done. Luther and Hannah entered side by side, looking like a couple on a shopping spree while Westy shadowed them at a distance. Hannah lost sight of him immediately.

She paused before the mall directory and located a cosmetics shop. "This way," she said to Luther, who stepped into place beside her. His expression appeared relaxed but his eyes scanned the area alertly, missing nothing.

"You can leave this to me," Hannah assured him as they entered the shop. She approached the saleswoman setting up a makeup display in a glass cabinet. "Hi," she said, brightly, "my husband and I are going to a Halloween party next month . . ."

The saleswoman expressed delight with Hannah's plan to disguise herself as "the other woman." She drew Hannah toward the rear of the store to try on wigs. Hannah glanced toward Luther, who'd found a chair by the exit and was pretending to read a magazine.

After several false starts, Hannah found a winner. The ash-brown, shoulder-length wig transformed her from a redhead to a light brunette. It fell to her shoulders in soft, natural-looking layers.

"Let's get rid of these freckles," the cosmetologist suggested, layering Hannah's face with foundation. She applied a heavy makeup around her eyes. Glancing in the mirror, Hannah hardly recognized herself.

"What do you think?" she said, returning to Luther half an hour later.

He stood up, slowly, his gaze critical as he took in her new look. "Very effective," he said.

"This is just a start," she informed him. "I need glasses and a wardrobe."

He crossed to the cashier's counter and handed over a credit card. Hannah wondered if the FBI was funding this shopping spree, or whether Luther himself was paying for it. He signed his name on the credit card slip, telling her nothing.

She resolved to wait.

Leading the way to the optometrist office four stores over, Hannah selected a pair of prescription-free lenses with silver frames. Luther paid again, casting her a side-long glance as she continued to shape shift on him.

"You're having fun," he observed as they left the shop on a mission to buy clothes.

"A little," she confessed. Half the fun was watching him watch her. "SEALs wear camouflage; operatives wear disguises. There's not much difference in what we do."

"That's true," he said thoughtfully.

"Which way now?" She glanced toward the department stores at either end of the mall.

"Hechts has the best fall sales."

Hannah sent him a wry smile. "Now *that* was a telling statement. You must have a wife or a girlfriend who loves to shop." She was openly fishing, now.

His expression hardened subtly. "No, I don't," he said, leading the way.

Ooh, ouch. Hannah caught up to him. He'd obviously *had* a wife or a girlfriend recently or he wouldn't have responded that way. Her step felt curiously lighter. Knowing Luther was single made this outing feel more like a date and—wow—she hadn't had a date in years!

"Do you even see Westy?" she inquired, using the glass at the front of the stores to see behind them.

"Not right now," Luther admitted. "And we're not going to see him till he wants to be seen. But then again, neither will anyone who might be following us."

Being reminded of the Individual took the fun out of adventure. This wasn't a date. These were steps she had to take to protect herself from a powerful and unknown entity.

Entering the department store, she stopped before the Ladies section and eyed the conservative fashions with distaste. "Here we go," she said, plunging in. "This is going to cost a fortune. I don't even own underwear."

From the corner of her eye, she saw Luther's conjecturing gaze drift over her.

"You can help me," she told him. "See this look?" She held up a satin blouse with a hideous ruffled collar and balloon sleeves. "This is what you call frumpy. I'm looking for frumpy in size ten, long."

He backed away with his hands up. "I think I'll have a seat over there," he said, gesturing to a set of waiting chairs.

"Coward," she called. Fortunately, there was plenty of frumpy clothing to choose from. Five minutes later, she carried her selections to him, draping the items on the seat beside him.

"You're done already?" he asked, in disbelief.

"I still need shoes and underwear," she answered, heading toward the lingerie and footwear departments. "Be right back."

She chose two pairs of shoes: gray pumps that went with everything and tennis shoes in the hopes that she'd get some regular exercise. Breezing through the lingerie department, she was hit by a perverse impulse to rattle Luther's equanimity. The key to altering one's identity, she reminded herself, was to feel like a different person, right down to the undergarments. Her new alter ego just happened to wear the sexiest lingerie imaginable, unlike Hannah whose taste ran toward cotton and jog bras.

She bore down on Luther with her scandalous selection. "All set," she announced.

His deer-in-the-headlights look made her ribs ache with the urge to laugh. He turned away abruptly, and she trailed him to the checkout counter, biting her lower lip.

"Do you need any jewelry?" he asked, fixing his gaze on an earrings display.

"Oh, yes," she said, selecting big, gaudy earrings to complement her new wardrobe.

"How about a watch?"

"No, I think that's enough," she said, reluctant to impose upon him further. "How am I going to pay you back?" she lamented when the cashier named a price well above the one she'd tallied mentally.

"You already are," he said, and she realized he was thinking of Lieutenant Renault's predicament. She hoped she didn't let him down.

"Where's that photo booth Westy wants me to use?" she asked as they reentered the mall.

"Across from the public restrooms. You can change in there."

She took the pumps, undergarments, earrings, and a shapeless dress into the restroom with her.

Luther stood next to the water fountain holding the rest of her bags. No sign of Westy anywhere.

But then, "Excuse me." There he was, bending over the water fountain. He'd been in the restroom, one step ahead of them.

Luther grinned in appreciation.

"Know what it means when a woman shows you her underwear?" Westy asked, smirking as he wiped his mouth.

Luther's smile faded. "It means she intends for you to pay for it," he countered cynically.

"Means she's hot for you," Westy corrected him.

Luther grunted noncommittally, though his heart beat a little faster. The thought of Hannah hot for him was intriguing—he couldn't deny it. She was beautiful, even with a dowdy wig and glasses on. More than that, she was fun to be with—quick, witty, and unpredictable. But not for an instant would he get involved with a woman who couldn't wait to pack her bags and run off to a foreign country to do intel. He knew the kind of woman he was looking for, and Hannah wasn't it.

Movement in the corner of his eye had him glancing toward the restroom. If he hadn't been with Hannah for the last hour, she could have walked right by him and he wouldn't have noticed. She looked about a decade older than she really was, wearing a shapeless baby-blue dress with lace trim, big pearl earrings, and nondescript pumps. Wispy brown hair framed her bespectacled face.

She walked right past them. Even her walk was different, not loose-limbed and confident as it had been before, but stiff and contained. She looked like the nuns back at his Catholic high school. But then he thought about the sexy lingerie she had on . . . and, oh boy, he couldn't get his thoughts to surface again.

Hannah was headed for the mini-photo booth. He caught up to her, taking a bag out of her hands. "Westy needs you to pick a name," he relayed. He fed the booth a five-dollar bill and drew the curtain for her. "Make sure you'll answer to it."

"I know the drill, Lieutenant," she drawled, pushing the button and taking her picture. She regarded the digital version on the screen, privately amused that she could look so geeky, and selected it. The machine cranked out a strip of photos. She handed the strip to Luther and stepped out.

"So who are you?" he asked, glancing with approval at the picture.

"Rebecca was my mother's name. Hearing it always makes me turn my head."

"Last name?" He pulled a pen from his shirt pocket.

"Lindstrom," she said, half teasing.

He looked at her sharply.

"If I'm family, you'll be able to get me in and out of restricted areas more easily," she reasoned. "I can be your little sister." She smiled at him, innocently.

His gaze skated over her, betraying less-than-brotherly thoughts. "Rebecca Lindstrom," he repeated. "Date of birth?"

She used her mother's month and day, keeping her own year.

"Westy's going to mail this to his contact. We'll have a driver's license delivered to us in a couple of days."

Westy strode by at that exact moment, and Luther handed off the photos and information surreptitiously. "Hungry yet?" he asked.

"I thought we were going to search my car."

"Valentino said to wait until dark. It's in an impound lot. He doesn't want us to be seen or heard."

Her stomach tightened. Rule number one in avoiding capture was never to return to the scene of the crime—or in this case the vehicle involved in a crime. But if the notebook was still hidden in her car, it was worth the risk to look for it. "I'm starving," she admitted, "for anything but rice, chicken, or beans."

Luther cut her a compassionate look. "I take it that's all they fed you back at the fortress. How's a burger and a milkshake sound?"

"Now you're talking," she exclaimed.

With a smile, he put a hand on her back, steering her toward the food court. But then he removed it self-consciously.

Someone had left Luther wary, Hannah reflected. For a breathless second she wondered if she might be the one to test his restraint. But then she dismissed the thought as superfluous.

She had big plans that she'd been guarding for three long years, and they didn't include any kind of amorous relationship. She was headed for a life of intrigue, glamour, and, yes, a little bit of danger. Nothing was going to get in her way this time.

Chapter Four

"I want to go with him," Hannah insisted as Westy stepped from the truck, wearing nothing but black, his face smeared with paint. "What if he can't find the key?" She'd kept a spare key in a magnetic box under the front fender.

"He'll break a window if he has to. You're not going anywhere near the car," Luther insisted.

Like Westy, Luther had donned a black T-shirt, but he hadn't painted his face. He handed her a headset. "Sit tight and listen. If you hear or see anything, say my name and I'll materialize. I won't be more than fifty feet away."

"Oh, for God's sake, I'm not helpless. Can I at least have a gun?"

In the shadows, it was hard to read Luther's expression. "Sorry," he said. She couldn't tell if he was sorry for treating her like an amateur or for not giving her a gun. "Test the headset."

She thumbed the mike. "Testing, one, two."

"It works. Now sit tight. We'll be right back."

Hannah dropped her head against the headrest and sighed. This wasn't exactly what she'd had in mind when it came to searching her vehicle. Ernie was *her* colleague. Finding his notebook was *her* responsibility, not Westy's, not Luther's.

But resisting Luther's instructions could feasibly jeopardize the objective, so she remained where she was, supremely uncomfortable in her dowdy dress. Her lace bra itched and the wig was making her scalp sweat.

For duty, God, and country, Hannah thought with a scowl.

Whatever the men were doing, it was taking them forever. Supposedly Westy was the only one entering the lot. Her vehicle was somewhere in the fenced-in area, surrounded by other impounded and abandoned vehicles. Luther's job was to defend the periphery while Westy searched Hannah's car for the notebook she'd hidden underneath the console.

She strained her ears to hear either man. The windows of the truck were down, but the only thing she could hear were crickets chirping in the grass. The wind gusted occasionally, blowing a cooling breeze through the window. Hannah lifted her arms to cool her sweating armpits. She toyed with the thought of taking her wig off. It was then that a set of headlights strafed the field.

She watched the vehicle until she was certain it was coming closer. Then she thumbed her mike. "Heads up, guys. We have company. Looks like . . . military police coming to secure the lot."

"Roger," said Luther easily, but she could hear him running toward her. "Stay put. I'll be right there."

He jumped into the backseat with her just before the white sedan pulled alongside the truck. To Hannah's astonishment, Luther gathered her into a loverlike embrace.

An MP got out of the sedan and walked cautiously toward them, illuminating the interior of the truck with a flashlight. Hannah and Luther blinked into the glare, playing the part of lovers caught unawares.

"You two are in a restricted area," said a female officer. Stepping closer, she panned the flashlight around briefly, not seeing the headset Luther had kicked under the seat along with Hannah's. Nor could she tell that Luther's gun was wedged between the front seat and the door.

"Sorry, Sergeant," Luther said with a sheepish smile. "Just looking for a little privacy."

"Yeah, well, get a room," said the woman, unsympathetic. "Can I see your IDs?"

Luther sighed and dug into his back pocket, releasing Hannah who pretended to search for her purse. "Oh, I left my purse back at the club with Janie," she cried.

The sergeant frowned at her disapprovingly while casting an eye over Luther's identification. Her demeanor changed subtly as she no doubt took note of his rank. "Take yourself out of here, sir," she warned.

"Yes, Sergeant," he said, clambering out of the backseat to get behind the wheel. "You want to come up front, babe?" he asked Hannah.

She got stiffly out of the vehicle and into Westy's seat. Luther fired up the truck and waved at the MP before easing away.

"Don't ever call me babe again," Hannah warned him.

He threw her a quick grin. "Just wanted to see you bristle."

They drove until there was no way the MP could see them. Luther turned the lights off first, slowed to a halt in a grove of trees, and groped for his headset. "Westy, do you copy?"

"I'm at the back of the lot, sir. Found the vehicle. No need for the key. There's nothing here. Car's all torn up."

Hannah moaned, picturing her beloved Mustang shredded to pieces. "Did he look down by the hand brake?" she inquired.

Luther relayed the question.

"Roger, sir. Nothing there. If Valentino didn't find the notebook, then the Obradovitch woman found it."

"Copy. You need to head toward our location. I can't go back with the MP still around."

"I'm coming your way," Westy replied.

Luther gave him more specific directions, and in just a minute or two, Westy was opening the passenger door. "Oh, sorry, ma'am," he said, seeing Hannah there. "I'll move."

"No, no. I'll take the back." He slipped into the rear seat, still breathing hard from his sprint across the field. "What now, sir?" he asked Luther.

Luther put the truck into drive and headed for the gate. "Back to Virginia Beach, I guess," he said, sounding disappointed.

"What about the copy in my office?" Hannah asked.

"Valentino had your office searched, remember? He didn't find it."

"He didn't know where to look," Hannah retorted, meaningfully.

Luther gave her a double take. "You think they missed it," he guessed.

"I know they did. And if we head into Bolling Air

Force Base tonight, I can get us into the DIAC to look for it."

"Bad idea," said Westy in the backseat. He was scrubbing his face with a towelette. "I can guarantee you someone's just waiting for you to show your face at the office."

"Look, I'm as cognizant of the dangers as you are," Hannah argued, "but I'm not showing my face, am I? No one's going to recognize me in this getup."

"Then how do you propose to get in?" Luther asked. She could tell by his tone of voice that he didn't like the idea any better than Westy did.

"My godfather is the director, remember? I can ask him to escort us."

The men lapsed into thoughtful silence. "Valentino warned you not to contact any of your associates. How do we know your godfather isn't the Individual?"

Huggable, lovable Uncle Caleb? The thought was preposterous. But Hannah knew both men were right. This wasn't the best time to search her office. "So how are we going to prove Lovitt's crimes?" she asked.

"How much of the notebook's contents do you remember?" Luther asked.

"Some of it. I can tell you the types of weapons that were stolen and from where. Thing is, Ernie managed to connect Lovitt to each one of the thefts. He showed that Lovitt was informed of each SEAL mission in advance, making it possible for him to get to the interdiction sites first."

"Maybe we could do the work all over again," Luther suggested. "We have access to mission information at the Spec Ops building."

"Maybe," Hannah relented, "but it's going to take a

while. How long before Lieutenant Renault's Article 32 hearing?"

"I don't know. His first meeting with the defense counsel is tomorrow. We'll bring you with us and you can tell the lawyer what you know. Maybe they can request a delay, give us some time."

"We'll need it," Hannah said.

They slowed at the gate, holding a collective breath as the Marine on duty eyed their vehicle. To their mutual relief, he waved them through.

Whether disappointed by their failure to find the notebook or depressed at the thought of her car totaled, Hannah slouched in the seat, weary to the bone.

"Why don't you put the seat back and close your eyes?" Luther suggested as she lifted her glasses to rub her eyes.

Westy shifted his legs to give her more room.

"Thanks." She put the seat back, curled onto her side, and pretended to sleep. The hum of the tires filled her ears.

A long time later, she overheard Luther speaking to Westy in a hushed voice. "Chief, you think we could all stay at your place for a while?"

"No problem. Guess your house is still empty, huh?"

"Yes," said Luther on a dampening note.

Hannah pricked her ears. There were overtones to this conversation that she wasn't understanding.

"Shouldn't have let Veronica run off with everything," Westy said. "It was your money she spent on it."

"Thanks for reminding me."

An odd sensation swept through Hannah as she lay there, eavesdropping. Veronica. So, she'd been right; Luther had suffered a recent breakup. *Wife or girlfriend?* she wondered, though it really didn't matter, did it?

Holding her when she'd needed to be held was an act of kindness. He'd have done the same for anyone in need of reassurance.

She and Luther weren't together for romantic reasons. He was a defensive lineman standing between her and the faceless Individual that had come out of nowhere. The only thing they had in common was a mutual desire to make Lovitt answer for his crimes.

Sebastian was dressed completely in black: black boots, black slacks with zippered pockets, a long-sleeved black T-shirt, and black gloves. He didn't need face paint. Thanks to his Mexican heritage, his skin was brown; his wavy hair was black as pitch. He didn't worry that the two sailors stumbling past him en route to the elevator would even see him. After twenty-two years as a SEAL, Sebastian had perfected the art of blending into shadow.

But never alone.

Still, this needed to be done. If they could show that Miller hadn't killed himself, that Lovitt had ordered him silenced, it just might tip the scales of suspicion in Jaguar's favor.

Regrettably, Sebastian had to break the law himself to get the evidence they needed. Jason Miller's regular entrance was roped off from the hallway with yellow security tape, the door double bolted. He couldn't get in that way.

The elevator doors closed with the late-night arrivals

inside it. Sebastian stepped from his hiding place and onto the guardrail that ran the perimeter of the parking lot. He notched his gloves tighter and looked up.

Miller had enjoyed an ocean view on the fifth floor. Since the building's roof was secured, climbing from balcony to balcony, up the face of the building, was the only way in.

Praying that his forty-year-old body wouldn't betray him, Sebastian jumped. His fingers closed around the iron bars on the first balcony. Finding them rusty and easy to grip, he performed a chin-up and crooked his knee over the ledge, moving with stealth to avoid unwanted notice by the room's occupants.

By the time he clambered over the railing of the fifth-floor balcony, his fingers were stiff, his biceps shook with fatigue, and a light sweat had broken out under his T-shirt.

But he'd made it. Squatting by the sliding-glass door, Sebastian pulled a penlight from his pocket to examine the lock. What he saw drew a shiver up his spine. No need to put his lock-picking skills to the test, here. The catch on the door had been sawed in half.

Someone had come this way before him.

He reached into another pocket and extracted a compact digital camera used for reconnaissance. Since it relied on infrared light, there wasn't any flash to betray him. The military police on Dam Neck were vigilant, cruising the empty streets below. Sebastian took a picture of the compromised lock, stood up, and slid the door open.

A heavy curtain blocked the entrance. He skirted it and found himself in a dark living room. The putrid odor of stale organic matter assaulted him. It was quiet inside, the pulsing roar of the ocean muffled by the drapes.

With the hairs threatening to rise on the top of his head, Sebastian clicked on the penlight. He panned it around the room, taking in the serviceable furniture—all Navy issue, nothing personal. Miller had lost more than a wife in his divorce, apparently.

The beam of light slid over a desk opposite the balcony. The stains on the wall riveted Sebastian's attention. He stood there a moment, looking at the pattern of blood and gray matter. He hadn't gotten to the rank of master chief without seeing some terrible stuff, but this was bad.

Supposedly, Miller had shot himself in the forehead. In order for his brains to hit the wall like that, he would have had to have been sitting in his desk chair, facing the sliding-glass doors.

The authorities had stated that Miller left behind a suicide note. If *that* had been left on his desk, it would have been covered in gore.

Struggling for detachment, Sebastian took several pictures of the stains and the desk's sticky surface. He reached for a drawer and opened it. Aside from a box of nine-millimeter pellets, the desk stood conspicuously empty.

Taking a final look around, he slipped outside to clear the stench from his lungs. He stowed his camera and penlight and glanced down, finding the area around the BQs quietly deserted.

The aura of death surrounded him, making his skin feel tight. He looked to the stars for relief, taking comfort in their glittering presence.

The biggest mistake a man could make, Sebastian mused, was to live his life as Miller had, estranged from his family, giving all he had to the SEALs. There was more to life than that. And if God was merciful, Sebastian would soon know the joys of having his own family, becoming a father.

Only first he would have to convince Leila Eser to trust her heart to him.

They had an agreement, he and the Turkish-American woman who'd danced into his life last spring, changing everything. Suddenly he'd seen a future for himself that he'd never before envisioned—a life apart from the SEALs, as a husband and a father.

But Leila, who'd been abandoned by her spouse and left financially destitute, wanted nothing from Sebastian but a baby. At thirty-eight, her biological clock was winding down. And so, Sebastian had agreed to give her a baby in exchange for the pleasure of her company, once a month.

Only it wasn't enough. And with the reminder of how transient life could be, it seemed suddenly imperative that Sebastian make an effort to change Leila's mind.

To do that he would have to unsettle her safe existence, to interrupt her staid routine. He smiled just thinking of her outrage. She was as passionate in her anger as she was in bed.

As the moon skated out of sight behind a cloud, Sebastian threw a leg over the railing and began the perilous climb down.

Chapter Five

Hannah rolled onto her back and sighed. She'd obviously confused her inner clock by staying up nights in her cell in Santiago, watching the movement of the guards. It didn't seem to matter that Westy's guest bed was a thousand times more comfortable than her cot at the Spanish fort. With a headboard that Westy'd carved himself, the bed took up most of the space in the spare room, tucked into the eaves of his 1940s bungalow-style house.

The whitewashed house was quaint and comforting, with a front porch, dormers, and a black Labrador retriever named Jesse. Hannah ought to be able to sleep just fine. God knew she was tired enough.

Except that every time she closed her eyes, memories of the last three weeks crept over her. Ernie's jovial laughter echoed in her head, and her heart broke anew to think that she would never see him again. In the chaos following his death, there'd been no time to miss him. Now grief hit her squarely in the chest, bringing reminders of the devastating loss she'd suffered three years before.

Ernie had been more than a colleague. He'd been a surrogate father, like Uncle Caleb, taking her under his wing to help familiarize her with the DIA. In the mornings, they drank coffee and shared concerns about world issues. Ernie brought in clippings from the comic section of the newspaper for her to pin up on her pegboard. Hannah would look up from her tedious research, read the comic strip, and smile.

She'd had no idea Ernie was so close to exposing Commander Lovitt. The last time she'd seen him, he'd been anticipating his upcoming "vacation." While on vacation, Ernie must have come too close to exposing Lovitt's culpability. Perhaps he'd found Lovitt's stash of stolen weapons.

Hannah punched up her pillow, thinking. Since they hadn't found Ernie's notebook in her car and since entering the DIAC wasn't a safe option right now, what if they went to Ernie's so-called vacation spot? They just might find what it was that had made Ernie such a threat to Lovitt.

She threw back the covers, eager to bounce her thought off of Luther. She could hear him in the kitchen now, given the muted sounds coming up the stairs. The men were taking turns keeping watch.

She glanced down at her oversized T-shirt. Neither she nor Luther had thought of buying her pajamas while purchasing her new wardrobe. Westy'd scrounged up an extra T-shirt with a Harley-Davidson logo on it and a pair of running shorts. Figuring she was decent enough, Hannah headed down the creaking steps.

She found Luther at the table cleaning his weapon. He lifted an ever-watchful look at her, one that skittered over her and jumped away. Awareness leaped between them like a flare, though the only actual light was the one hanging over the table.

"Come on down," he invited in his easy baritone. "I'm just doing a little housekeeping."

She approached the table, taking in the components of his disassembled weapon. Parts had been placed on a towel to keep the gun oil from staining the tabletop. "Do you really prefer an MP-5 over a pistol?" she asked, taking the seat across from him.

He glanced at her sharply. "You know your guns?"

"Sure. It was part of my training."

"With the CIA," he guessed, glancing at her for corroboration. "Pistols are for cops. SEALs prefer submachine guns. There's less loading and more power, which is what all of us need."

"But Westy shoots with a SIG Sauer."

"Not in the field. He's our master sniper. He uses a Remington 700 with bolt action."

Hannah nodded. "And you prefer the MP-5."

His eyes gleamed with appreciation. "Ever unloaded one?"

"No," she admitted. "Case officers are encouraged to carry pistols. They're easier to hide."

"I bet you're a sharpshooter, too," he said, his mouth lifting in a reluctant smile.

She shrugged one shoulder in acknowledgment.

"Is there anything you can't do?"

She propped her chin on one hand and thought about it. "I can't sleep," she admitted.

His smile faded. As he studied her face, she knew he was seeing all the signs of stress and fatigue that she was too tired to hide. "A lot of SEALs have trouble sleeping," he confided.

"Do you?"

He looked down, hiding the ghosts that drifted briefly across his eyes. "Sometimes. Especially after a messy encounter."

In those words, she heard everything he wasn't saying, and she realized the toll it took on him when things didn't go as planned. "Like when you killed those men for me."

"I said I'm okay with that," he said, polishing the dust off the gun's casing. "Are you?" He looked up at her, his gaze steady and concerned.

She recalled the awful contortions of the general as he struggled for air. The urge to burst into tears rose up with formidable pressure. "I'll be fine," she said quickly.

His patient gaze encouraged her to push a few more words through her tight throat. "What bothers me most is that Ernie was killed. He was such a good guy, you know? He didn't deserve to be hunted down, no matter how much Lovitt has to hide."

"A great deal, apparently," Luther commented, muscles jumping in his jaw.

"It occurred to me that we should trace Ernie's last steps," Hannah added, sharing her recent insight. "I don't know if you've picked up on this, but Valentino's not going to help you put Lovitt behind bars, not until the Individual is arrested. That's why the FBI didn't investigate Ernie's death, at least not overtly. Some guys in suits cleaned out his office, but I'm not sure who they were," she added, frowning.

Luther dropped the rag in his hand, sat back, and crossed his arms. Biceps bulged beneath the smooth tanned skin of his upper arms. Hannah swallowed, recalling how gently those arms had cradled her.

"First we'll look through records at Spec Ops," Luther decided. "If we can piece together Ernie's research, then there's no need to retrace his footsteps. If not, we'll look into it. What do you know so far?"

"Not much. Only that he was on a so-called vacation in a place called the Northern Neck, three hours from D.C. His car was discovered just outside of Sabena, Virginia. He'd been run off the road." She blinked away the vision of Ernie crushed between his seat and the steering wheel.

"If we have to, then we'll go to the Northern Neck," Luther agreed. "I know where it is."

Hannah nodded. Their gazes locked. For a long while, no words were spoken. Hannah was the first to look away, her eyes drawn once more to his upper arms. "No tattoos?" she asked, curious to know more about him. "I thought all you Navy guys had tattoos."

"I've got two," he admitted. Humor flickered in his eyes like fireflies at dusk.

Her eyebrows rose. "Two?" she said disbelievingly. "Where are they?"

He shrugged. "Stick around long enough, maybe you'll find out."

Her heart beat faster at the loaded statement. Awareness crackled between them. "Where are you from?" she asked. "I don't hear an accent when you talk. You sound like a Harvard graduate."

"I was accepted to Harvard," he admitted without arrogance. "But I went to Texas A&M."

"You are *not* a Texan," she insisted.

"Indeed I am. Born and raised."

"Indeed I am," she repeated, mocking his upper-middle-class accent-from-nowhere.

"My mother's an English professor at the University of Houston," he enlightened her. "She brought us up to speak a certain way—no dialect, no slang, no cursing. I'm a slab of white bread, boring as hell," he mocked himself.

"You just cursed," she pointed out. "And you're not boring." If anything, he was amazingly complex, a man born with a silver spoon in his mouth, apparently, who'd chosen a rigorous, not to mention deadly, occupation in order to keep the world safe.

"You've heard Westy talk," he added. "That's what I'm supposed to sound like."

Hannah looked around. "I don't see your mother here."

He tapped his forehead. "She's here. Every time my grammar slips I get a lecture."

Hannah laughed, amused by his predicament. "So where was your mother when you were getting your tattoos?" She raised her eyebrows at him.

"I knew you'd get back to that."

"I'm as tenacious as a pit bull," she admitted. "My brother could tell you that."

"Then you'll just have to learn some patience," Luther countered. This time there was caution in his eyes, as if he was growing wary of the frisson between them.

"Were you married to Veronica?"

Oh, Lord, she couldn't believe she'd just asked that.

He looked at her, his eyes like dark blue marbles. "You keep your ears open, don't you?"

"I told you, I can't sleep," she said, breaking eye contact.

"She was my fiancée," he surprised her by admitting.

"What happened?" she dared to ask.

"We weren't compatible," he said, simply. "Call me old-fashioned, but I expect fidelity in a relationship."

"Of course," she said. She couldn't imagine any woman wanting to cheat on Luther, but the word "compatible" reminded her that she wasn't exactly wife material either. She pushed her chair back, determined to get some sleep before dawn cracked. "I'd better sleep while I can," she said.

He made a point to catch her eye. "It's safe here," he reassured her. "Westy and I won't let anything happen to you."

She smiled at his earnest reassurance. "My heroes," she sighed, pressing her hands to her heart briefly.

He chuckled at her as she turned away.

Slipping between the sheets a moment later and listening to Westy's soft snores in the room next door, Hannah thought about Luther's confession. He'd actually been engaged! A breakup that close to marriage, on the grounds of unfaithfulness, would leave any man wary of commitment. So despite the bubbly feeing she enjoyed in Luther's company, he wasn't going to let his guard down, which meant she'd never get to see his two tattoos.

Now wasn't that annoying.

Portsmouth Naval Medical Center, Portsmouth, VA
22 September ~ 06:42 EST

As the elevator doors closed with mother and daughter inside, Helen Renault reached for Mallory's hand. Mallory not only held on but sidled closer so that they stood shoulder to shoulder. At fourteen, Mallory had surpassed her mother in height.

Helen could feel the tremor in her daughter's hand and the clamminess of her own palm. They weren't supposed to be here. Since Gabe's arrest four days ago, they hadn't been allowed to see him at all. But Doctor Shafer had treated Gabe a month back when he'd been medevaced from the South Korea Peninsula. He'd befriended Helen and Mallory when they'd come to collect the husband and father who'd been declared dead.

At four A.M. this morning, Dr. Shafer had wakened Helen with a phone call. If she wanted to see her husband, Gabe was currently under his care at the Portsmouth Naval Hospital. He would let her in, providing she managed to get over there before the guards showed up.

Helen hadn't wasted more than a minute to brush her teeth and drag a comb through her long, blond hair. She'd gone to wake her daughter and found Mallory in the kitchen grabbing two granola bars from the pantry. "Let's go," Mal had said.

Obviously Helen wasn't the only one having trouble sleeping lately.

With a warning chime, the elevator doors swooshed open. Helen and Mallory peered warily into the hallway of the psychiatric wing. It appeared deserted. They scurried furtively down the hallway to room 314, where Dr. Shafer had said Gabe was undergoing medical tests.

The door to the room stood partly open. Helen pushed it wider and they both peered in. The curtains at the window were drawn back, revealing a sky the color of peach sorbet. Dr. Shafer looked up from a machine that was connected by wires to Gabe's head. Gabe's eyes were closed. At Helen's indrawn breath, his lids sprang open. He glanced alertly in her direction, his tense body conditioned to expect the worst, thanks to the cruelty of his captors in his twelve months spent in North Korea.

He was visibly astonished to see them. "Helen. Mal!" He struggled to sit up. With an impatient mutter, he peeled the suction cups off his forehead and chest and tossed them aside, scrambling out of bed to greet them. He held his arms open.

Be strong, Helen commanded herself as they both rushed forward. *Be like Mallory.*

But Mallory pushed her face into Gabe's shoulder and couldn't look up again. Seeing Mal so distraught made it impossible for Helen not to cry. As she leaned against her husband's familiar body, hot tears gushed from her eyes.

"Come on, ladies," Gabe chided, holding them tightly. "It's not that bad."

"We've missed you," Helen confessed in a strangled voice.

"I've missed you, too."

"No one will let us see you. I don't understand!"

"That's just the way the Navy operates, sweetheart. No visitors while I'm under medical evaluation. Dr. Shafer knows I'm not dangerous, though, don't you, Doc?"

Through tear-blurred eyes, Helen noted Dr. Shafer's compassionate smile. He crossed the room and busied himself with paperwork, giving Gabe and his family a modicum of privacy.

"What's going to happen, Gabe?" Helen whispered. It wasn't fair that her newfound happiness was being threatened by outside forces. Gabe had been accused of succumbing to paranoia and killing two innocent sailors. But Helen had been there when the incident aboard the *Nor'easter* came to a frightening and potentially tragic end. There was nothing innocent about the way the third sailor had wrestled an anti-tank round on his shoulder, intending to fire it into the belly of the boat.

Helen had shot him, using the gun Gabe had left at home. That shot had only slowed him down. If Gabe hadn't shot him two more times, the result would have been an inferno out at sea with massive casualties.

He deserved a medal of honor, not this.

"Listen to me. Both of you," he urged, cupping their faces to regard them one at a time. "Nothing bad is going to happen to me. This will all be over soon. It's just a big misunderstanding, and my men are working it. I'll be home before you know it."

There had once been a time when Helen preferred Gabe gone. But that was before his captivity, back when being a platoon leader was more important to him than being a husband, and he'd been more machine than man. Seeing him now, with gentle encouragement beaming in his gold-green eyes, his features taut with determination, she'd give anything to have him safely home again.

"I have a meeting with my lawyer this morning," he added. "The guys are all behind me. There's nothing to worry about."

With several more optimistic comments, he managed to summon smiles from both of them. He joked about the food being even worse than Helen's cooking. He kissed Helen lingeringly, right there with Mallory watching. Helen had just started to feel like it would all work out when two security personnel stormed angrily into the room.

"This man has not been cleared for visitation," the younger one barked, pointing an accusing finger at Dr. Shafer.

"Oh, really? I didn't know that," the doctor mildly replied.

"Out," barked the guard at Helen and Mallory.

"Jesus, Leonard, give 'em a second," the old man growled, as Helen stepped reluctantly from the circle of Gabe's arms.

She and Mallory made their way to the door, and Gabe's reassuring look was the only thing that kept their tears from gushing a second time.

"Love you, girls," he called, blowing them both a kiss.

Helen held fast to hers, clasping it close to her heart. Mallory took her hand, and together they headed back to the lonely house they'd come from.

Oceana Naval Air Base Trial Services Building
22 September ~ 08:10 EST

Jaguar's defense counsel turned out to be a lieutenant commander in her late twenties with little experience as a Judge Advocate General, or JAG. Lieutenant Commander Curew wore her brown hair in a fraying bun and had a harried look on her face that did nothing to hearten Luther or any of his teammates.

Afternoon sunshine pierced the lowered blinds in the window of the counsel chamber, making the room as warm as it was stuffy. Six SEALs edged one side of a long table, with Commander Curew sitting in the center, opposite. Hannah occupied a chair at the end, to Luther's left.

Jaguar sat immediately across from his lawyer, flanked by platoon members. Wearing his dress-white uniform, he looked nothing like the deranged POW Lovitt had made him out to be. The rows of pins above his left breast pocket indicated the vast number of missions he'd taken part in since enlisting in the Navy, eight years before becoming an officer. The resolve in Jaguar's gold-green eyes and the strain etched in his sharp-featured face sent Luther's admiration for the man up another notch.

Commander Curew worried her lower lip as she gathered her thoughts. "Don't get me wrong, gentlemen," she began, her hazel eyes troubled. "There is benefit to the fact that your testimonies are nearly identical. All of you state that the two remaining seamen jumped overboard to keep from being arrested, but without information regarding their motives, it comes down to your word against Commander Lovitt's, and frankly that's not going to be enough to win this case."

Her troubled gaze touched on Master Chief, who'd offered up photos suggesting that Miller, Lovitt's executive officer, had been terminated, possibly for knowing too much. "As for the circumstances surrounding Miller's death"—she drew a sharp breath at the implications suggested by the photos—"if this case goes to court-martial, then of course I'll do whatever it takes to prove Lieutenant Renault's innocence, but this is far too inflammatory to be brought up at an Article 32 hearing."

Her gaze drifted to the end of the table, where Hannah

sat in her wig and spectacles. Her lilac-colored polyester suit with its large mother-of-pearl buttons looked stifling in the warm chamber. To Luther, however, Hannah managed to look calm, intelligent, and oddly appealing, even in her dowdy disguise.

"Miss Lindstrom's testimony, on the other hand," the commander added, "could tip the scales in Lieutenant Renault's favor, provided you can find the evidence to corroborate it," she said to Hannah.

Hannah had been introduced as Rebecca Lindstrom, though it had been made clear that the name was an alias. The defense lawyer knew that Hannah's colleague had been killed while probing into Lovitt's affairs. His notes detailing Lovitt's crimes had apparently been seized by Lovitt's protector, an international arms dealer called the Individual.

"Ma'am, if we can petition for a delay," Luther urged, "we could really use the time. Once the FBI arrests the Individual, Lovitt's activities are bound to come to light."

Commander Curew scribbled herself a note on the pad in front of her. "I'll ask, Lieutenant, but I can't guarantee that the request will be met. The powers that be are bringing this hearing before a judge as quickly as possible," she added, lips thinning with disapproval.

The men shared dark looks. Lovitt had friends in high places. They were doing their utmost to keep him above the fray, to keep the Navy from taking a blow to its dignity.

Commander Curew began gathering up her notes. "Unless the delay is granted, gentlemen, we'll meet again on Monday at eight hundred hours, prior to the Article 32. At that time, each of you will offer the testimony you've given me today." She darted a rather desperate look at Luther and Hannah. "If you find anything remotely damaging to Lovitt's reputation, please let me know at once. You have my card."

With that, she stood up, causing all six men to come respectfully to their feet. They bid her good day, listening to her heels tap the linoleum tiles as she retreated.

Within seconds, two military guards stalked into the chamber to take Jaguar back into custody. Luther watched with his stomach burning as they slapped cuffs on Jaguar's wrists. Jaguar kept eye contact with his platoon members up to the moment he was hustled from the chamber.

As the door swung shut behind him, the men turned wordlessly to Luther and Master Chief, seeking their guidance.

Luther was the first to speak. "Miss Geary and I are going to visit Spec Ops tonight and go through the paperwork," he conveyed in a confidential voice. "Master Chief, if you could talk to the duty personnel and convince them to let her in . . ."

"Yes, sir," said Sebastian without hesitation.

"We'll find what it takes to keep Jaguar out of jail, guys," Hannah said, giving Vinny and Bear a reassuring look.

Luther liked her immensely in that instant. It was easy to forget that she'd been traumatized for her part in this drama, already. She stood next to him, undaunted, determined to bring corruption to heel and to seek out justice. She was a lot like him in that regard.

He thrust the random thought from his head. "Let's go," he said, urging her toward the exit.

As she and Luther pushed through the double doors of the Trial Services Building with Westy immediately behind them, Luther swept an eye over the parking lot. Hannah was their best chance at rediscovering the evidence they needed to prove Lovitt's perfidy. God forbid Lovitt caught word that she was alive and helping them. He'd do whatever it took to keep her quiet.

And Luther was just getting used to having her around.

Naval Air Station Annex Dam Neck
22 September ~ 23:03 EST

Hustling Hannah into the Spec Ops building at twenty-three hundred hours proved ridiculously easy. Master Chief had left word with the duty officer that the woman escorted by Lieutenant Lindstrom should have access to the building, with or without identification.

It was late at night, the building deserted with the exception of the duty officer, a young ensign new to Team Twelve. He'd snapped Luther a smart salute and waved him through the checkpoint, not bothering to divest him of his weapon when the alarm went off.

Luther carried Westy's pistol, not that he expected to use it in this highly secured building. Westy, in turn, was armed with Luther's MP-5, keeping an eye on the building's doors from the vantage of the parking lot.

"This way." Luther urged Hannah down the empty hallway. The new, high-pile carpeting muffled the sound of their footsteps. He shivered with cold and an unusual case of the jitters. No one had bothered to turn off the air-conditioning, and with the temperatures moderate outside, the air in the building was downright chilly.

Seeing a light at the end of the hall, Luther hesitated. He realized with a sense of foreboding that someone was working near the archives room, even at this late hour. And the only soul who had a habit of working late was the CO's secretary, Veronica.

Talk about your worst-case scenario. Well, God damn! He cursed under his breath, drawing a curious look from Hannah as he came to a dead stop.

"What?" she inquired.

"We need to come back later."

"Why?"

But it was too late. The chair in the office squeaked, and there was Veronica, peering around the corner to see who was whispering in the hallway. She looked back and forth between the two of them. "What are you doing here?" she demanded of Luther, darting a disdainful look at Hannah's attire.

Luther ground his back molars together. "We have business in the file room," he stated, heading doggedly toward it.

Veronica's pretty face reflected skepticism. "Really?" she mocked. "And I suppose your friend, here, has top-secret clearance."

"Actually, I do," Hannah said calmly.

"She doesn't have her CAC card," Luther interrupted, making reference to the Common Access Card. "I'm letting her in with mine."

"I don't think so," said Veronica with that smile that meant she was going to be a royal bitch.

"She's cleared," Luther insisted.

"Not if she isn't in the system," Veronica retorted, her dark eyes flashing.

"This system?" Hannah indicated the thumbprint scan mounted next to the archive door. "Depends on whether it's synched to the larger database." Stepping closer, she inputted in her PIN and pressed her right thumb against the screen. It matched her print to the database, requesting that she insert her CAC card. "Like he said, I don't have my card, but it recognized me." She sent Veronica a pointed look.

Veronica's eyes narrowed as Luther scanned his own thumbprint and inserted his card, releasing the lock on the secured door. He hustled Hannah inside before his ex-fiancée found a way to interfere.

"Does she always work this late?" Hannah asked as Luther flicked the light switch. Soft halogen lights winked on, exposing row upon row of filing cabinets.

"Only when she's going home with the officer on duty."

Hannah gave him a long, perceptive look.

"Forty-eight file cabinets," Luther commented, diverting her focus from him to the task at hand. "And two computers."

"Do you have an account on these computers?" Hannah inquired.

"All officers and senior enlisted have accounts."

"Then we'll start by finding a comprehensive list of all the weapons stolen. That's got to be listed on a Navy Website somewhere. We'll cross-reference the list with all the missions that Lovitt was involved in or knew about. If his name comes up more often than any other commander's, we've at least got supporting evidence. I'll search through records the old-fashioned way."

Luther sat at the nearest computer and powered it up.

Hannah turned toward the filing cabinets and pulled out the first drawer. "So that was Veronica," she said, without inflection.

"Yes," he said shortly.

"She's pretty," Hannah observed.

He stared at the hourglass on the monitor. "You think?" He was tempted to reply that Hannah was a lot prettier, only what was the point of that? "Here we go," he said instead as the desktop popped up. He went into search mode while Hannah riffled through the files, scouring earnestly for information linking Lovitt's name to the weapons stolen from warehouses, frigates, and air terminals all over the world.

Veronica tossed down the document she was editing, unable to get the verbiage straight. Thoughts of Luther in the archive room with that dowdy-looking woman had her thoughts churning. What were they doing in there? Was it work-related or was Luther actually seeing someone so soon after throwing her out? If so, his taste in women had obviously veered off course.

Whoever the woman was, she had access to information that Veronica didn't, and that rankled. After working as a government servant at Spec Ops for six years, she ought to be allowed in the archives room. It wasn't like anything going on around her was really kept secret. She had ways of getting a man to talk.

For that matter, James, the security officer, had shown her how to validate the users of the thumb scan. Why sit here wondering who the woman was when all she had to do was to punch in a code to find out?

She'd jotted down the procedure on a sticky note and stuck it in her desk. Ah, yes, here it was.

Crossing to the scanning device, Veronica entered the code James had used and waited. The machine bleeped and beeped before listing names in the order of its most recent user. Luther's name was right at the top. Below that was the name Hannah Geary, along with her date of clearance and place of employment.

Veronica stared at the strangely familiar name, wondering where she'd heard it before. *Geary, Geary, DIA.* She cleared the screen and returned to her desk where she gnawed on the end of her pen.

Wasn't Geary that analyst who'd found incriminating information about Commander Lovitt? Hadn't the woman gone missing when she was supposed to surrender her evidence to the Quantico police?

Well, well . . .

Apparently she wasn't missing, after all. Either that or she'd been found. What would old Eddie do if he learned the woman was a threat, still, to his reputation?

Poor man, he'd been removed from Spec Ops and given an administrative job over at Oceana. His marriage was on the rocks, as he'd confided the last time they'd been together. He certainly deserved to know that Luther and this Hannah woman were conspiring against him. And wouldn't he be grateful to Veronica for tipping him off?

The last time he'd been grateful, he'd bought her a tennis bracelet!

With a smirk of self-satisfaction, Veronica leaped up to find a more secluded office. Whatever happened to Luther as a result of her meddling was his concern. He deserved a chunk of misery for breaking their engagement.

Edward Lovitt's hands shook as he placed the phone back in its cradle. He crossed to the kitchen sink to splash water on his face, keeping his movements quiet so that he wouldn't awaken his wife.

Oh, Jesus, was this never going to end? The Individual had assured him in their last correspondence that Ernest Forrester's findings would go no further. His office had been wiped clean, and his office mate had been dealt with. Eddie didn't need to get involved.

If that was the case, then why was Hannah Geary snooping through files in the archives room at Spec Ops? Not that she would find anything. He'd gone through every inch of paperwork and computer data, making certain his name couldn't be linked to any of the weapons he'd stolen.

But the last thing he needed was some intelligence analyst showing up at the last minute with incriminating information.

Damn the Individual for getting Eddie involved in this business in the first place!

He tossed down the towel and stalked to the living room, where he'd been relegated to sleeping on the couch.

Whoever the Individual was, he'd known enough about Eddie's past to blackmail him. Eddie had sold secrets to the Russians in the Cold War—big deal. It was harmless stuff, all of it. But if the truth went public it would have ruined Eddie's career. So to ensure the Individual's silence, Eddie had agreed to steal and store weapons for him.

The arrangement had functioned without a glitch until a nosy DIA officer started snooping near Eddie's warehouse. He'd had to eliminate the man before he could expose him.

A quick hit-and-run in a rural area seemed the best solution. Only the Individual had railed that the measure was a big mistake. He'd announced that he was backing away, apparently through with his demands.

Thank God, Eddie had thought. He'd quickly applied his energies toward cleaning house, eliminating anyone with the least inkling of his activities.

Jaguar, who should have perished in a North Korean warehouse last year, was Eddie's biggest concern. But like a cat with nine lives, Jaguar evaded him again, frustrating what ought to have been a quick and easy elimination out at sea.

Killing Miller had been easier.

The fiasco with Jaguar was now in the public eye, where Eddie's rank and Jaguar's PTSD were the only things protecting him. This Hannah Geary woman could potentially ruin his chances of getting his career back on track.

With sweat making his T-shirt cling, Eddie reached for his laptop. He fingered the keyboard to rouse his computer and then hesitated. What was he doing? Did he really want to involve the Individual in a matter he could resolve himself?

He closed his laptop decisively.

No, the last thing he wanted was to invite the Individual back into his life.

He would deal with Hannah Geary himself.

And then he'd order his brother-in-law, the sheriff of Sabena, to dump the remaining stores of weapons on the bottom of the Rappahannock River. They could rust away to nothing for all Eddie cared.

The only thing he wanted now was to have his life back, the way it was before the Individual made his terrible demands.

Chapter Six

Sebastian sat straighter in the driver's seat. The woman who occupied his every waking thought had finally stepped out of the building.

Leila Eser owned a dance studio called Impressions. It was well past six P.M., and every store owner in the strip mall where her studio was located had closed up shop for the day. Only Leila, who was a slave to her business, lingered long after her final client departed. Sebastian had nearly lost patience and gone in after her, only he didn't want to miss the look on her face when her car failed to start.

Leila headed toward the red Camaro, shielding her eyes against a brazen sunset. Even from a distance of a hundred feet, she was strikingly beautiful, as dark and exotic as her Turkish heritage implied with slender lines and black hair hanging down to her hips. She didn't see Sebastian, who was parked in a used-car lot across the street, camouflaged by passing vehicles. He tingled with anticipation as Leila unlocked the door of her car, using her remote lock. He'd lifted an identical set from her condominium the last time they'd been together, more than a week ago.

She swung the door wide and eased gracefully inside it, leaving one leg exposed from the hem of her very short skirt all the way down to her high-heeled sandals. It was a wonder that every driver on the road didn't steer out of control.

She inserted the key in the ignition, no doubt eager to turn on the air-conditioning before shutting herself inside. He imagined what she was probably hearing—a ticking sound and nothing more.

Guilt pricked him as he sensed her dismay. He watched her sit a moment, confused and indecisive. But then she popped the hood and got out of the car, circling warily toward the engine. The tension in her body had him reaching for his own keys. It was time to come to her rescue.

Yes, it was pathetic that he'd had to incapacitate the woman's car to get her to acknowledge him. But as they said in Mexico, *El Amor se desespera.* Love makes you desperate, and he was more in love than most. Only by putting her squarely at his mercy would she get to know him better.

Leila was peering, mystified, at the components of her engine when he pulled up alongside her Camaro. She looked up, distress turning to relief as she recognized him.

"Problems?" he asked, leaning casually upon his steering wheel. He drove a blue 1960 Ford Falcon with a loud rumbling motor and one door still covered in primer.

"It won't start," she admitted, flicking a disdainful glance at his ride.

"Really?" He put his car into park and turned it off. Getting out, he noted the way her gaze skittered over his attire—desert camouflage BDUs and boots. He'd rolled up the sleeves of his jacket to counteract the Indian summer heat, baring the smooth muscles of his upper arms that were bronzed a deep copper-brown, much like hers only he'd seen more sun. "Let me have the keys?"

"They're in the car."

He eased inside and turned the key. *Click, click, click.* "Sounds like a bad alternator or an electrical problem."

She stamped a foot in vexation. "Wouldn't you know it! My warranty just expired a week ago."

Yes, he'd picked up on that information when she'd mentioned it in passing. That's what had gotten him thinking in the first place.

"Can you fix it?" she asked hopefully.

He got out and moved to the front of the car. "No, they cover new engines with casings. Only a mechanic can get to the parts." Or a SEAL who'd made a hobby of tinkering with engines, but she didn't need to know that.

"What am I going to do?"

She was already wringing her hands. Sebastian pulled his cell phone off his webbed belt and flipped it open, calling on his mechanic, who was waiting on standby. "Mike? Sebastian here." He summarized the problem, listened to Mike tell him that he'd tow the car to his shop and have it ready for him in the morning.

"You need to get it towed," Sebastian relayed. "My mechanic, Mike, will have it ready for you in the morning."

Leila's silver bracelets jangled musically. "What time in the morning? How will I pick it up?"

"Don't worry. I'll give you a lift."

Given her stricken expression, she was clearly very worried. He had her completely off balance because the only way to get through this difficult moment was to accept his help. "No, I can't impose on you."

"It's not a problem." He was getting uncomfortable again, being the cause of her distress. "I can go into work a little late tomorrow. The new CO won't be in until noon."

She eyed her ballet studio. "Perhaps I should just stay here."

It was everything he could do to give a careless shrug. "Wasn't there a break-in at this mall last week? It'd be safer if I took you home and picked you up in the morning."

She looked from him to the studio, as if choosing the better of two evils. "Okay," she said, making her decision. "Thank you."

"Leave your key for Mike under the floor mat. He'll be here within five minutes."

She pulled the key off the key chain, struggling not to break her long pink fingernails. Then she stuck her head into her car to hide the key and to retrieve her purse. Sebastian raked a gaze over the curves exposed to him but turned toward his car before she noticed. She wasn't at his mercy yet.

He waited for her to settle into the bench seat beside him, fumbling to fasten the archaic seat belt. "All set?"

"Yes, thank you."

If she thanked him one more time, he would beat his chest and cry mea culpa!

"You just happened to be passing by?" she asked with belated suspicion. He worked at Dam Neck Navy Base and lived not too far from its back gate, making a trip to her studio quite a detour.

"I was called out to Oceana," he said, referring to the

naval air base closer to her shop. It wasn't exactly a lie. He'd been out there last week.

She hummed her understanding, then turned to look out the window. And that was it. He knew from experience that if he didn't force her to engage in conversation, she wasn't going to say another word to him.

A slow-burning anger heated him from the inside out. He could feel it spreading insidiously through his body, galvanized by a healthy sexual appetite.

Sebastian was renowned for his supreme patience, but for some reason Leila robbed him of his usual self-control. Which was probably the reason why he took a sudden left at the intersection, tires squealing to beat the yellow light.

"This isn't the way to my condo," Leila informed him, one hand braced on the seat, the other clinging to the seat belt.

"Yes, I know."

He kept it at that, punishing her for her reticence, for her damnable, icy poise.

"So where are we going?" she asked, seconds later. There was an edge to her tone this time.

He slanted her a look. He was so tempted to say something that would cause her to fall apart, to rip the world out from under her feet, to make her feel the way she made him feel. "Are you hungry?" he asked, instead.

"No."

"No?" He let his gaze drift over her deliberately. "You look hungry. You look like you starve yourself."

"What business is it of yours?"

Her cheeks turned faintly pink. Sebastian took it as a

good sign. "It is my business," he insisted. "If you intend to have my baby you'd better feed him."

"Him?" She made a sound of disgust. "I guess you assume that just because you ooze masculinity you could only have a boy child." Her magnificent eyes began to flash.

He *oozed* masculinity? "You need some good Mexican food," he continued, ignoring her jibe. "I'm going to cook for you."

Her jaw grew visibly slack. "Excuse me? This isn't part of our deal."

"I think you failed to read the fine print," Sebastian retorted, though they'd forged no written contract. "The part that says I have every right to insist on the best health and welfare of my child—"

"There isn't even a baby yet!" she cried in disbelief.

"Do you know that for sure?" They'd made love just over a week ago. He guessed it was too early to tell.

She pressed a hand to her forehead and briefly closed her eyes. "Allah, you make me crazy," she muttered. "Fine, I'll eat your food, if it'll make you happy. But then you are going to take me home."

He gave her his best enigmatic look. No need to tell her that the only place she was going tonight was to his house. He wouldn't put it past her to jump from his vehicle at the next intersection.

Instead, he put a leaden foot on his accelerator, getting her to his ocean-front cottage as fast as possible. He'd whip up his favorite dish of *mole poblano,* feed her until she was groaning with repletion, and then he'd make certain they became more intimately acquainted.

✦ ✦ ✦

Leila jammed her hands under her thighs so she wouldn't wring them. What was happening? All this had the earmarks of an abduction. Sebastian had said that he would take her home, only now she was headed to *his* house, where he claimed he intended to feed her. Bad, bad idea.

His house was where he'd taken her the night they'd met. It was May back then, the night she'd turned thirty-eight and realized she wasn't going to have the baby she'd always dreamed of, not unless she did something absolutely out of character.

She'd rented a car for anonymity's sake, and with her friend Helen's help, she'd been cleared at the gate of Dam Neck Navy Base. She'd headed straight to the Shifting Sands Club where Helen had assured her she'd be the focus of male attention.

The moon had been full. A cool breeze, redolent with the smell of the ocean, had wafted through the open windows. She'd been swarmed by men, but when Sebastian made his way toward her, the others had backed away, in deference to his rank, she later learned. But one look at him, and she'd already made her selection.

She remembered thinking Sebastian would make the perfect father for her baby, his dark coloring so like her own. With a glass of wine coursing her bloodstream, she'd danced with him on the patio, thrilled by his grace and by the look of intensity in his espresso-colored eyes.

She'd let him take her home, to his A-frame cottage by the sea. And with the ocean throbbing in the background, she'd relinquished herself to blinding passion. She'd lost count of the number of times they'd made love. The experience had been so intense, so frightening, that she'd slipped away when he fell into exhausted slumber. She hadn't even told him her name.

Nor had a baby been conceived that night. The experience had only left her with a gnawing hunger for human touch and a profound curiosity to know more about the man.

She'd ignored both impulses. Her husband, Altul, had left her after years of marriage—destitute and bankrupt. It had taken every ounce of willpower to put her life back together. She wasn't about to risk her fragile heart again.

But Sebastian was like a magnet of opposing force, drawing her inexorably to him. And when Helen had called in turmoil over Jaguar's supposedly imaginary fears, Leila had intervened to speak with him. At the time, Jaguar had been living with Sebastian with the belief that his family would be safer without him. Leila had known she would run into Sebastian again. She'd told herself she only intended to apologize.

And apologize she had, offering him a stammering explanation that had resulted in his offer to give her the baby she still desired—no strings attached.

So why was he speeding her toward his home, with a glitter in his eyes that told her he was angry, though he appeared relaxed?

The sky had mellowed to violet by the time they pulled into the carport of his home. Sebastian cut the engine. "Come in," he invited, getting out.

Keeping her panic subdued, Leila followed him up the wooden steps. At the front door, he stepped aside to let her in, flicking on a light switch. Recessed lights lit the exposed timbers of the pointed ceiling. The house was small, with a great room and kitchen area downstairs and a loft and bedroom above, where Sebastian slept. He'd built the house himself.

She took in the depressingly clunky furniture. The cushions and carpeting were a muted gray. The pictures on the wall were uninspiring. The home's only saving grace was the kitchen—a culinary artist's dream, with graphite countertops and gleaming stainless-steel appliances.

"Relax," Sebastian invited. Glancing his way, she found him unbuttoning his shirt jacket. Her panic spiked. *Relax?* How could she relax with him undressing before her?

He shrugged off the jacket, revealing a tan T-shirt underneath, one that clung to his chiseled torso. She watched, dry-mouthed, as he unbuckled his belt, then tugged his T-shirt free. To her great relief, he turned away, pulling it over his head as he turned away. "I'm going to change. I'll be right back," he said, taking the steps two at a time, muscles in his naked back rippling.

Leila tore her gaze away. She headed to the kitchen on wobbly knees and poured herself a glass of water, gulping it down. Ignoring the sounds coming from the loft, she cast an envious gaze around his cooking space. The man's priorities were in the right place, apparently.

She dared a peek into his refrigerator. He was also immaculate. The shelves were all wiped down. She glimpsed an array of health and ethnic foods that only made him that much more appealing.

"I assume you've heard the latest about Jaguar." She jumped guiltily and shut the refrigerator door. Sebastian was coming down the stairs in an impossibly white crew neck shirt, black shorts, and bare feet. He looked like a domesticated panther.

"Oh, yes, he's been arrested. Helen's going out of her mind. Do you know what's going to happen?"

Sebastian struck her as grim as he paused by the counter that divided the kitchen from the great room. "An Article 32 is scheduled for Monday. Lieutenant Lindstrom and Westy are working with a DIA analyst to find something that'll prove Commander Lovitt was responsible."

"Poor Helen," Leila sighed, mourning her friend's plight. No sooner had Helen rediscovered love in her husband's arms than it was being put to the test. It just proved the fact that love was painful. "Do you think they'll find the evidence they need?"

A crease appeared briefly between Sebastian's dark-as-night eyebrows. "They have to," he said simply.

She knew a sudden and powerful urge to comfort him.

"Have you ever heard of *mole poblano*?" he asked, before she found the right words. He moved into the kitchen and started pulling ingredients from the refrigerator, brown sugar and what looked like a hunk of chocolate from the cupboard.

"Yes," she said, "but I don't believe I've ever tasted it."

"It takes hours to prepare," he divulged. "I've found it easier to make the nut-chili puree in advance." He unscrewed a glass jar, releasing a savory aroma.

"What's in it?" she asked, curious despite herself.

He slanted her a look with one dark eyebrow raised. "You really want to know?"

"Yes."

"Stir-fried almonds, pecans, peanuts, and shelled *pepitas* are blended with chilies in a turkey broth."

"That sounds simple enough."

His eyes glinted. "Then you sauté a ripe thick-skinned plantain, setting it aside. Next, you sauté tomatoes, adding raisins and the sautéed plantains at the last minute. Run this fruit blend through a sieve before adding it to the chili puree."

His voice had a sensual, hypnotic effect on her. Leila felt herself falling under its spell.

"After that," he added, "you brown an onion and garlic clove in a clean skillet. Add peppercorn, chickpeas, and anise; a cinnamon stick, Mexican oregano, dried thyme, and sea salt. This, too, is added to the puree."

He held up the glass jar before dumping it in a blender. "But I do all that in advance."

Watching him at work in his kitchen was fascinating, almost magical. He fried a hunk of bread in oil as well as five coarsely chopped tortillas, adding them to the blender with the chili puree and a cup of turkey broth.

Warming strips of turkey breast in the oil he'd used for the bread, he poured the sauce from the blender over it, leaving it to simmer. He measured out a half cup of brown sugar and stirred it in. And then came the chocolate.

Leila had a weakness for chocolate. She watched it melt into the fragrant, spicy-sweet smelling sauce, and her mouth watered.

"When did you learn to cook?" she wondered aloud. How could he have had time as a SEAL in charge of so many men?

"My mother needed help in the kitchen," he replied, reminding her that he was the oldest of eight, that his father had died, postponing his dreams of college, making it necessary for him to join the Navy. "Fortunately," he said with a half smile, "I enjoyed it." He ran his rather elegant-looking hands under the faucet, while gazing at her. "And you?"

She shrugged. "I was made to learn. Turkish women are expected to toil in the kitchen," she mocked.

"And when did you learn to dance?" His eyes warmed with appreciation.

"School dances," she admitted, looking away. "I was forbidden to go, but I found a way. The cheerleader sponsor saw me on the dance floor and begged me to join the dance team. By the time my parents found out, I was too involved to quit. When I went to college, I majored in it."

Having revealed that much, she felt suddenly exposed to him. There were some things Sebastian didn't need to know about her, even if he did become the father of her child. She turned abruptly toward the sliding-glass doors and unlatched them, stepping outside onto his balcony.

She took a breath to clear her head, to gather herself.

The sun had set, leaving the Atlantic Ocean looking like a giant pot of ink. Tonight the moon was not in sight, but the stars winked on, one by one. The scent of seafood wafted on a breeze that carried the sound of laughter. It would be so easy to lose herself, to let her guard down as she had before.

As if to prove just that, the melodic notes of piano music greeted her ears. Sebastian had turned on the stereo. Leila closed her eyes, lured helplessly into the romantic atmosphere.

She sensed Sebastian stepping onto the deck behind her and her breath caught as she anticipated his arms going around her. He would pull her against his lean male body. His touch was all it would take to shatter her resistance.

"Qué bella la noche," he commented.

She opened her eyes to find him propped against the deck rail, regarding her.

"It is beautiful," she admitted, striving for a conversational tone.

"Not half so lovely as you."

The compliment snapped her out of her trance. "Okay, stop," she said, propping her hands on her hips. "If you brought me here to feed me, Sebastian, then that's one thing. But you're not going to seduce me. We have a deal, and it doesn't include seeing each other whenever whim dictates, do you understand?"

To her discomfiture, he merely looked at her, making her feel like she'd displayed unseemly emotion for nothing.

"Would you care for a glass of wine?"

"No," she said. "Thank you." Wine was the last thing she needed; his company was intoxicating enough.

"Come and see what I have, though," he offered, gesturing with his head.

Recalling the fabulous Crest Chardonnay he'd shared with her on a picnic a month ago, she trailed him back into the kitchen. The aroma of chocolate and chilies filled her senses as she stood beside his wine cabinet.

He pulled a bottle out for her inspection. "Château Lafite Rothschild Pauillac, 1996," he announced, handing it to her. "It conveys an essence of limestone, honeysuckle, and pear. But a dark wine would be best with our meal. This is Swanson Cabernet Sauvignon, 1997. It blends cassis and black raspberry, with cedar and ash, sage, thyme, vanilla, and bittersweet chocolate."

Chocolate again.

"Are you sure you won't try it?" he asked, avoiding eye contact.

"Perhaps just a small glass," she conceded.

She sipped the Cabernet with secretly profound appreciation as he stirred their dinner. For a man who wielded a gun for a living, Sebastian had such sensitive-looking hands, with handsome knuckles and long, slender fingers that knew just where to touch her and just how.

Before she knew it, her wineglass stood empty. They'd discussed their favorite music and the best places in the world to see. And those to avoid.

With a start, Leila realized that she was feeling relaxed and warmly alive. She'd let her guard down. Sebastian had ignored her warning earlier. He was slowly, inexorably drawing her in.

Before the night was through, she was certain he would peel her clothes off in that very deliberate manner of his and kiss every inch of her, beginning with her lips, her neck, her breasts, and so on, moving down the length of her body until she was nothing but a pool of liquid need.

Only then would he tell her how much he wanted her and what he was going to do to her, interspersing lilting Spanish phrases into his whispered predictions.

"Let's eat on the balcony," he suggested, oblivious to her carnal thoughts. "Would you light this for me?" He handed her a candle in a glass dome and a box of matches.

"Of course," she said. "I'll set the table," she added, desperate for some mundane task to take the edge off her traitorous anticipation.

It took her six attempts to light the candle. She blamed

it on the ocean breeze, but her fingers shook as she laid place mats and silverware on the glass top of his wrought-iron table.

Sebastian brought the food out with a flourish. As they sat down across from each other, an awkward silence fell between them. "I like to say grace," Sebastian admitted.

"Yes, me, too. Go ahead."

He hesitated. "What faith will we raise our child?" he asked very seriously.

Leila narrowed her eyes at him. He made it sound like they'd be living together. "I don't think we need to face that right now, do you?"

He shrugged, closed his eyes, and gave a simple blessing, and the moment passed.

Leila found herself ravenous. A whimper of delight escaped her as she dug into her food. The exotic blend of spices teased her taste buds. The chocolate took the edge off the chili peppers, and the tender fare melted in her mouth. "You're very good," she admitted, forking up another bite. Her face heated as she considered just how very good he was, at *everything*.

Sebastian's eyes held the candlelight as he regarded her. "Next time you can cook for me."

She wanted to retort that there would be no next time, only that seemed awfully rude under the circumstances. Her car had broken down and he'd rescued her. Not only that, but he'd been a faultless host, going to great lengths to feed her. Of course, she mustn't forget his ultimate intentions.

A pleasant shiver rippled over her.

Conversation moved to other topics, and before she knew it, she'd imbibed a second glass of wine, causing her to stagger as she rose to help clear the plates. Sebastian flashed a hand out to steady her. "Careful."

It was all she could do not to turn into his arms.

"Let's walk on the beach," he suggested, unexpectedly.

They put the dishes away and descended the myriad steps to the ocean. Leila lacked the will to protest when he took her hand, anchoring her to his side as they slogged their way through the dense sand to the rushing waves.

"Your hair will tangle," he observed, pausing to gather the long strands, twisting them in a loop, and drawing the ends through it.

She swayed against him, then, loving the feel of his hands in her hair. It was inevitable that he would make love to her tonight. She might as well be reconciled to it, and if she was honest with herself, she'd admit that she was looking forward to it.

But then he took her hand, and they began to walk. He talked to her. He told her the names of all his brothers and sisters, where they lived, what they did. His words filled her mind with vignettes of happy moments and warm-hearted people. His youngest sister was the last to be mentioned. She'd just had her first son and named him Sebastian. "We are fifteen years apart, Marianita and I. Who would have thought she'd have a child before me, hmm?"

Leila's heart did a funny flip-flop. Why hadn't she considered when she'd made her bargain with Sebastian that he might want to be involved in their baby's life?

She had underestimated him, she realized. She hadn't predicted what a wonderful father he would be. But how much time should she allow her baby to spend with him? It depended on Sebastian's work, of course, but—oh, dear, just the thought of giving up her baby, even for a week-end, made her frantic. Perhaps if she came to visit also? But then she'd fall in love with Sebastian, and every time his team called him away, her heart would freeze in fear.

She lost track of how far they'd walked and when they'd turned around. There was only the velvety tenor of Sebastian's voice, the cool, moist sand between her toes, the wind caressing her body, and the warmth of his hand cradling hers.

She looked up and blinked, surprised to find them at the steps to his cottage.

"You must be tired," he said, still holding her hand. "What time did you get up?"

"Early. Six o'clock."

He chuckled at her answer. "That's not early."

Despite her weariness, all she could think about was sliding into Sebastian's bed to relive the night they'd met. It was taking forever for him to get around to seducing her.

They reentered the house together. He found her a towel, a washcloth, a new toothbrush, and ushered her into his bathroom right off the loft. As she stood under the shower, soaping herself, she felt lonely. A couple of hours in his company and she was already used to him.

When she ventured from the shower wearing his robe, she found the bed turned down waiting for her. Sebastian was downstairs, tidying up the kitchen. She gazed down at him, uncertain of his motives.

"The bed is yours," he called up, catching sight of her. "I'll be fine on the couch."

She stood there, not believing the words coming out of his mouth. Desire, still sparking through her veins, sput-tered and dimmed, leaving her achingly unfulfilled, not to mention rejected. "Thank you," she said, though what she really wanted to say wasn't nearly that polite. "Good night, then."

She eased between the crisp, clean sheets and listened to the hushed sounds coming from below, waiting, hoping Sebastian would mount the steps and join her. But it soon fell quiet, meaning he'd fallen asleep on the couch.

She drew the extra pillow across her chest and put her nose to it. It smelled just like him.

This is what it would be like whenever he is called away, she thought, seeking to ease the ache in her chest. It was a good thing he was a man of integrity; that he hadn't taken advantage of her, after all. How awful it would be if he'd made her fall in love with him!

She closed her eyes and slept, at last, his pillow clutched to her heart.

Chapter Seven

Their second night in the Spec Ops building was even less productive than the first. Last night, Luther had finally located a summary of the stolen weapons, which he lifted off the Navy-Marine Corps Intranet, complete with descriptions, serial numbers, dates stolen, and circumstances surrounding the thefts. He copied the information and stored it for personal reference on his Palm Pilot.

Analysis of the data showed that both East and West Coast SEALs had been tasked to interdict weapons from places like the Gulf of Siam, the Gulf of Oman, and the Bering Straits, only to find the weapons already seized. There was nothing to indicate that Lovitt had prior knowledge of any of the missions, however, which would have allowed him to extract the weapons ahead of the SEALs.

"This is crazy," Luther admitted, following three hours of unrewarding search. He swiveled the rolling chair to face Hannah, who was draped over a filing cabinet skimming the contents of a packet.

She wore a calf-length canvas skirt with panty hose and full-sleeved white blouse. Not an inch of her fair skin was exposed. Yet somehow, the gaze she sent him over the top of her glasses struck him as erotic.

"Which part?" she asked, straightening. "Staying up all night or beating our heads against a brick wall?" She stretched her back, arching like a graceful cat.

"Both." Luther massaged his stiff neck while trying not to notice the material of her blouse growing taut over Hannah's breasts. He could just make out her nipples. "Don't you find it curious that Lovitt's name doesn't appear anywhere? It's almost like he's come in here himself and wiped his name out of the documents we're looking at." He froze in reflection. "Wait a minute. If he did that, an administrator could find it in the user logs."

Hannah slid the filing cabinet shut and approached him. "That's still not as effective as linking him to the actual thefts. I'm telling you, Luther, we need to go to the Northern Neck and find whatever Ernie found." The choked quality of her voice had him looking up sharply. He thought her eyes might be misting behind her glasses.

"He's the real reason you're here, isn't he?" Luther asked, considering her motives. Why else would she be willing to stay up all night? "What was Forrester like?" he asked, wondering if Hannah'd had a thing for him.

She paused to reflect. "Fat," she said with a strained chuckle. "Poor man, he ate like a rabbit and he couldn't lose weight. He loved his work; he was devoted to it, going above and beyond anyone's expectations, which is probably why he discovered Lovitt's involvement in the first place. You know, it really ticks me off when people die before they've accomplished what they set out to do," she added, pulling up a second rolling chair and thumping into the seat.

Beneath the note of frustration, Luther sensed a deep river of grief. He suffered the craziest impulse to pull her onto his lap and wrap his arms around her, giving her permission to let go of the pain she held in check.

"You're right," he said, suddenly determined to make things better for her. "If Lovitt killed your colleague then we need to prove it. Enough of this. Let's go to the Northern Neck and see what Forrester was up to. Any idea where he was staying while he was there?"

"No," she said, scooting closer.

He typed Forrester's name into a search engine and found a newspaper article reporting his death. Luther and Hannah skimmed it together.

"It says he was visiting from the D.C. area and staying at the Magnolia Inn in Sabena," Hannah observed.

"Upon investigation of the accident," Luther read out loud, *"Sheriff James Blaylock deemed it an unfortunate incident. Forrester may have lost control of his vehicle, swerving off the road and into trees. His air bag failed to inflate fully."* He glanced sidelong at Hannah's tense profile. She sat back and folded her arms across her chest.

"I want to know more about this Sheriff Blaylock," she said in a hard voice.

Luther entered his name in the search engine, not surprised to come up with dozens of hits. "We need to limit the search."

"Add Lovitt's name," Hannah suggested. "Who knows? Maybe we'll get lucky."

He followed her suggestion, expecting no results. Much to his surprise, there was a match—an article linking the names Lovitt and Blaylock together. "Check this out," he exclaimed as a wedding announcement popped onto the screen. "*'Sheriff James Blaylock marries Anna Lovitt.'* It's two years old."

Hannah sat forward, her expression brightening. "Do you think she's related?"

"Here." He pointed to a paragraph near the end of the article. "*'The bride is the daughter of the late Marshall and Dotty Lovitt. Her older brother, Commander Edward Lovitt, United States Navy, gave the bride away.'* Got you now, you son of a bitch!"

"No we don't," said Hannah, keeping him from giving her a victory hug. "All we have is circumstantial evidence. So Lovitt's brother-in-law is the sheriff of Sabena. What does that prove? Nothing."

"You're right," he conceded. "We'll go to Sabena first thing in the morning."

"Do you think we can find what we need in two days?" she asked dubiously.

"We don't have much choice, do we?" Luther cleared the screen and logged off. As he reached under the desk to depress the power button, his shoulder brushed Hannah's thigh. He managed to follow through and to straighten as if the contact hadn't affected him like a bolt of lightning.

Physical awareness clawed through him, sharp and all-consuming.

Working in close quarters for two nights straight had only increased his awareness of her. The way Hannah moved, her intelligence and insight, and the feminine scent that she gave off were slowly undermining his determination to keep her at a distance.

And now he was going to the hub of Lovitt's illegal operation with Hannah right beside him. They'd probably have to stay in the bed and breakfast where Forrester had stayed, if only to get a true picture of the DIA officer's last hours.

How was Luther going to do that without snatching the wig off Hannah's head? More than once, he'd fantasized about running his fingers through her soft, glorious hair, of removing her glasses and watching her eyes flare with awareness.

It was going to be a test of his resolve—that much was certain.

Hannah groaned into her pillow. Was it possible to have slept so little in the past seventy-two hours and *still* find sleep elusive?

She pushed herself into a sitting position, brushed the hair off her cheeks, and gazed at the now-familiar four walls of Westy's spare bedroom.

She could only guess what time it was—three in the morning, perhaps. They'd be leaving for Sabena in just a few short hours, taking their investigation to new heights. It was never more imperative that she recharge her batteries.

But images of Ernie's flight from Sabena kept flashing through her mind. Perhaps, having found proof of Lovitt's crimes, he'd hastened to the B and B to collect his things, only to be driven off the road as he raced out of town.

With Lovitt's brother-in-law being the sheriff of Sabena, it may have been a police car that pursued him, forcing him off the road. In that split second, as he hurtled toward the trees, he must have experienced a horror similar to her parents'. Only theirs had lasted longer.

Don't think of that! But it was too late. If she fell asleep now, she would dream about the plane crash.

She blew out a weary breath. *I need help,* she thought. Luther was immediately downstairs, dozing on the couch in the living room. With dismal certainty, she knew that she would sleep just fine in the circle of his arms. Only what kind of case officer would she be when she couldn't sleep alone?

She delayed the inevitable nightmare by rearranging her twisted sheets. A thump on the roof made her freeze. Perhaps it was an acorn falling off the immense oak tree that stretched its branches over Westy's house. But then it came again, too stealthy to be an acorn.

And this time, it sounded closer.

Hannah rolled out of bed. In two steps, she crossed the small room and pressed her back against the wall, peering beneath the flimsy curtains of the dormered window to see outside.

A shadowy figure ducked out of view, perhaps catching sight of her. Fear jolted Hannah's system, propelling her out the open door and into the hallway. She gasped in fright as she ran straight into Westy's powerful and practically naked body.

"Shhh," he said, whisking her around the corner. "Get down into the stairwell and stay there," he commanded, pushing her head down.

Hannah obeyed, wishing fervently that she had a gun like his. His SIG Sauer glinted in the darkness as he drifted soundlessly into her room.

Just then, the dog let loose a warning bark downstairs. Luther hushed him. Quick footsteps signaled his response to the alarm.

The noises on the roof came again, this time retreating. "Fuck." Westy threw up the window, batting the curtain aside as he attempted to peg the intruder before he got away. The attempt obviously failed. In the next instant, he was flying past her, his steps remarkably quiet on the creaking stairs. "Don't move," he ordered.

"Okay." Hannah's heart thumped unnaturally loud. She couldn't hear what Westy was saying to Luther, probably that they should split up and go out either door. But if they did that, then she'd be left all alone here, without a weapon.

Sure enough, she heard the kitchen door squeak open. It had to be Luther slipping out the back because Westy was stealthier.

A scrabbling noise greeted her ears. Hannah tensed, but it was only Jesse. The black Lab climbed to the landing and whined at her pathetically.

You think you're scared? she conveyed telepathically. *They left me here without a weapon.*

If the intruder had a partner, working in pairs like the Obradovitch couple, then one of them would lead Westy and Luther away while the other sneaked through an upstairs window to blow her head off.

No, this wasn't good. Hannah eased down the steps, scooting on her bottom. She needed to arm herself, and a knife was better than nothing.

The kitchen was full of shadows. Through the French windows of the addition Westy had built on the back of the house, she could see his backyard, with its shade trees conveniently placed for snipers to hide behind.

She went down on her hands and knees, crawling across the heart of pine floor, keeping well below the countertops as she made a beeline for Westy's knife rack. Peering up at it, she selected the largest blade. The haft felt reassuring in her palm. She'd done some hand-to-hand training back at CIA camp.

For what seemed an excruciating amount of time, she crouched in the kitchen expecting the worst. If the Individual was after her, he wasn't going to let her live this time, not when she'd killed his Cuban presidential hopeful.

Without warning the back door flew open. Hannah sprang to her feet, launching an offensive that could not have been predicted or countermeasured with a gun.

"Hey, hey, hey!"

It was Luther, not Misalov Obradovitch, who stood at a similar height. In three quick moves, Luther disarmed her. He slammed the knife down on the counter and jerked her against him, the muscles in his body rigid with anger. "What the hell do you think you're doing?" he raged through his teeth.

"Sorry, I thought you were—"

"I'm not. I'm here to protect you." His arm was a band of steel trapping her against his naked chest. "Stop going offensive and let me do my job," he added.

His chest was warm and smooth and faintly damp from the humidity outside. Hannah stood nose to nose with him, her mouth so close that it would take no effort at all to steal a kiss.

So she did, not really intending to. The instinct to soothe his agitation and comfort herself overrode her common sense for the moment.

His lips were soft and warm. She knew exactly how it would feel if he kissed her back. She drew a breath as desire coiled around her. "Sorry," she whispered, pulling away.

She wasn't really, but he didn't need to know that.

His grip didn't slacken. He stared down at her, stunned. She could feel his body quickening against hers, growing hard.

But then he released her, letting her heels fall to the floor. His gaze flew to the windows. "Let's get out of this room," he muttered. He pulled her with him into the living room, closing the drapes so they couldn't be seen.

"Did you see who was on the roof?"

"Yes, running away. He got into a car and took off. Westy's parked behind a bush hoping he'll come back, but I think it's safe to say he won't."

"Was it Misalov Obradovitch?" She quailed as she recalled the impassive look in the European's eyes. The thought of him and his ruthless wife after her unnerved her completely.

"I don't think so. This man was slim, light on his feet. Something about the way he ran looked familiar, but I couldn't see his face."

"Someone knows who I am," she concluded. She collapsed on the couch as her knees gave out suddenly.

Luther turned and looked at her. "How?" he said, his voice rough with frustration. "How could anyone know already?"

"There has to be a leak," she said.

Luther shook his head.

"Your fiancée," Hannah suggested.

"Don't call her that." His abrupt tone told her she'd struck nerve. "She's not my fiancée. She never should have been."

The words released a certain tension in her chest. "Could she have figured out who I am, though? Does she know enough of what's going on?" Hannah pressed.

He sat down next to her. "I don't know."

"Who else knows me? There's the defense lawyer and the men in your platoon."

"Not one of them is loyal to Lovitt," he reassured her. "Shit, it has to be Veronica," he admitted darkly. "Maybe she found out who you were from the ID scanner."

"Only a security officer could do that."

He gave a humorless laugh. "Or the secretary screwing the security officer," he countered. "I wouldn't put it past her to play some kind of game with me. She has no idea the seriousness of it all." He put one hand behind his neck, squeezing it. "If Veronica told Lovitt, then he'd probably come after you himself. I think that's who it was," he said, looking at her sharply. "That was Lovitt's run. I thought I recognized it."

"He'll tell the Individual where I am," Hannah added, her mouth growing dry with fear.

"He'll also try to clean things up in Sabena."

They sat shoulder to shoulder, reeling with the implications. "We need to leave for the Northern Neck tonight," Hannah urged.

"No, we should wait for your ID to come tomorrow," he argued.

"No one's asked to see it yet."

"They're not going to let you into the Trial Services Building again without it," Luther insisted.

"Fine." She collapsed against the cushions. It was either that or launch herself at Luther and steal another kiss.

"Why don't you go upstairs and catch some sleep before we go?" he suggested.

"Right, like I'm going to sleep up there when Lovitt was just trying to shoot me through the window."

He rolled to his feet, disappointing her. "Lie down here then," he offered. He crossed to the window to peek outside.

Hannah swung her feet onto the couch and nestled into the blanket Luther had been using. It smelled like him, like sportsman's soap and ironing starch. "What about you?" she asked, wishing he would join her.

"I'll catch a few winks in the chair here."

Hannah turned her face to the pillow and closed her eyes. She knew she wouldn't sleep. Her ears were cocked to the sound of Luther easing into the armchair. The springs protested his weight. He stuck his long legs out in front of him.

"Can I ask you a favor?" Hannah asked ten minutes later. It was sheer desperation that made her say it. Her eyes felt like they were hard-boiled. If she didn't get some sleep soon, she'd have a mental breakdown, and men in straitjackets would have to be called in to cart her away.

"Depends," he said warily.

"Would you mind laying down beside me for a little while?"

"Lying down," he said, correcting her grammar, but he didn't immediately answer her question. Finally, he rolled to his feet. "You're going to have to scoot way over."

She did, giving him most of the space. When he was finally on his back, she settled against him, holding in her sigh of relief. He was long and muscular. She fit against him like a long-lost puzzle piece, shoulder tucked under his arm, her head on his chest. Closing her eyes, she listened to the steady pumping of his heart.

Exhaustion tugged at her. "Thank you," she mumbled, drifting toward sleep.

Luther said nothing at all. Either he was too tired himself to speak or she wasn't welcome.

Chapter Eight

The sun had been well past its zenith, imbuing the air with late summer heat, by the time Luther, Hannah, and Westy took off for the Northern Neck in Westy's car. Hannah's ID had not arrived until noon, which hadn't bothered Luther at all. It gave him time to plan for whatever contingencies the mission might entail.

As a result, Westy's Nissan 300ZX was loaded to the gills with diving gear, reconnaissance equipment, and their overnight bags. Hannah's new ID was safely stowed in the purse Luther had bought her on their way out of Virginia Beach. Sitting in the backseat, with her disguise once more in place and the old-lady purse in her lap, she looked nothing like the woman who had woken up in his arms this morning. She looked like a Catholic School teacher with a secret fondness for sexy lingerie.

He preferred her the way she'd awakened with her red hair tousled, wearing none of the heavy makeup that disguised her as Rebecca Lindstrom. With morning sunlight framing Westy's window, he'd allowed himself to be dazzled by the color of her hair and the way her eyelashes rested against her freckle-dusted cheeks. Her mouth, so wide and soft in her sleep, had him thinking about the kiss she'd given him the night before.

Why the kiss? he'd wondered. Had she figured out that he was rich? Was she after his money as Veronica was? Or had she simply needed a reassuring touch?

He had to suspect that it was reassurance that she needed. Why else would she have asked him to join her on the couch and then fallen asleep on him? She liked him for who he was, not what he used to be. But did she know that spending time with her was undermining his resolve to resist her appeal. How many times did he need to repeat to himself that she was not the tame, uncomplicated woman he was looking for?

With an imposition of will, Luther brought his thoughts to the present and the mission at hand. They'd driven a couple of hours now, leaving the congestion of the ocean-front behind without any sign of being followed. If Lovitt had been the one stalking Hannah last night, they'd apparently convinced him to keep his distance.

To further mislead him, they'd decided to leave Luther's truck as a decoy.

As the afternoon dragged on, they traversed several bodies of water—including the James and York Rivers. Congestion thinned as they forged up Route 17 until there was nothing but fields of withered cornstalks, tapioca, and peanut plants as far as the eye could see. An occasional farmhouse dotted the flat terrain. Here and there, a tractor harvested crops.

"Lordy, we are out in the hicks!" Westy commented with sudden glee.

Hannah roused from semisleep in the cramped back-seat. "It must remind you of home," she commented in a drowsy voice.

Westy was from Oklahoma. That was really about all Luther knew of his past. The chief wasn't exactly forth-coming about his history, so how did Hannah know? "What part of Oklahoma are you from, Chief?" he inquired, suddenly curious.

"Broken Arrow," Westy said succinctly.

"His grandfather was a full-blooded Creek Indian," Hannah volunteered.

Westy kept his eyes on the road and said nothing.

Luther considered him sidelong. "You never told me that," he accused.

Westy shrugged. "Sabena, two miles," he announced.

Luther pulled the map from the glove compartment and shook it open. "Take a right on Country Route 110. Left on 45."

Westy took the next right, which bore them through a dense copse of woods, past a big white church and sprawling graveyard. Luther glanced back. There was no one behind them.

The trees ended abruptly, and the road spit them out over a two-lane bridge. According to the map, the channel of water beneath them was just one of the many branch-ings of the Rappahannock River, deep enough for large vessels to navigate. The car's tires hummed over grates, indicating that this was a swing bridge.

The picturesque town of Sabena sprang into view. A marina with a waterfront restaurant was tucked against the opposite shore. Nineteenth-century stores and houses lined the street, each charmingly distinct from the next and interspersed with century-old boxwoods, oaks, and maples just beginning to flush into an autumn hue.

Hannah wedged herself between the two front seats to take it in. "There's the sign for Magnolia Manor," she pointed out, seeing it up ahead.

Westy turned the car down a shady side road. With the sun beginning to set, the Victorian houses lining the streets looked eerie, with their turrets and towers and dark, watchful windows.

The road dead-ended at the head of a driveway flanked by brick pillars. A plaque had been nailed into the whitewashed bricks.

According to the article they'd read online, this was where Ernest Forrester had last laid his head. MAGNOLIA MANOR, read the tree-shaded sign. And underneath that, in smaller script, barely legible in the dusky light: A LOVERS' RETREAT.

Uh-oh. Luther swung a startled look at Hannah, who was also reading the sign, her mouth slightly agape. "Forrester didn't have a girlfriend, did he?" he inquired.

"No." She shook her head. "Definitely not. He must have stayed here for a different reason."

Westy shifted into neutral and pulled up the hand brake. "I'll leave you lovebirds to it," he smirked, fetching his gun from the glove compartment.

As they'd previously discussed, Westy's mission was to act like a loner, soliciting work at local warehouses. "Your cell won't always work out here, sir," he reminded Luther. He popped the hatch and fished his duffel bag out of the rear. As he zipped his gun into the bag, he caught Hannah's eye and winked at her.

Then he turned and sauntered down the road, duffel

flung over his shoulder. He definitely had the look of a roamer, right down to his flannel jacket, the hole in the butt of his jeans, and his worn work boots.

Hannah gazed after him, impressed. Luther got out, popping the seat forward so she could move up front.

With inexplicable butterflies in her stomach, she rose from the car and stretched, while Luther adjusted the driver's seat to accommodate his legs. She drew a deep breath, then took the seat beside him.

They sat for a minute, focusing on the mission, one that was suddenly a bit stickier, given the description of the bed and breakfast as a lovers' retreat.

"We should probably share a room," she pointed out, darting him a quick look. The shadows of the pine trees had fallen over the car, leaving his face in shadow.

"Right."

"Don't forget to call me Rebecca," she reminded him. "Maybe we should say that we just got married."

"Makes more sense than you being my sister," he drawled in agreement.

"But we're not wearing rings," she said, looking down at her bare left hand.

"We haven't found the right set yet," he suggested. "We're hoping to find something in the antique shops."

"That works."

Luther shifted into first and the car crept forward. Down the long, pine-shaded driveway they crawled. On the carpet of fallen pine needles, their tires were almost silent.

Hannah's eyes widened as the mansion came into view, glowing like a ghost in the dark, with spotlights illumining its facade. The two-story, federal period structure looked like something out of *Gone with the Wind,* complete with tall Doric columns and a portico. The only thing missing were live oaks dripping with Spanish moss. They were too far north for that.

Luther parked their car in the designated area. He retrieved their bags from the back, ignoring her offer to help.

Hannah sniffed the cool air. "Do you smell that?" she asked under her breath. "We're close to the water." The air was rife with the sulfuric tang of river mud.

Minutes later, the proprietress of Magnolia Manor huffed up the sweeping stairs ahead of them, chiding them subtly for not making prior reservations. The lantern she carried cast flickering light over the whitewashed walls. "You would have loved the honeymoon suite," she lamented, her large hips swaying, "but of course it's taken. People call up to two years ahead of time to make sure they can reserve it."

"Our marriage was sort of impromptu," Hannah confided. "Good thing you still had one room available. Though I hope it's not haunted." The proprietress had warned them that the only vacant room had last been used by a patron who died while on vacation.

"Oh, I assure you it isn't," the woman replied.

"Did anyone ever find out what caused that man to drive off the road?"

"No, but it was quite late at night. The poor soul must have fallen asleep at the wheel. Such a shame," she added, catching her breath at the top of the stairs. The lantern cast an unkind light onto her jowly face.

"So you don't think that someone just gave him a nudge," Hannah added.

The startled woman nearly dropped her lantern. "Oh, heavens, no," she cried. "This isn't the city, dear. We don't have crime like that out here." She turned abruptly away, leading them to the last room on the right. "The key sticks a little," she admitted, jiggling the key in the lock. Pushing the door open, she hit a light switch. Hannah sighed in relief. She was beginning to wonder if the place had electricity.

"I trust you'll enjoy the view, come morning. Breakfast is served from six to ten. If you need anything at all, you just let us know. Enjoy your stay, now."

The proprietress backed away with her lantern, shutting the door behind her.

Hannah took the bag Westy had loaned her out of Luther's grasp. "Beats the hell out of the last place I stayed," she commented, breezing in to have a look around. "Oh, wow, we even have a balcony."

"I don't know if that was—"

She put a finger to her lips and began sweeping the room for bugs, not expecting to find any. She had to believe they were still one step ahead of Lovitt.

The room was small but tastefully decorated to reflect early nineteenth-century design. Hannah ran a hand up the posts of the canopy bed. She looked under the marble-topped vanity. "This furniture is old," she commented, "early nineteenth century."

Luther, who'd joined the search, cast her a wry look. "You know your antiques, too?"

"This one's a reproduction," she said, searching the bedside table. "No dovetail grooves on the drawers."

Luther lifted the cranberry-and-black Kurdish carpet, laid over the oak floorboards. He peered under the cushion of the plush reading chair, a modern concession to comfort.

"Place is clean," Hannah determined.

"I'll take the chair," Luther volunteered, stowing his bag, along with his weapon, in the wardrobe.

Hannah peered into the bathroom, taking note of the footed bathtub, brass fixtures, and the elaborate wallpaper. She crossed to the window to look outside. The river, if it was there, was camouflaged by trees. It was nearly dark out. "So what do we do tonight?" she asked.

"We go into town and play the part," Luther suggested.

"If the locals are as naïve as Mrs. Dodd, we're not going to learn a thing," Hannah sighed. "Though I had a feeling she knew more than she was letting on."

"So did I. We'll learn something," he said. "I have confidence in your information-gathering abilities."

"Really?" His comment made her smile at him.

"Westy sure opened up to you," he added on a strange note.

Hannah's smile faded. Why didn't that sound like a compliment?

The sound of footsteps outside had them both looking at the door. Sure enough, whoever was out there gave a tentative knock.

Luther pointed at the bed, and Hannah threw herself onto the mattress. Luther stripped off his shirt and messed his hair up. Stalking to the door, he cracked it open. "Yeah," he said, with just the right amount of irritation.

"I'm so sorry to interrupt," Mrs. Dodd effused, "but I forgot to give you our complimentary coupon. We give it to all our newlyweds. A free dinner at the Waterside Inn, the restaurant next to the bridge."

"Thank you," he said, shutting the door with a forced smile. He retraced his footsteps, frowning down at the coupon.

Hannah took advantage of his distraction to ogle his naked chest. The lamplight highlighted the bulging pectoral muscles that the darkness had disguised last night. Brown chest hair tapered into a line of fuzz bisecting his tautly muscled abdomen. No tattoo anywhere, she noted.

"Are you hungry?" he asked, catching her staring.

She ripped her gaze upward. "Yes, actually." Though not necessarily for food. She wanted to feel Luther's arms around her, this time when they were both wide awake.

But what was she thinking? There was no allowance in her plans for any intimate relationship in the next few years. Her career would demand everything of her.

"Let me freshen up," she said, rolling off the bed and snatching up her bag. She disappeared into the bathroom.

The woman gazing back from the bathroom mirror brought her back to reality. If she, for one second, believed Luther was drawn to her in this disguise, she was the naïve one.

Strolling hand in hand along Main Street, Hannah was conscious of how gently Luther clasped her hand.

The display of intimacy was for the benefit of the locals, of course. And yet the link between them felt oddly comfortable. In contrast to the cooling air, Luther's hand felt warm. His lightly callused palm reminded her that much of his job was physical. Like her, he'd chosen a profession that put him on the defensive edge of the free world.

Perhaps, cognizant of his deadly training, he took pains to handle her so gently.

It was hard not to surrender to the atmosphere of romance as they struck out toward the riverside restaurant. Age-old cedar trees lined the crumbling brick of Sabena's courthouse wall. In the windows of an antiques shop, a collection of Tiffany lamps cast a kaleidoscope of color.

If only there were time to poke around the shops, Hannah lamented. But then again, her town house was crammed with furniture from both her parents' and grandmother's estates. There wasn't room for any more.

Organ music floated on the breeze, escaping a Friday night church service. This quaint old-fashioned town seemed like the perfect place to raise a family, not a hotbed of corruption—which was probably why Lovitt had gotten away with hiding his weapons here as long as he had.

As they turned the corner toward the restaurant, Luther's grip tightened. Hannah looked around, catching sight of the six marked police cars parked beneath the lampposts.

"Do you get the feeling they're expecting us?" Luther asked under his breath.

"Mrs. Dodd must have sent us here intentionally," she agreed. "We have to play it off."

"If anything goes down, get behind me," he advised.

She clicked her tongue in annoyance. "I wouldn't have to, if you'd given me a gun," she whispered back.

"What do you need a gun for when you have me?" he purred, holding open the door for her. His gaze lingered on her upturned face as he slipped into the role of doting husband.

Hannah swept inside, looking casually about. Waterside Inn touted outdated carpeting, gaudy light fixtures, and laminated furniture in dire need of replacement. But given the mouth-watering aroma and the scarcity of seating, there was no better place to eat in Sabena. And with its large-paned windows overlooking the river, it had the potential to be a fine-dining establishment.

"Two, please," she told the hostess. Trailing the girl to a corner table, she counted the law enforcement officers seated in the center of the room. There were eight of them, all pretending not to notice their entrance, which was obviously an act, as Luther wasn't the kind of man to walk into a room unnoticed.

"Here you are," said the hostess, laying their menus on the table for two.

Luther held out the chair that put Hannah's back to the wall.

"Don't you want a view of the room, dear?" she asked him.

He glanced at the window. "I can see just fine."

The window behind her mirrored the interior of the restaurant, she realized. Luther could still be a gentleman, while keeping an eye on the cops.

As they took their seats, the hostess filled their glasses with ice water and told them their waitress would be along shortly.

"The seafood must be fresh here," Luther commented.

Probably, but thinking that one of those cops had run Ernie off the road had stolen Hannah's appetite. She made a quick selection and put her menu down. A policeman was eyeing them over his coffee cup.

The waitress appeared with a basket of bread. "What can I get you tonight?" she asked brightly.

Hannah chose the flounder. Luther opted for crab-stuffed clamshells. He handed the waitress the coupon Mrs. Dodd had offered them, and with a puzzled look, she moved away.

Hannah took note of the waitress's confusion.

"How come Westy never told me about his grandfather?" Luther asked her, harking back to their earlier interrupted conversation.

"Probably because you never asked him," she replied.

He just looked at her. "I've worked with him for three years," he said. "He never talks about himself."

"That's because there's a lot in there that he doesn't want to face."

Luther regarded her thoughtfully. "I think you're right."

"What's your code name?" she asked him abruptly. It had just occurred to her that Lieutenant Renault was called Jaguar and Chief McCaffrey was called Westy. So what was Luther's code name?

"Little John." He helped himself to a roll from the breadbasket.

"Little John?" She looked him over, her eyes widening. "Is there possibly some part of you that's little?" she inquired, raising her eyebrows.

Luther buttered the lower half of his bread very carefully. He took great pains to avoid eye contact, but to her amazement he appeared to be blushing.

"Well?" she prompted.

"John is my first name," he explained. "John Luther Lindstrom. I was the youngest guy on the team. Hence,

Little John, you know, from Robin Hood. The name lost its meaning after I was promoted to lieutenant."

Hannah frowned in concentration. "Why does that name sound familiar?" she asked. "John Lindstrom."

He leaned forward, pitching his voice discreetly. "You should know this already, sweetheart. We're married."

The deep blue depths of Luther's eyes captured her. She leaned in, too, so that their faces were mere inches apart. "Know what?" she asked, giving herself permission to study his strong-boned face, his nicely shaped lips. She remembered how they'd felt against hers, tender and restrained.

"I played football for the Dallas Cowboys. That's why I sit with my back to the room."

Hannah gaped at him, harkening back to Westy's observation several days ago. *You don't know who he is, do you?* he'd said. "Guess I picked a lousy partner to go undercover with," she muttered. Then, because she knew she could get away with it, she stroked the hard curve of Luther's jaw.

Her touch so obviously unsettled him. She could tell by the wary look that stole over his features. With reluctance, she released him, noting the approach of the waitress again.

"We serve a complimentary bottle of wine to all the newlyweds stayin' at Magnolia Manor," announced the girl. She displayed a bottle of white wine and commenced to fill up their empty wineglasses.

"None for me, thanks," Luther said, sliding his wineglass to the wall.

"Is there something else I can get you?" the waitress asked.

"No. Water's fine.'

"Your dinners will be right up then," she said smiling.

Hannah took a sip of the wine, which was tart and unremarkable. "Tell me why you became a SEAL," she demanded.

He glanced at the room's reflection. The police were still eating.

"Come now, I'm your wife," she cajoled, unsettling him further. "Football is so lucrative, so glamorous. Why'd you quit?"

"I got into a car accident," he admitted shortly.

Hannah eyed him with concern and waited for more.

"I'd had too much to drink," he added, glancing toward his empty wineglass, "which is why I don't drink anymore. I couldn't breathe. One of my ribs had punctured a lung. I was pretty sure I was going to die. But I didn't. I was stuck in the car for hours. It gave me time to think about . . . what I was doing with my life."

She suffered an almost-overwhelming urge to grab his hand. "What happened?" she prompted.

"I promised myself I'd make changes in my life; do something to make the world a better place."

She nodded with approval. "So you became a SEAL."

His smile was wry. "Not exactly. First I spent six months in traction. I trained for a year after that. Then I joined the Navy, went to Officer Candidate School in Pensacola. Then I went to BUDs—basic underwater demolition and SEAL training in Coronado. I had to roll out the first time around because my back wasn't up to it. I finally graduated with class 235. That's when I became a SEAL."

"Any regrets?" she asked.

A few bleak memories flickered in his eyes but he shook his head. "Not about quitting football, no."

They fell quiet as the waitress reappeared bearing their meals. "Flounder and stuffed clam shells," she announced. "How's the wine?"

"Delicious," Hannah replied with an innocent smile.

"Enjoy your dinner," said the girl, moving away.

"You know, if you weren't so famous," Hannah remarked, cutting into her flounder, "you'd be great for the Agency."

"Thank you," Luther said, "but I'll stay where I am." His expression darkened. "Unless Jaguar loses his case."

"He won't," she promised him.

They fell quiet as they savored the food. Luther nudged her under the table, bringing her gaze up sharply. One of the cops was coming toward them. A fish bone lodged itself in Hannah's windpipe. She snatched up her water and chased it down.

"Evening, folks," said the bewhiskered cop with a shallow smile. "How're you doin' tonight?"

"Just fine, Officer. Yourself?" Luther dabbed his mouth with his napkin.

Hannah's gaze dropped to the officer's name tag. *Duffy.*

"You must be from out of town," the officer wagered.

"Yes, we are." Luther's tone was affable.

"Where you from?" the man persisted.

"Virginia Beach area." The restaurant seemed to have gotten awfully quiet. "We're on our honeymoon."

"Congratulations. I don't suppose you own that little Nissan parked over at Magnolia Manor?"

Luther betrayed no reaction to the question, even when it was blatantly obvious that the cop was fishing for information. "No, actually, the car belongs to a friend of mine."

"Ah, well. I happen to run a check on all the cars that come to town, and I come to find that car's got an unpaid speeding ticket."

"Does it? I'll have to remind my friend to pay it."

"You do that. We run a pretty tight ship up this a'way. Bein' in the Navy you ought to appreciate that."

"Navy?" Luther shook his head.

"Your friend has military stickers on his car," the cop explained.

"Ah," said Luther, admitting nothing.

"You mind showing me your driver's licenses?" he asked. They'd come to the point of this conversation. "Just in case you're the owner of the car and you're shy 'bout tellin' me," he added with an oily smile.

Luther tugged his wallet out of his rear pocket and handed over his license, taking care to hide his military ID. The cop seemed more interested in seeing Hannah's ID. She was grateful that they'd waited a day for it. As the police looked at her photo, then her face, then back at the card, turning it over to assess its authenticity, she held her breath.

"Good picture, Miss Lindstrom," he finally said, handing their IDs back. "Can't say the same for you, though," he added, needling Luther. "Ya'll enjoy your stay. Ma'am." With a final nod, he moved away to join his buddies who, in one accord, stood up to leave.

Luther kept an eye on the window.

Hannah cut out another piece of her fillet and chewed it slowly, covering up the fact that her heart was beating fast. They waited until the chatter in the restaurant resumed its normal volume to discuss the confrontation.

"What do you think?" Hannah asked.

"Lovitt gave them a heads-up, but they're not sure it's you," Luther guessed.

"We need to move fast," Hannah suggested.

"No. They'll be watching us tonight. We go straight back to the B and B and we stay there. Tomorrow we'll sightsee," he added, "keeping our eyes peeled. Don't forget Westy's out there making inquiries."

"I guess you're right," Hannah conceded.

At the same time, it occurred to her that it might just be more dangerous to lock themselves in their room—just the two of them—than to be out and about, scrounging for evidence. Spending time one-on-one with Luther was quickening something inside her, something that demanded her attention. If she wasn't careful, her feelings for him would threaten the plans she'd nurtured for years now. She was growing less obsessed with returning to the CIA and more interested in spending time with Luther. Right about now, she'd give anything for a second kiss.

Chapter Nine

Luther floated in a semiconscious state, resisting the pull toward a deeper sleep. With the cops in Sabena so suspicious, it was safer to stay awake. He dozed sitting up in the sofa chair, his MP-5 propped within reaching distance.

For the first hour he listened to Hannah toss and turn as she fought to fall asleep. Every sigh she made had him recollecting how soft her hands were, how long and slim her fingers. The rest of her body would be softer still.

She'd said and done things tonight that had ratcheted his awareness of her to a whole new level.

Is there possibly some part of you that's little? she'd asked with a teasing smile that had made him realize that sex with Hannah would be downright fun. He'd envisioned himself pinning her to the wall, sliding himself up inside of her, and saying, *Does that feel little to you?*

Luther shifted in the chair. Thoughts like those weren't going to get him anywhere but into trouble. Hannah was hot, yes. He'd known that the minute he'd laid eyes on her, and he'd been wary of his attraction ever since.

But she wasn't the woman for him. She wasn't going to keep the home fires burning while he went out doing what he did. In fact, she would rather be on the front lines, fighting alongside him. Therefore, regardless of how pleasant he found her company to be, how tempted he was to slip into bed with her and exorcize his burgeoning need for her, he wasn't going to do it.

His cell phone vibrated, doing a dance on the bureau. Luther leaped out of the chair, snatching it up before it wakened Hannah. He carried it into the bathroom and shut the door. "Lindstrom," he said.

"Sir." It was Westy reporting in. "I've talked to several people this evening. I think I have a fix on Lovitt's warehouse. It belongs to another Blaylock, the sheriff's brother."

Bingo. "Where is it?" he asked, staring at the whites of his eyes in the bathroom mirror.

"Just across the river from where you are, sir. You'll see it when the sun comes up. I'm going in for a job interview in the morning. I'll bring the camera, in case I see anything." Master Chief had handed off the infrared camera he'd used to recon Miller's apartment.

"Good work, Chief. Keep me posted."

A strangled sound had Luther spinning toward the bedroom. He severed the call abruptly, wishing he'd brought his MP-5 into the bathroom with him.

Cracking the door, he peered into the room. To his relief, there was no intruder. Hannah lay rigidly upon the bed. She'd kicked the sheets off, caught in the grips of a nightmare.

"No!" she cried, bringing her fists up as if holding on to something.

He went to rouse her. "Hannah," he said, shaking her shoulders lightly. Even in the dark, her hair shone a deep, dark red. He was dying to run his fingers through it.

To his astonishment, she threw her arms around him, seizing him in a headlock. He had one knee up on the bed, and as she rolled, she took his head with her. He ended up flat on his back with Hannah straddling his hips, pinning him to the mattress.

He was immediately aware of her crotch, positioned over his hips. She smelled of the French milled soap that came courtesy of the B and B. And the only thing between him and her naked skin was Westy's Harley-Davidson T-shirt and a pair of running shorts. His ears started ringing for the blood that surged abruptly.

But there was just enough moon glow coming through the gauzy curtains to illumine Hannah's dazed expression. She wasn't trying to seduce him. She was caught in a state between dreams and reality. He'd seen that look on the faces of exhausted SEAL candidates during Hell Week.

"What's happening?" she asked, disoriented.

"You were dreaming," he explained, wriggling out from under her.

"Oh," she said, brushing her hair out of her eyes. "Yes, it's always the same damn dream. I'm so tired of it."

Her vulnerability tugged at him. The Hannah that he knew was amazingly strong, intelligent, fearless. This was the side of herself she kept under lock and key.

"You want to talk about it?" he invited. It couldn't hurt to alleviate some of the pressure she was under.

She rubbed her eyes and sighed. "For some stupid reason, I'm in the plane with my parents. I'm the copilot, trying to help my father recover the plane, only it keeps going down."

Jesus, he hadn't realized this was about her parents. He didn't have the words to comfort her on that level. "Oh, sweetheart," he said, smoothing a lock of hair behind her ear. The endearment startled him, rolling off his tongue so easily. But then, he'd been calling her that all evening as a part of their role-playing.

To his dismay, tears welled up in her eyes. She twisted away and dropped her face into her pillow. She lay there as still as a statue, not making a sound.

Luther heaved a silent sigh. *Shit.* He couldn't ignore her upset just because she threatened his self-control. That would make him an ass.

He lay down cautiously beside her. Keeping several inches between them, he swept a comforting hand up and down her back. Her chest convulsed. God, he hurt for her. He didn't even want to imagine what it would be like to lose both parents at once.

And then to be the oldest child, to put her dreams on hold in order to care for her sibling. It took a special kind of person to get through that, still capable of smiling.

Without warning, Hannah rolled toward him. She threw an arm around his neck and held on tight. And just like last night, her trim, athletic body conformed to his. Last night he'd had jeans on. Tonight he wore pajama pants that did nothing to conceal his mounting awareness of her. But Hannah seemed oblivious. She sniffed, wiped her eyes, released a shaky sigh. And then she fell asleep.

Again.

Luther regarded the flecks of moonlight dancing along the ceiling. Honestly, this had never happened before. He'd had women drooling over him for years, practically begging him to get in bed with them, and here Hannah had fallen asleep on him, not once, but twice. He felt a little chagrined.

On the heels of chagrin came flattery and gratitude. She must really trust him. Nor did she tempt his restraint by trying to seduce him. He knew what would happen if they made love: He would like her even more than he did now, which was a hell of a lot.

Hannah wasn't for him—no way. In fact, aside from her unfaithfulness, Ronnie had come closer to fulfilling his idealized version of the perfect mate. Hannah was a future case officer, eager to put her information-gathering skills to work and to head out overseas. She was the last woman in the world who'd want to settle down and live a simple life.

So, come morning, he'd be glad that he didn't slide a hand up under her T-shirt. But all night long, apparently, he was going to have to battle the impulse.

Hannah hummed in her sleep, reveling in her starkly sensual dream. Her arms were locked around a massive chest, one leg crooked over a muscled thigh. This had to be Luther she was touching. No other man in the world had a body like this.

She smoothed a hand over a flexing pectoral muscle. His skin was velvety smooth, sprinkled with crisp chest hair that tickled her fingers as she sifted through it. Remembering the line of fuzz that arrowed over his abdomen, she traced it with her fingertips, driven by female curiosity.

The fuzz grew softer, less distinct. To her disappointment, she encountered the barrier of an elasticized waistband. But, wait, this was a dream, so the only true barriers were those in her mind, right?

She slipped her fingers under the elastic band and . . . *oh, my.*

He was as hard and smooth as a fantasy ought to be. And that code name, Little John, was a serious misnomer.

Thrilled by her obvious effect on him, she banded the offering and he jumped against her palm.

"Do you know what you're doing?"

Luther's rough inquiry had her questioning reality. She cracked her eyes open and found herself lying hip to hip with him, her mouth pressed to his shoulder, her hand inside his pants.

She snatched it free, looking up at the same time into his dark blue, highly alert gaze. "Sorry!" she exclaimed. She rolled away so fast that she fell off the bed.

"Careful."

"I'm fine." She jumped up, too mortified to look his way. Throwing open her suitcase, she snatched up the clothes she would wear that day, along with her disguise. All the while, she could feel Luther's brooding gaze on her.

With her hands full, she raced for the bathroom, shu the door between them and put her back to it, humiliated.

Now he knew that she found him h-o-t, hot. Not only was his body incredible but he was hero material right down to the bone. He'd held her all night long because she'd needed him. He was appealing enough to begin with—earnest, honest, all-American. But his kindness was the clincher. It made him irresistible.

Only Luther couldn't make it more obvious that he didn't want to get with her. Sure, he'd offered comfort when she needed it, but there was a look in his eyes that warned her to keep her distance. She could only guess that he wasn't over Veronica yet. Or maybe he found Hannah revolting in her disguise. Or, more likely still, he figured she'd make a lousy lifelong partner.

That last possibility bothered her the most, though of course it was probably true. What kind of wife took off to the other side of the world, giving everything to her career and feeding leftovers to the man she loved?

Loved? Holy cow, where had that thought come from? Hannah turned abruptly toward the shower and cranked on the hot water. She wouldn't waste another moment thinking of her and Luther.

He was standing at the window when she reemerged wearing a mauve pantsuit that was a decade out of style. In the guise of Rebecca Lindstrom, she felt considerably less exposed.

"I think we found Ernie's lover," he drawled, glancing at her briefly.

Hannah crossed to the window to peer outside. Magnolia Manor stood on a hill overlooking a line of cedar trees and a wide, snaking river. On the opposite shore stood a large, clapboard warehouse.

The building boasted a substantial pier, wide enough for loading and unloading cargo. Half a dozen men milled about, enjoying cigarette breaks in the early morning sunshine.

"The water looks deep enough for big boats," Luther observed. He glanced at her sidelong. "They rent canoes here," he added. "I think we'll take one out."

"Yes," she said, eager for exercise.

He turned toward the bathroom, making no comment on what had happened earlier.

Grateful, Hannah turned to straighten up the bed. If he could forget about her behavior this morning, then so could she. If only this lingering yearning would go away also.

Luther had just discarded his shirt when his cell phone rang. He dug in the rear pocket of his jeans, careful not to disturb the balance of the canoe.

At the other end of the craft, Hannah shaded her eyes against the noon sun as she glanced over her shoulder. Her gaze touched briefly on his naked chest, then jumped away.

"Lindstrom."

"Sir, you look pretty conspicuous without a shirt," Westy drawled, telling Luther that he was close by.

"Yeah, well, it's hot," Luther countered. Not only that, but he had a perverse desire to see Hannah blush the way she'd blushed that morning.

Once out on the canoe, she'd become an uncomplaining helmswoman. They'd forged the river for hours, studying the activity at the warehouse. Luther acquainted himself with the water's temperature and tidal current. There was a chance he'd have to swim across the river tonight to get a closer look. Hannah wielded her paddle with the same skill and determination that she did all things. She'd retreated behind her disguise, leaving him feeling confused and dangerously aroused.

"Where are you?" he asked Westy.

"In the woods, a hundred yards upriver. Look for a sock on a tree branch."

"Be right there. Out." Luther slid his phone back into his pocket. "We need to talk to Westy," he said to Hannah. "He's waiting upriver."

Without a word, she swiveled in her seat and stuck her paddle into the muddy blue water. So much for unsettling her. He wasn't even sure exactly what he wanted—a civilized discussion as to why they shouldn't get involved . . . or more of the same.

"Do you mind watching the canoe?" he asked, pulling one end of it ashore a minute later.

She looked put-out but resigned. "Fine," she said.

Luther left her glaring after him as he stepped into a deserted bit of forest, leaves crunching under his tennis shoes. It was broad daylight. He was determined to spot Westy before the man had a chance to scare him, which was how he got his kicks.

Aside from a darting squirrel, the forest appeared deserted. Luther turned in a slow circle and nearly jumped out of his skin when Westy materialized beside him, having stepped from behind a tree. "Jesus!" he swore.

Westy, who was wearing a khaki-colored T-shirt with the sleeves ripped off, clicked his tongue in mock disapproval and handed him a piece of paper.

"What's this?"

"Sketch of the warehouse. I just finished my interview. Don't think I got the job, though. They're leery of outsiders. But at least I got a look around."

"Did you see anything? Take any pictures?"

Westy shook his head. "There was nothing to see. I drew this, though." His idea of a sketch was an elaborate drawing with details that only an artist would notice.

"This is great. Any chance we can walk in?"

"Nope. The locks on the doors are complex, and there's an alarm system. We'll definitely have to swim in."

"Sorry about that." Westy's distaste for diving was no secret, but as a SEAL he'd learned to deal with it. What made this particular dive so dangerous was the fact that they didn't know the river well at all. Neither one of them had swum in it before. Doing so in broad daylight would only draw suspicion, which meant that it was going to be a night dive.

Fortunately, they had their diving gear with them. Their wet suits, complete with Draeger Rebreathers, were crammed into the back of Westy's car.

"Meet me at the Manor, down by the canoes, at zero three hundred hours," Luther decided, "ready to dive. Put your stuff in the car first in case we have to take off."

"Yes, sir."

"Questions?" Luther asked.

Westy peered off in the direction of the river. "How'd it go at the lovers' retreat?" he asked, that devilish smirk on his face.

The memory of Hannah's lusty palm on his joystick brought heat to Luther's face. "Fine," he said shortly.

"Have we heard from Valentino?" Westy asked, astute enough to change topics.

"He's still out of the country." Luther had tried to reach the agent several times. "Presumably on a very hot lead. Wouldn't it be great if Lovitt and his boss could go to jail together?" he mused.

Westy muttered something about Lovitt getting it up the ass for the next twenty years.

"Keep your sketch, Chief. Use it to come up with a COA."

"Yes, sir," he said, content to plan their course of action. "So, what's Hannah going to do?" he inquired.

When had Westy started calling Hannah by her first name? "She'll sit tight," Luther replied, disliking the jealousy that nipped at him briefly.

"She won't like that."

Luther'd already guessed as much. "Well, unless the CIA trains their people on how to dive, she's not coming with us," he countered.

Westy just looked at him.

"I'll see you at zero three hundred hours, Chief," Luther said, releasing him. "Call me if something comes up."

"Yes, sir." Westy turned and melted into the forest.

Swear to God, the man hadn't taken five steps before he disappeared.

Returning to the canoe, Luther found Hannah swatting a fly from her head and flapping air under her knit top. Her face was flushed from the heat, and she looked more than just a little irritated. "What's the plan?" she asked.

"Westy and I have to swim into the warehouse through

the berthing area," he said, pushing the canoe off the shore. "All other points of entry are secured."

Hannah faced forward. "And what am I going to do?" she asked over her shoulder.

He pushed the boat into the water, stepping in at the last second. It kept him from having to answer.

Hannah didn't paddle. She waited, one ear cocked in his direction as she sat there with the paddle on her lap. "Luther," she said on a warning note.

"We have to swim in, Hannah," he repeated, "using Draeger Rebreathers." He doubted she even knew what they were—special diving gear that eliminated bubbles, allowing for more clandestine insertions.

"That doesn't mean I can't take a canoe out. How are you going to bring the camera over?"

"It's waterproof."

That silenced her, at least for a moment. She sat there in her ash-brown wig, scratching an itch under her sweat-stained top, glasses fogged with perspiration. And she still looked gorgeous.

"You left me in the car at Quantico," she said, her voice taut with frustration. "You left me in Westy's house to chase down my would-be assassin. Now you want to leave me at the Manor twiddling my thumbs?"

"Hush," he urged. "Sound carries over water."

She growled at the reprimand. Luther swallowed a chuckle. He found her temper as interesting as everything else about her. Most women would be grateful to be shielded from danger. Not Hannah. She wanted to be right there in the thick of things. His respect for her crept one notch higher. "I'll let you help next time," he promised.

"Next time?" She sent a glare over her shoulder. "If we find what we need, there won't be a next time!"

He was counting on it. "Look," he soothed, still paddling alone, "Westy and I do this kind of thing all the time. We can read each other's minds. We don't need any added distractions."

"Now I'm a distraction," she said to the cloud-ridged horizon.

Heck, yeah. It was bad enough that he couldn't get this morning's interlude out of his mind. Her temper right now was turning him on. It made him want to prove to her just how much of a distraction she really was, how much of a woman. He thought of the hours they had left before tonight's planned insertion.

Time for a marathon of afternoon sex, came the undisciplined thought.

Hannah tossed a glare at him. "Is that really all I am?" she demanded. "A distraction?" Her gaze dropped to his gleaming torso.

He decided to go with honesty. "You distracted me pretty well this morning." He watched with satisfaction as her cheeks flamed pink.

She faced abruptly forward, for once at a loss for words.

Luther's pull on the paddle lagged. He realized suddenly that his arms ached, so he laid the paddle across his knees and let the current carry them.

The scent of brackish water filled his lungs. An osprey winged overhead, eyeing the river for darting fish. A breeze set the leaves to flutter on the approaching shore. It was lovely. But thunderclouds piled high on the horizon, promising foul weather.

Luther wiped the sweat from his brow and started paddling again. As they approached the other side, Hannah joined the effort, sending vicious strokes through the water as if she couldn't get to shore fast enough—or away from him.

She said nothing to him as they dragged the canoe onto land and turned it over.

"We need to stow our stuff in the car this afternoon," he said, "without being seen."

"We're leaving tonight?" she asked, glancing at him quickly.

"If we have to. It's just a precaution."

"If we stay, you can sleep in the chair," she announced. And with that, she hurried ahead of him, knit pants clinging damply to her thighs as she all but ran for the entrance.

You'd better run, little girl.

He tamped down the impulse to chase after her; to throw her onto the bed and prove how thoroughly distracting he found her. That was what Veronica would have wanted. Taunting and running were standard operating procedure for her.

But not for Hannah. He didn't know exactly how he knew that, only that he did.

Entering the room in her wake, he heard her in the bathroom, showering. Her knit top and wig were on the bed; her clothes lay in a heap on the floor.

Luther's heart beat thick and heavy.

He tossed aside his shirt and kicked his own shoes off. His fingers settled on the zipper of his jeans.

Stop, he commanded of himself. *Think. Are you ready for this?*

He knew his weaknesses even better than he knew his strengths. Once he made Hannah his, he wasn't going to want to give her up.

So, no, he wasn't ready. This wasn't going to happen.

His relationship with Veronica had taught him a lesson he couldn't afford to ignore. Finding the right woman was crucial. Until he met a woman whose goals in life meshed with his, right to the names of their unborn children, he wasn't going to get involved. What was the use of making mistakes if you failed to learn from them?

He'd done a lot of tough things in his three years as a Navy SEAL. Walking away was one of them.

It was a perfect night for insertion. Thunder rumbled continuously as thunderheads swept over Sabena, drenching the landscape. Lightning stabbed fiery fingers toward treetops and the roofs of buildings. No one in his right mind would go out on a night like tonight.

Hannah hung over the balcony rail, watching Luther disappear into the dark as he jogged toward the river. Supposedly, Westy was waiting down by the canoes, wearing the second diving rig. Luther had donned the first here in their bedroom, giving Hannah a fascinating glimpse of how the rebreather worked, recycling the diver's own air to eliminate bubbles.

Dressed in a wet suit with his gear slung over one shoulder, he'd left, dropping over the balcony, into the silvery rain. Hannah quivered with the need to follow. But as Luther had bluntly pointed out, there was nothing she could do.

She sighed, rubbing away the goose bumps that prickled

her skin. Temperatures were plummeting, bringing a distinctly autumnal chill. Sometimes, it was the woman's destiny to wait, she reasoned. Or was it?

Her spirits rallied as an option occurred to her. Actually, there *was* something she could do, she realized, turning toward the room to find her shoes. Luther had underestimated her capabilities for the last time.

Chapter Ten

"Here, sir."

He did it again. Luther jumped at the sound of Westy's voice, practically in his ear. The chief stood against the tree trunk next to him, camouflaged in his black wet suit.

Luther glared at him. He checked over Westy's equipment, and the chief did the same for him, wordlessly and with efficiency that came from regular practice.

Westy's favorite knife was strapped to his webbed belt. They would take no other weapons with them, their purpose being simply to photograph anything suspicious with the camera that was stowed in Luther's belt pouch.

Securing their masks and popping the mouthpiece between their teeth, both men waded into the water at their insertion point. They sank into mud up to their calves.

Even in the dark, Luther noted Westy's shudder. They walked in until the water was up to their waists, nodded, and went under.

Their masks were designed for nighttime dives and

equipped with state-of-the-art infrared screening capabilities. What appeared from the surface to be a solid body of water was, in fact, a world of darting fish, sunken branches, hills and troughs, and shimmering organisms that were probably shrimp.

Luther consulted his underwater compass, and they struck out, crossing the creek that was surprisingly deep. After a hundred yards or so, they'd crossed the channel, and the complex network of pilings on which the warehouse was constructed. Neither man had surveyed the area from their current perspective.

They headed into the forest of sunken pilings, following the channel that had been dredged to allow big boats to dock inside. The muddy river bottom was only a few meters below them when they swam beneath the warehouse's outer wall. They came up against a bulkhead, and they were in the berthing area.

To their mutual dismay, the interior of the warehouse was illuminated. They would have preferred operating in the dark. If anyone was up there, they'd be seen.

Luther signaled that he would surface first. Keeping close to the bulkhead, he poked his head out of the water and lifted his mask to look around. A dozen naked lightbulbs dangled here and there, casting a paltry glow over stacked wooden crates, dollies, and huge refrigerators.

Not a soul in sight. He signaled the all-clear to Westy and they moved to the only ladder. Removing their flippers, they stowed them behind the ladder and climbed out stealthily in rubber booties.

The warehouse was immense. This berthing area alone was big enough to house a boat of substantial dimensions.

Luther glanced at Westy, who gestured toward the nearest wall. Their movements were muted by the drum of rain on the tin roof overhead.

Luther opened the door of the closest refrigerator. The smell of fish and oysters assaulted him. The place was an authentic seafood warehouse, no question of that. Imagine working here all day, Luther thought, finding the floor slippery under his booties.

He and Westy moved methodically along the wall, peering into each container they came upon. They found catfish, croaker, flounder, sea bass, and enough oysters to feed the entire population of Virginia, but nothing suspicious.

Luther moved to a mound of crates. Either they'd just been unloaded or they were left here in anticipation of being shipped off soon. He tried to tug one open but it had been nailed fast.

Westy found a discarded hammer and, at Luther's nod, wrestled the nails free. One gave a squeak that echoed off the ceiling. Both men held their breath.

The quiet that followed reassured them enough to proceed. At last Westy was able to lift the lid. Luther pushed aside the straw stuffing. What he saw there made his scalp tighten.

Amid the stuffing lay a collection of AK-47s, just like the ones that had disappeared off a frigate bound for Somalia a month ago. Hot damn, they'd found Lovitt's hidden stash! He brushed aside the stuffing, hunting for serial numbers, anything that would link these weapons to the stolen ones.

He had to break out a penlight to find the numbers. With

a tremor of excitement, he took pictures of the weapons and several close-ups of the numbers etched into them.

They moved to another crate, taking less care to keep silent as they struggled to open it. A scuffling sound caused them to freeze like thieves and turn their heads. What they saw made Luther's blood run cold.

A Doberman pinscher stood not twenty feet away, regarding him through eyes that glowed yellow.

Westy reached slowly for his knife. Luther knew the chief could peg the animal in the heart if he had to. They both eyed the distance to the water, gauging their ability to dive in before the dog could rush them.

"Easy boy," Luther crooned, backing slowly toward the water.

The dog growled low in its throat.

"Hold it right there!" The voice came out of nowhere, echoing off the high ceiling. Beyond the watchdog, an elderly man stepped out of the shadows bearing a shotgun that was aimed at Luther's chest. "Who the hell do you think you are trespassin' on private property?"

The man wore a security officer's uniform. Turning themselves over to him was not an option. Luther nudged Westy's arm, signaling for them to get the hell out. They both leaped into the water, jamming their mouthpieces into their mouths as they sank as deep as possible.

A sudden explosion coincided with a burning sensation in Luther's back, near his right shoulder blade. He flinched from it, twisting down and away, as he'd been trained to do to avoid taking another bullet. Two more pellets strafed the water close by. He glanced at Westy, relieved to see the chief beside him, unhurt. He reached for Luther, tugging him in the direction they needed to go.

A barnacled column scraped the right side of Luther's face as he veered too close to it. He fumbled to don the mask that was drifting off his head.

He'd been shot. He couldn't let the realization slow him down, but they'd had to leave their flippers behind, making their exit that much slower. Westy kept one hand on the strap of Luther's rebreather and propelled him forward, kicking hard for the both of them. Luther could see blood forming around him in a neon-green cloud.

By the time they reached the opposite shore, he felt too weak to slog through the mud. Westy propped a shoulder under him, urging him through it.

"My fault, sir," he panted. "I assumed the place was locked down at night. Didn't do my homework."

"We got what we needed," Luther answered, willing away the pain that radiated from his shoulder and down his spine. "We need to leave before the police get on it."

"Roger that."

He was about to give more detailed suggestions when a twig snapped ahead of them. Both men froze, peering into the inky darkness, expecting the worst.

"Luther? Westy?" A woman's voice sang out softly over the patter of rain.

It was Hannah. The men breathed a sigh of relief and moved in her direction, staying behind the trees. "Here," Westy called. "What are you doing outside?" he demanded.

Gee, that was the same question Luther had.

"I thought I heard a gunshot. What happened?"

"Lieutenant's been hit. It doesn't look too bad, but we need to leave now—"

"Luther!" And there she was, her spectacles flashing in the dark, her hands touching him lightly. "Where were you hit? Oh, your face is bleeding."

"It's just a cut."

"We need to keep moving," Westy reminded them.

Hannah went to prop herself under Luther's other arm. "We're all set. I pushed the car to the head of the driveway."

They looked at her for a stunned second. "You what?" Luther said.

"You're out of control, ma'am," Westy said with a chuckle.

Hannah's forethought would keep their departure from being overheard. Luther should have thought of it himself.

Right now it was all he could do to put one foot in front of the other. Every step jarred his shoulder. He leaned on his companions, counting on them to guide him through the pine trees to their vehicle. Over their laboring breaths came the wail of sirens as police presumably raced to the warehouse, hailed by the ancient night watchman.

Sabena's finest would know right away who was behind the break-in. It wouldn't take long for the flippers to be found. To protect their dirty secret, the police would do whatever it took to keep the interlopers from getting away.

Hannah opened the passenger door and dove into the back. Westy lowered Luther into the passenger seat. It hurt more to sit in the low-slung car than it did to stand. Luther swallowed a moan and put his hands over his face.

"Find a shirt," Westy told Hannah. "Put pressure on his back here."

As Hannah hunted for a clean shirt, Westy jumped into the driver's side and was pulling them away before he'd even shut his door.

"This isn't the way we came in," Hannah said from the back as Westy hung a left. At the same time, she put pressure over the place where Luther had been shot and he almost went through the roof.

Shit, shit, shit! Luther forced his eyes back open, using willpower to thrust aside the pain. He saw Westy hand a map to Hannah.

"I'm taking a back way out. See if you can find a naval installation within an hour from here. They'll expect us to head south toward Virginia Beach. Find something to the north."

Westy was all business when the going got tough. He accelerated, sending them screaming along a wooded road at a speed that made Luther long for his seat belt. The road was slick with the rain that had finally ceased, just like the night he'd driven into the scrub oaks in his Lamborghini.

Hannah must have read his mind. "Here, hon." She leaned over him, breasts brushing his shoulder as she drew the seat belt harness across his chest. With a grunt, she locked it into place.

Hon? "Thank you."

There wasn't a single other vehicle on the road, but there was plenty of wildlife, including a family of deer grazing at the roadside and a possum waddling straight into their path.

Westy swerved expertly and missed it. He slowed as they approached an intersection and came to a stop, his car idling loudly. Deserted roads trailed into darkness in three different directions. "I have no idea where we are," he admitted. "Let me see that map."

"We're here," Hannah said, handing it to him and pointing. "The only way out of the area will take us east about thirty miles. If we're going to travel in that direction, we might as well haul it to Patuxent River Naval Air Station. It's a ways away, but they'll never think to look for us in that direction."

Westy studied the map for a second, no doubt memorizing the route. "Pax River it is," he determined. "Hold tight," he said, extinguishing the light.

Luther braced himself for takeoff. His shoulder blade throbbed with every heartbeat. He'd started to shiver, despite the wet suit that was supposed to prevent hypothermia. He shifted, trying in vain to get comfortable.

Hannah peered under the shirt that stanched his wound. "It isn't bleeding too badly," she told him. "You'll make it another forty-five minutes or so, right?"

She sounded anxious.

"I'm fine," he lied. To help combat the pain he reminded himself that they had what they needed to prove Lovitt's guilt. Surely it would undermine his testimony against Jaguar.

They needed to inform Valentino right away. If he thought they'd wait for him to arrest the Individual, he was crazy. They needed to get these pictures to the NCIS so that Lovitt could be made to answer for his crimes.

With painstaking movements, Luther flipped open Westy's glove compartment to find his cell phone. They were still in a rural area, and the signal strength was paltry, but he held down the 7 all the same to speed-dial Valentino, and—hallelujah—the call went through.

"Valentino." The agent sounded wide awake, even at this ungodly hour.

"You're back," said Luther. "I hope you found what you were looking for."

"Who's this?" the agent asked.

"Luther Lindstrom."

"You sound different."

"Yeah, well, I've been shot. We found weapons in a warehouse in Sabena, and we took pictures."

He'd managed to shock Valentino into silence. "Are you going to be all right?" he asked.

"I think so. When are you going to arrest the Individual? I want to turn these pictures over to NCIS."

"Soon," Valentino promised. "In the meantime, I could use a duplicate set. Where are you?" he asked.

"North of Sabena. We're heading to Pax River. There's a hospital on the base."

"I'll meet you there," said Valentino.

"Yes, sir. Out." Luther dropped his arm, hoping the FBI would support them in something they should have handled all along. Pain shot down his spine, making him moan.

He sensed Westy's look of concern. "We'll be there soon, sir. Oh, fuck, maybe not. There's a cop behind us."

The pressure on his shoulder eased as Hannah turned to assess the situation. Luther used the passenger side mirror to see behind them. Sure enough, there was a trooper gaining on them, blue lights flashing.

"What's our COA, sir?" Westy queried.

Luther cursed his injury. If he could hold a gun and angle himself out the window, he'd opt for shooting out the cop's tires. "Keep driving," he said.

"I'll get rid of him," Hannah volunteered, her tone confident. "Westy, where's your gun?"

"Can you shoot the tires?" Westy asked, sounding hopeful.

"No problem."

"Just a second," Luther interrupted. "We don't need any casualties on our hands."

"You promised I could help the next time," Hannah reminded him. "Where's the gun?"

"In my duffel bag. Zipper on the right side," Westy said.

She needed to free the hand that was putting pressure on Luther's wound. "Lean back," she ordered him, wedging the cloth between him and the seat. *Oh, Jesus God in heaven that hurt!*

Through the ringing in his ears, Luther heard her thumping around in the back, wrestling with their luggage. "Got it." She slid the magazine out of Westy's SIG and checked the chamber for a round. "Can you open the hatch from the inside?" she asked.

"Permission, sir?" Westy fell back on protocol.

"Granted," Luther growled with great reluctance. "Whatever you do, don't miss!" he begged. If she killed a state trooper, he could kiss his career good-bye.

"I won't," Hannah promised.

Westy popped the hatch. Hannah had to push it open, battling the force of the wind. "Slow down!" she shouted as a cold, wet breeze rushed into the vehicle, chilling Luther to the bone. "Bring it down to thirty-five and hold it steady."

Westy obliged, easing off the accelerator. Luther watched through the passenger side mirror, his heart in his throat as the blue lights bore down on them. No siren, he noted. The officer didn't want to alarm them, wanted to make it look like he was citing them for speeding.

The car drew closer, close enough for Luther to note its white paint. He squinted at the logo on the hood, doing his best to see it through the haze of pain that clouded his vision. "Sabena Police," he gritted.

"Shoot," Westy instructed. He'd slowed down to thirty-five, but the car behind them was doing at least seventy. The driver obviously intended to ram them. "He wants to hit us!"

Just as Westy shifted a foot toward the accelerator, his SIG exploded. The sound of squealing rubber assured Luther that Hannah had found her mark. She fired again, filling the car with the smell of cordite.

In the mirror, Luther watched the pursuing vehicle swerve out of control. Spinning up gravel, it fishtailed wildly before veering into the drainage ditch. The driver would probably be fine.

Westy floored the gas pedal, picking up speed. "Damn good shooting!" he praised. "How'd you like that, sir?" he asked, grinning like a madman. The hatch slammed shut under the force of the wind.

"Couldn't have done better myself," Luther acknowledged. The pain seemed suddenly to have magnified, making it impossible to keep his eyes open. It was all he could do not to howl like a baby. He heard himself moan.

Suddenly Hannah was close to him, looping one arm across his chest in a comforting embrace. He thought about yesterday morning, when she'd reached for him so enthusiastically. He wished he'd taken her up on the invitation. At least he'd have the memory of that pleasure to take his mind off the pain.

Dizziness catapulted through him, dragging darkness in around him. "I'm going to pass out," he warned them.

Hannah reacted immediately, pressing a lever to tip his seat backward. Instead of smashing his nose into the dashboard, he slumped back into her lap.

Chapter Eleven

"Welcome back, Lieutenant."

Luther pried his sticky eyelids open. He found himself in what appeared to be a hospital recovery room. The sterile space was crammed with IVs, tubes, and medical implements bleeping and beeping away. In fact, one of the IVs dripped into his own left hand. His right arm was bound to his chest. He couldn't feel any pain, so he supposed he was doing fine.

"I'm Rexanne," said the large black woman checking his pulse. She had jowls like a pit bull's and hair growing on her chin. He wondered where Hannah was.

"How are you feeling?" she asked in a no-nonsense tone.

He tried to sit up. He couldn't afford to loiter here.

"Oh, no. Unh-uh!" Rexanne halted his ascent with a man-sized hand. "You're not going anywhere just yet. Give yourself a day or so."

"I need to check out," Luther insisted. Jaguar's Article 32 hearing was tomorrow.

Rex raised penciled-in eyebrows at him. "Those pellets

may not have struck any vital organs, but you have twenty-two stitches that will tear right open if you move too fast. I've dealt with your kind before," she warned him, her dark eyes bulging. "Don't you even think about leaving this hospital until the commander gives the all-clear."

Luther closed his eyes and waited for her to go away.

"Of course, you'll have to explain how you got shot," Rex added archly. "As soon as you're up to it, an officer from Patient Safety will be in to see you."

Luther cracked his eyes open. "Where's my chief and the girl that was with him?" He didn't like having Hannah out of his sight any longer than necessary.

"We only let family into Post-Op," the nurse informed him. "They're waitin' in the room we've set up for you."

"What'll it take to get me out of here?" he asked testily.

To his horror, Rexanne pursed her lips in a sly, considering manner. "I'll let the commander know you're feeling better," she said, jotting down his pulse. She moved away at last, and he breathed a sigh of relief.

What seemed an eternity later, Nurse Rex wheeled him down the hallway toward a room. This military facility, unlike the one near home, had yet to be renovated. It still touted hanging halogen lights and the infamous dark green tiles that had been put into every square foot of government-owned property fifty years ago.

The nurse pivoted his gurney expertly through an open door. He was relieved to see Westy conked out in the lounge chair. Hannah was sleeping on his bed.

She sat up at his entrance, too groggy to contain the look of melting relief she sent him. "Luther!" she cried. He glimpsed a shimmer of tears behind the lenses of her crooked glasses. Maybe it was the painkiller coursing his bloodstream, but her concern left him feeling good enough to jump from the gurney and run a 5K.

"Out," Rex commanded, ordering Hannah to evacuate his bed.

Westy rolled to his feet, looking shaggier than ever with his hair mussed and his beard poking out like a pincushion. He'd found time, at least, to change out of his wet suit into regular clothes. "How do you feel, sir?" he asked, sending Rex a wary glance.

"He needs to rest for forty-eight hours," the nurse replied on Luther's behalf. "No excitement. No moving around." She drew the gurney alongside the bed and transferred the IV solution to the hook above it. Luther scooted over quickly, afraid that the nurse might actually try to pick him up. "If you need to use the restroom," she added, "hit the call button and I'll bring you a bedpan."

Luther gaped in horror. "You're joking, right?"

"Do I look like I'm joking?" She shot him that look with her eyebrows raised.

"No, ma'am."

She heaved a ponderous sigh and shook her head in lament. "That's the problem with you officers. You have no sense of humor. You got two legs, don't you? Walk to the bathroom." She glowered at Hannah and Westy. "You two make sure he rests. I'm holdin' you accountable."

"Yes, ma'am," Westy countered, giving her a squinty-eyed look of determination. "I think she likes you," he added the moment that Nurse Rex turned the corner.

Reaching into his back pocket, Westy pulled out a folded square of paper. "Master Chief faxed this over to keep us from having to answer any questions."

"What is it?"

"A statement saying you were injured in a live-fire train-ing exercise."

"Amen to that," Luther said, scanning the paper's contents. This would keep the Patient Safety people out of his hair. "Have we heard from Valentino?"

"Not yet, sir."

"What time is it now?"

Westy glanced at his watch. "'Bout eleven thirty. How's the shoulder, sir?"

"It's fine," Luther replied. "Can't feel a thing. Listen, we need to be out of here within eight hours if we intend to make the Article 32. And we still have to brief Jaguar's lawyer on everything we know. Christ, maybe I should call her first." He ground the heel of his hand into his left eye, feeling suddenly dizzy.

"I'll call her," Hannah promised. "Are you cold, Luther? Do you want this blanket?"

"Sure."

He watched her pull up the covers, tucking them here and there. It was almost as if she were fussing over him, he thought, enjoying her attention. Despite the IV in his left hand pumping liquids inside him, his stomach rumbled. "I'm hungry," he admitted. He hadn't eaten since the night before.

"I'll check on lunch, sir," Westy volunteered, heading out the door.

Which left Luther alone with Hannah. She'd turned toward the window to adjust the drapes. "How are you supposed to rest with all this light shining in the win-dow?" she said, yanking on the stubborn curtains.

"I'll be fine." The sunlight framed her figure in a blinding halo. She made the unlikeliest of angels, but right now he wasn't thinking straight.

Giving up on the drapes, Hannah returned to his bedside. Luther groped for ordinary words, but nothing about her was ordinary, so why bother?

"I was worried," Hannah admitted. She looked away, nonplussed by her confession.

"I'm fine," he reassured her.

"Seems like everyone I . . . care about dies," she added, her eyes suspiciously bright.

She cared about him. The admission rushed over him like a Caribbean breeze. "I'm still here," he said. Their gazes met and held. He realized his close call had connected them at a deeper level, one of friendship and trust, not unlike the connection he shared with his teammates.

"I saw your tattoos," Hannah admitted with a sudden smile. "They had to cut off your wet suit in the emergency room."

Two words in Arabic script were inscribed on the backs of his calf muscles, which meant he'd been lying on his stomach while they cut his gear open. He wondered what else she'd seen.

"What do they mean?" she pressed.

"Liberty and Justice." The bond grew stronger with the admission.

"Oh, your sisters' names."

He was pleased that she remembered. "I got the tattoos right before Operation Iraqi Freedom, in case the worst thing happened. I wanted the enemy to know what I stood for."

Her expression warmed and softened. "It's pretty obvious what you stand for, Luther," she said.

He felt as if she'd reached inside him and caressed his soul. None of his teammates had ever done that. He cleared his throat, desperate to shift the conversation elsewhere. "You saved our lives last night," he said, "with your superlative marksmanship."

"I was trained just like you," she answered.

The reminder brought him up short. That's right. She was trained by the CIA to be a case officer. She wasn't going to be the next woman in his life because she was going overseas, to some scurvy little country, where she'd use her charm, wit, and, yes, maybe even her body to gather information.

So why did he even tolerate the tender feelings swirling through him? They were a waste of time.

"Here we go, sir." Westy pushed into the room, interrupting Luther's muddled thoughts. "Lunch isn't ready yet, but they still had some food from breakfast. I had them warm it up." He placed a tray laden with scrambled eggs, sausage, toast, grits, and three cartons of milk on the table by his bed.

"Thanks, Chief. This is great." Westy pushed the rolling table closer. With the IV in the only hand left to him, Luther reached awkwardly for his fork. He stabbed at a breakfast sausage and popped it in his mouth. Hannah and Westy stood there, looking at him. "Why don't you guys find yourself some food and check into temporary quarters," he suggested, stabbing the other link. But then he thought about Westy and Hannah occupying the same room, and jealousy prompted him to add, "To sleep."

Westy smiled his evil, little smile. "Yes, sir." He pulled an envelope out of his shirt pocket. "If Valentino shows up, you can give him these duplicates of the pictures we took. I put the originals on a CD." He put the envelope by Luther's bed.

"Good thinking," said Luther. The last thing they needed was for Valentino to whisk away their evidence in order to protect his own investigation. "We have to leave sometime tonight," Luther added.

"Are you sure you're going to be up to that?" Hannah asked dubiously.

"I don't have much choice," Luther countered. "If we miss the Article 32, then Jaguar's case will go to court-martial. We can't let that happen."

"I'll call," Westy promised. "The cell phone is still in my car. Rest easy, sir." He was suddenly efficient, hustling Hannah out of the room.

On her way through the door, Hannah looked back. Was that regret or concern coming out of her eyes? Luther wondered. It was hard to tell with those damn glasses on.

Not that it mattered.

Luther finished his food. With his stomach pleasantly full, he pushed the table on wheels away and settled onto his side. The IV in his left hand bothered him more than the bullet wound in his back. He tugged the blanket higher, closed his eyes, and in seconds he was sleeping, caught up in dreams.

He dreamed that Hannah came back.

I couldn't leave without doing this first. She slipped the wig off her head and shook out the short, silky waves of her hair. She took off her glasses, revealing grass-green eyes that shone with desire. Her slim, delicate fingers went to work on the buttons of her blouse.

One button at a time, the blouse eased open, revealing the sexiest demi bra he'd ever seen. The blouse slipped from her shoulders to the floor. Dry-mouthed, Luther gazed at the tops of her creamy, white breasts. Hannah climbed up over him, letting him caress her. Her nipples jutted through the silk, making his mouth water.

She kissed him with such impossible sweetness that he shuddered with need. She was giving herself to him, and it didn't matter that she'd be gone tomorrow, off to save the world. He needed her now. And if he didn't lay claim to at least some part of her, he'd regret it forever.

She slid herself against him, stroking him. And then she spread her legs, keeping eye contact. *Sweet, Jesus.* The only thing between them was the crotch of her silk panties.

"Lieutenant!"

The forceful summons jarred Luther violently from his dream. He reached out instinctively, fearing he'd nodded off on a mission and the enemy was looming over him. His right arm was oddly uncooperative. A burning sensation seared his left hand.

Who? What? Where? He blinked at the face frowning down at him, recognizing it without placing it right away.

Not a terrorist. Oh, crap, he was grabbing the lapel of Valentino's long, black trench coat.

His fingers sprang open. He sat up to utter his sincerest apologies. It was the wrong thing to do. Pain stabbed deep between his spine and shoulder blade. With a shout, he arched and collapsed on his side, as Westy's favorite five-word curse resounded in his head.

"Breathe," Valentino instructed.

Luther sucked in a breath, and the pain slowly subsided. He forced his eyes open. "Sorry," he whispered, holding up a hand to gain himself an extra second. He'd pulled the IV halfway out of his vein. With an irritable mutter, he yanked it the rest of the way out and left the IV dangling.

Valentino waved away the apology. "Been there myself," he said. Beneath the trench coat, he wore a white silk sweater with a crew collar. Paired up with the lightweight coat, he looked like an Italian priest. He held up the envelope of pictures Westy had left for him. "Where are the originals?" he asked, very gently.

Luther suffered a sudden, sharp awareness of just how incapacitated he was at the moment. "Westy has them," he said carefully.

"You can't turn them over to NCIS just yet," Valentino warned. His black eyes looked as hard as polished onyx.

"We can't let our platoon leader go to jail for something he didn't do," Luther countered.

"Understood," said Valentino. "That isn't going to happen. But we play this thing out my way, Lieutenant, or no way at all."

It was suddenly clear why Valentino had infiltrated the Italian Mafia and survived. He played the game like one of them.

Luther considered the threat, wondering what it meant, if anything. A righteous fire ignited inside of him, giving him the courage to speak his mind, given that he was lying in a hospital bed, scarcely capable of moving. "I hope you're a man of your word, sir," he retorted, holding Valentino's gaze in a challenging manner. "You wouldn't want to screw over a whole platoon of Navy SEALs, I can promise you that."

To his relief, Valentino gave him a grudging smile. His eyes glittered with private humor. "No, I wouldn't," he agreed. "Just be patient, Lieutenant. We're very close to getting our man. I'll be making an arrest here, shortly, and things should fall into place after that. Whatever you do, do not let your guard down. This will be a test of your professionalism."

What the hell did that mean? Luther wondered, trying to think over the nagging pain in his shoulder.

"How's Geary holding up?"

It was almost as if Valentino asked the question to keep Luther off balance. The memory of his dream flashed before his eyes.

"Fine," he said shortly. "She's a strong woman," he added without exaggeration.

Valentino slid his hands into the pockets of his trench coat. "Tell her she can see her brother again as soon as the Individual is in my custody. Can I get you anything before I go?"

"No." Luther just wanted him to leave so he could brood over Valentino's interference. "Thank you." If they didn't warn the NCIS about the stolen weapons, then Lovitt would clean out the warehouse before the authorities could look into it. On the other hand, maybe the pictures of the serial numbers, matching those of the missing weapons, would be enough.

With a final enigmatic look, Valentino turned around and walked out. Luther sat there a moment reviewing what Valentino had said, trying to analyze it, while ignoring the excruciating throbbing near his shoulder blade. If he intended to leave the hospital tonight, he would need some serious painkillers. He depressed the nurse call button.

A familiar voice boomed out of the little speaker. "What is it?"

"I need something for the pain," Luther growled, swallowing his manly pride.

"Already?" Nurse Rex scoffed. "You SEALs ain't nothin' but big babies. Jus' sit tight one minute, and I'll be right down. Ol' Rex goin' ta take care o' you."

He cringed as he settled on his side to wait. "That's what I'm afraid of," he whimpered.

Chapter Twelve

Leila settled deeper into her pillow-strewn couch, scowling in concentration at the murder mystery book in her lap. She refused to think about Sebastian again tonight, mooning over the memory of their evening together like some love-struck teenager. Tonight she would lose herself in a book, proving she was not obsessed with the man. She was not falling in love.

Love. The word alone left her panic-stricken. She *couldn't* fall in love with a man who jumped out of airplanes at altitudes so ridiculous he required an oxygen mask! She would *not* love a man who leaped out of bed at any hour to answer the summons of his pager. His job thrust him continuously into danger, meaning he could die tonight, tomorrow, leaving her destitute. If her heart was broken a second time, she would not survive.

Leila blinked at the print. This wasn't working. All she could think of was her lovely evening with Sebastian two long nights ago. She couldn't recall a more satisfying evening spent with anyone. And he hadn't even kissed her, except on the cheek when he put her in her car at Mike the mechanic's shop the morning after. "Enjoy your day, *querida*," he'd murmured, his espresso-colored eyes warm with tenderness.

Allah, she *was* falling in love with him! No wonder she'd wandered about all weekend feeling lost, lonely. This never-ending ache was the cost she paid for letting down her guard.

She mustn't let these feelings overtake her! Leila slapped the book shut and jumped to her feet to prowl about her living room. The Turkish carpets underfoot kept her steps silent as she paced in her chintz-noir bathroom, wringing her hands.

At all costs, she must avoid Sebastian, though it galled her to no end that he'd called her only once. He'd left a phone message inquiring after her car—was it starting for her now?

Her car! Did he care more for her car than he did for her?

Oh, what did it matter? She was done with him— through. Only, no, that wasn't possible. If she hadn't conceived yet, then she'd be calling him in just two weeks, arranging for their next encounter.

Anticipation raised goose bumps as she envisioned Sebastian kissing her in that slow, enticing manner of his, penetrating her inch by inch until she practically wept with need.

She threw herself down on the couch and moaned, a hand sliding helplessly between her thighs. She wanted him now, tonight. She wanted him every night. He'd done something to her traitorous body, cast a spell over her, become her obsession. His gentlemanly behavior hadn't done anything to abate her desire. If anything, it had only made her want him more.

By the prophets, how could she protect her heart when her body betrayed her so?

A knock at the door had her starting guiltily. She pushed to her feet, gathering her robe more securely about her frame. The hope that Sebastian had come knocking gave way to the bitter certainty that it was George, the annoying Greek who lived in the condominium next door. He was forever knocking at her door at unorthodox hours, begging for olive oil or Parmesan cheese. Her cold reception had yet to curb his persistence.

"What now, George?" she snapped, rolling up on her toes to glare through the eyehole.

What she saw on the other side made her gasp as she dropped to her heels. It wasn't George the Greek. It was Sebastian the SEAL, the very last person her heart needed to see.

Oh, mercy! Should she open the door? No, he would undermine the tenuous grip she had on her emotions. But, if she didn't let him in, how rude would that look when he'd been so hospitable the other day?

She released the dead bolt and cracked the door a scant six inches. "Hello."

The look in Sebastian's eyes could have frozen boiling water. "You were expecting George?"

Jealous. He was jealous. She sought to repress the giddiness that bubbled up at the thought. "No, he lives next door. He's very annoying."

"I see," said Sebastian. His gaze drifted over her attire. "How are you?"

Breathless. "Fine. It's very late."

"Yes," he said. "I'm sorry."

She realized then that gloominess hung over him like a shroud. "Is something wrong?"

He touched his temple as if his head were aching. "Jaguar's Article 32 hearing was today."

Hearing dismay in his voice, Leila opened the door wider. She'd spoken with Helen earlier this afternoon. Having comforted her best friend for more than an hour, she felt it only fair that she comfort Sebastian as well. "Would you like to come in?" Her knees trembled with equal parts anticipation and dread.

To her surprise, he seemed to hesitate. But then he nodded and he stepped inside, casting an eye about her tastefully decorated home. He'd been here once before, sharing a bottle of wine with her before they'd climbed the steps to her room to make love.

That wouldn't happen tonight, Leila swore. To her relief, Sebastian lowered himself into the armchair. She sat across from him on the couch, trying not to recall how she'd been touching herself here just minutes before, dreaming of him.

"Helen told me what happened—that the prosecutor presented medical evidence of paranoia, something about raised levels of cortisol, I think it was."

Sebastian nodded again. "The prosecutor's name is Garret—Captain Garret. He's never lost a case."

"Oh, dear. Helen didn't say that."

"She doesn't know," Sebastian said with meaning. He rubbed his temple again. "It shouldn't have happened as it did," he added. "We have evidence to support Jaguar's innocence, but it wasn't presented in time. Lieutenant

Lindstrom—the big man at Jaguar's barbecue?—he was shot yesterday. He found the weapons Commander Lovitt's been stealing."

"He found them!" Leila gasped. "Is he all right?"

"He will be. But he couldn't get the evidence to court in time. We tried to cast suspicion on Lovitt by linking him to the XO's death, but there's only circumstantial evidence to indicate that Miller's death wasn't a suicide."

"Miller?" Leila cocked her head. "Do you mean Jason Miller?"

Sebastian looked at her oddly. "Did you know him?"

"No, but he practically stalked Helen after Gabe disappeared last year. He dropped by to see her all the time. He even wrote her a love letter."

Sebastian's gaze sharpened. "She wouldn't still have it," he guessed.

"No, but I do. I think."

"You? Why?"

"Because Helen was going to throw it away, and I thought, this is suspicious. Here is the last man to see Gabriel Renault alive and he's professing to love Gabe's wife. How weird is that?"

Sebastian sat forward. "Where's the letter?" he asked with controlled urgency. "We need samples of his handwriting to show that his suicide note was forged."

"Can't you find that at the office?"

"We could, but he cleared out his files the day he resigned. And a signature alone—which is all we have—is not enough. Do you think you can find the letter?"

"I'll look for it," she promised, hating to let him down.

"I save everything," she confessed. "It's probably at my shop. That's where Helen showed it to me."

"Can we go and look tonight?"

"Tonight?" Her gaze flew to the clock on the wall. "It's almost midnight."

He drew a breath. "You're right. I'm sorry." He pushed to his feet, causing her heart to drop with disappointment. "There's no hurry. We have a week to prepare for the court-martial. If you find it before then, be sure to call me."

He headed for the door.

Leila got up and trailed him, tamping down the desperate urge to beg him to stay. "Do you . . ." She stammered to a halt as he turned to look at her.

He stretched out a hand and stroked her cheek. The tender gesture took her by surprise. "I have to confess something to you," he said, looking unhappy with himself.

"What?" She froze, certain that he was going to break her heart, to tell her that it was over between them.

"You are going to be angry with me," he predicted, his eyes dark with regret.

Her eyes stung. Her knees began to tremble. He couldn't do this to her now—not when he'd made himself so appealing. He couldn't just break her heart so cruelly!

"There was nothing wrong with your car the other day," he told her.

What? Her car? What did her car have to do with anything? "I'm sorry?"

"There was no electrical problem." He reached into his pocket and pulled out her second set of car keys. "I compromised the wiring so that you would have to spend the night with me. I'm very sorry, Leila." He took her frozen hand and pressed the keys into her palm. "My conscience would not allow me to keep the truth to myself. I only pray you will forgive me."

Forgive him? He wanted forgiveness?

Tears of relief sprang into her eyes, blurring the vision of his handsome face. He wasn't going to break her heart, after all.

"You'll need time to think about it," he deduced. He turned sorrowfully away, headed for his car.

"Sebastian, wait!"

He turned around. The hope that burned in his eyes reassured her that he was still very much intent upon keeping her in his life.

"There is nothing to forgive," she reassured him, softly. At one time, she might have thought differently. His subterfuge would have made her question his character, would have shattered her trust. But he'd proven by his actions that his motives were pure. "I had a beautiful time," she added, going out on a limb.

The smile he gave her melted away the last drop of fear. "We must do it again soon," he called, stepping off the curb to return to his car.

A misty rain dusted his hair and shoulders in tiny diamondlike drops, clinging to him as her emotions did.

She watched him start his car, lifting a hand in farewell as he backed up and pulled away.

We must do it again soon.

She shut the door and leaned against it, weak in the knees.

Oh, Sebastian, she thought with a sigh. *That day can't come soon enough.*

Patuxent River Naval Air Station
28 September ~ 10:14 EST

"He's back."

Luther roused to those strange words, uttered in Hannah's voice. He cracked his eyes to see her hovering over him, her hair fiery red instead of light ash-brown, her pretty eyes no longer hidden behind glasses. She still wore a dowdy brown blouse with a clown collar, but the color looked good on her.

He blinked back the grogginess that threatened to suck him back into a black abyss. Was he dreaming? He would know if she started unbuttoning her blouse.

But there was Westy marching around the foot of the bed to scowl at him. "We missed the Article 32 hearing, sir," he said, not exactly in an accusing tone but certainly an irritated one.

"What?" Luther rubbed a hand over his face hoping to relieve the feeling that he'd been bound up in mummy cloth. "What time is it?" Sun was shining brightly through the window, turning Hannah's hair to flame. "Why aren't you wearing your wig?" he asked her.

She thrust a newspaper at him that was sitting on his rollaway table. "This is why."

Luther squinted at the print. Hannah pointed to the leading article at the top of the page. FBI ARRESTS BILL WESTMORELAND, DIRECTOR OF CIA. "Westmoreland!" he exclaimed. Recalling his conversation with Valentino, his gaze flew to the date at the top of the page. He met Westy's unblinking stare. "Oh, shit." He'd slept through the night. "I thought you were going to call me."

"Oh, I called, sir," Westy said, his jaw muscles jumping. "Several times."

Luther looked at the phone beside his bed. "I didn't hear anything."

"That's why I came looking for you, but your watchdog out there caught me trying to rouse you. I'd have taken the CD back to the beach myself, only I had Hannah to think about, and I didn't think you'd approve of me taking chances. I've never caught so much hell in my life, sir," he said, referring back to Nurse Rex.

Luther winced. No wonder Westy was pissed.

"Stop scolding him," Hannah interrupted, putting a restraining hand on Westy's arm. "It's not his fault the nurse drugged him."

Luther was grateful to Hannah for coming to his defense, but that hand on Westy's arm bothered him. They'd shared a room last night.

With a coarse mutter, Westy turned away and stalked toward the bathroom.

Luther's brain kicked in. "Rex drugged me?" he asked. Anger made him kick off the covers as he recalled how the nurse had smiled so cunningly when she handed him the painkiller yesterday. "She drugged me," he repeated, gripping the metal railing on one side of the bed. *Bitch,* he thought. "Damn it! What time is it? Did we miss the hearing completely?"

"We missed it," Westy said from the bathroom as he splashed water on his face. "It's ten hundred hours, sir."

"Shit!" He'd never sworn so much in so short a time.

"Oh, for God's sake," Hannah said, bending over to pull clothing out of Luther's suitcase. "Stop with the theatrics. It's not the end of the world. So Jaguar's case goes to court-martial. Big deal. We're still going to get him off the hook."

She laid a carefully folded dress shirt, jeans, undershirt, boxers, and a clean pair of socks onto the rollaway table. "This gives us more time to prepare our testimony. I say we swing by the DIAC and look for the copy of Ernie's notebook. With Westmoreland arrested, it's got to be safe to go there now."

Luther looked from the clothes she'd set out to Westy's face as he emerged from the bathroom. "Valentino said not to assume that Hannah's safe yet, and first thing she does is throw off her disguise," he said, chastising his chief.

Westy flicked a hot look at Hannah. "What'd I tell you?" he said. "Now he's blaming me."

"Don't blame Westy," Hannah said. "I'm tired of the disguise. It's pointless. Lovitt knows who I am or he wouldn't have sent someone after me the other night, and the Individual is in custody. I should be safe."

Bill Westmoreland, head of the CIA, was the Individual. Luther tried to wrap his mind around it. "Why would Westmoreland want you out of the way?" he asked.

She heaved a sigh. "I don't know. He was named DCI when my father died. Maybe there's a connection there. Whatever the reason, he's out of the picture now. I can be myself again."

Luther just looked at her. He saw reason in her argument, but his neck felt tight with apprehension. Valentino's voice droned in his head. *This will be a test of your professionalism.* "So what are we doing, Chief?" he asked Westy. "Are we going to the DIAC?"

Westy stuck his hands into his pockets. "Might as well."

"We'll find the copy of Ernie's notebook which we can use in Jaguar's court-martial," Hannah added persuasively.

Luther groaned at the mention of a court-martial. "I can't believe I slept for twenty-two hours."

"I'm jealous," said Hannah. "How are you feeling? Can you get up?"

Luther swung his feet off the bed and sat up experimentally. He had a lovely purple bruise on the back of his left hand from the IV needle. Feeling only a mild discomfort in his shoulder, he put one foot to the floor and stood. To his dismay, he realized that the gown he was wearing didn't quite close in the back and he had nothing on under it.

Hannah flashed out a hand to steady him. Westy moved to the other side.

"How're you doing?" she asked as he shuffled forward.

"Pretty good," he said, holding her tightly so she wouldn't get a glimpse of his backside. He'd feel better after he peed.

"Maybe Westy should stay in the bathroom with you."

They turned identical looks of horror on her. "No," Luther said, "I'll be fine. Just bring me my clothes. Please." He waited for her to turn away before sidling into the bathroom sideways.

Westy chuckled as he realized what Luther was attempting to hide.

"Give me ten minutes," Luther said as Hannah handed him his clothes. He shut the door in their faces, humiliated, feeling anything but heroic.

Defense Intelligence Analysis Center
Bolling Air Force Base
28 September ~ 14:49 EST

At the DIAC's security checkpoint, Luther suffered a body search at the hands of a retired Marine master sergeant, who clearly nursed a grudge against SEALs in general.

"He squeezed my nuts," said Westy, who'd suffered the same search. "I almost broke his fucking nose."

If he wasn't in such terrible pain, Luther would have laughed at the scowl on Westy's face, but laughter was beyond him at the moment. Voices echoed off the marbled floor of the DIAC's lobby. He leaned against the wall, waiting for Hannah's new ID badge to be laminated. The painkillers he'd forsaken by walking out of the hospital early would have come in handy right about now.

Westy gave him a searching look. "You okay, sir?"

"Fine."

"You look like shit."

"Thanks. I love you, too."

"My godfather's expecting me," Hannah conveyed, breezing up to them. "He's apparently been worried sick," she added breathlessly. "I'll have to take a moment to reassure him I'm all right. Then we'll fetch Ernie's notes. This way to the elevators."

Luther followed her blindly. A clammy sweat made his undershirt cling to him. The elevator ascended, and he widened his stance to keep his balance.

Hannah finally took note. "Luther, you don't look good."

"I'm okay. Just need to sit down soon."

"We're almost there." She linked her arm through his in a gesture of solidarity. The pleasure of her touch took his mind off the pain for a moment.

She didn't have to touch him anymore. They weren't role-playing like they'd been in Sabena. But they were friends now, buddies. While the thought bolstered him, giving him the strength to step out on the fifth floor where the director's suite was located, it left him wanting something more.

A middle-aged woman in a pin-striped suit looked up from her desk of stainless steel and graphite. "Welcome back, Miss Geary," she called out warmly. "Mr. Newman is expecting you." She gestured to the open door.

Hannah pulled Luther along beside her. Westy followed behind. "Uncle Caleb," she sang out, "I'm back!"

A handsome man in his late fifties was already rounding his desk with his arms flung wide. "Hannah, my girl!" he cried, sweeping her into a hearty embrace. He held her close for an awfully long time, but Luther could see that the man's emotions were genuine.

"Let me look at you," the director said, putting her at arm's distance, at last. He inspected her from the top of her head to the gray pumps she wore. "You don't look any worse for wear," he decided, "considering everything you've been through."

"How much do you know?" Hannah asked.

"Not much. I've had my own people looking for you, of course. The rumor is that you were in Cuba! You'll have to tell me what that's about. At least, you're back where you belong. I can't tell you how worried I was."

"I'm fine, Uncle Caleb," Hannah said, patting his cheek. "Really I am."

For a moment, Luther thought the man might actually cry. "If anything ever happened to you . . ." he choked.

"Nothing bad is going to happen. Look, I have my own bodyguards." She turned to introduce Luther and Westy. "These are the SEALs who rescued me. Lieutenant Lindstrom . . ." Luther awkwardly extended his left hand, which Caleb Newman vigorously pumped. "And Chief McCaffrey."

Newman turned to Westy. "I can't thank you men enough," he said, shaking Westy's hand as he looked back and forth between them. "Please, have a seat." He gestured to the upholstered armchairs. "Hannah, dear, tell me everything," he added, moving around his desk to his own chair. "Then I'll give you my own take on this business with Bill Westmoreland."

Luther eased into the armchair, grateful to be off his feet. As Hannah relayed how her colleague's death had led her to discovering Commander Lovitt's crimes, Luther drew deep, steadying breaths, pushing back the pain. Imposing mind over matter required most of his concentration, so that he absorbed only snatches of the conversation.

He was aware of Westy sitting silently on Hannah's right side, watching Newman closely, flicking Luther an occasional glance.

"So what do you think?" Hannah said when she'd concluded her story.

Newman laced his fingers together, giving her a troubled look. "Bill Westmoreland has always taken a radical approach when it comes to influencing governments abroad. It doesn't surprise me one bit that he's been meddling with the inner dynamics of other countries. What troubles me is that he's taken notice of you."

"Exactly. Why me?" Hannah wanted to know.

Newman shook his head. "I only know that he was jealous of your father's popularity, something he's never managed to gain for himself."

"But that doesn't explain why he'd want to get rid of me. Unless he was simply doing Lovitt a favor."

"Perhaps that's it," the director answered, looking satisfied with the explanation. "Dear heart, I hope you have second thoughts about returning to an organization that has betrayed you," he professed with feeling.

"One man doesn't make the whole organization corrupt, Uncle Caleb," Hannah argued. "I still plan to go back."

His hazel eyes darkened with disappointment. "Well, if that's your decision. You never promised me forever," he said sadly. "How is Kevin?" he asked, switching topics abruptly.

"He's fine. I spoke with him just today. He's nearly finished with his dissertation."

"Time to talk that boy into joining my agency," Newman said. "Have I got a job for him!" he added, pleasure bringing a sparkle to his eyes.

The conversation took a new turn when Hannah confessed that her Mustang was completely totaled.

"I'll buy you a new one," Newman promised. "Bright red this time, with a convertible top."

"Uncle Caleb," she chided, "you're not going to convince me to stay that way."

His eager countenance dimmed. "You can see straight through me," he lamented. "We'll talk more about this later. I can see Lieutenant Lindstrom isn't feeling well. But in the meantime, dear heart, if you wouldn't mind too much, it would put me at ease to assign my own body-guards to watch you."

Hannah glanced uncomfortably at Luther and Westy. "Oh, you don't have to do that, Uncle Caleb. I'm going to stay with the SEALs awhile to help them get a colleague out of trouble. Their commander killed Ernie," she reminded her godfather.

Newman gave her a long, pitying look. "I understand," he said finally. "By all means, help these gentlemen out. But if you could just humor me in this instance, you won't even notice my men," he promised. "They supply their own housing in the form of a Winnebago."

"Thank you," Luther said before Hannah could protest again. He, like Newman, didn't believe that just because Westmoreland was in custody, Hannah was safe. Valentino had warned him to stay vigilant.

"All right, Uncle Caleb, if it makes you feel better," Hannah agreed, coming to the edge of her chair.

"Where are you headed now, dear?" the director asked, even as he scribbled a note on a yellow Post-it.

"I think we'll stop by my town house so that Luther can rest," she decided.

This was news to Luther but he didn't have it in him to protest. Besides, he was curious to see where Hannah lived.

Newman's curious gaze flickered over Luther as he reached for a pen. There were two names written on the Post-it that he handed to Hannah. "Give these names to

Irma," he instructed. "Galworth and Stone will be waiting in the parking lot. You can't miss them."

Hannah leaned over the desk and kissed Newman's cheek as she took the note from him. "Thanks for caring," she murmured.

He clung to the note an extra second. "You mean the world to me, dear heart," he said quietly. "Please be careful."

"I will. I promise."

Luther struggled out of the chair before Hannah made him look completely useless by helping him.

"Thank you again," Newman called as they headed for the door. Luther lifted a hand in farewell.

"Can you make it to my office?" Hannah asked, sidling around him.

"I think so."

She looped her arm through his, just like before, handing Newman's Post-it to Irma as she led him to the elevator.

On the third floor, they disembarked. Hannah led them down a hallway buzzing with activity. The entire floor was dissected into cubicles. As they passed each one, Luther saw analyst after analyst typing away on keyboards, copying information, sorting through files. No wonder Hannah couldn't wait to leave her job here. This was definitely not the place for her.

"Here we are," she said, pausing at a cubicle near the end of the hallway. "See how Ernie's half has been cleared out?"

"By men in suits," Luther recalled, sweating copiously from the trek to her office.

"I was afraid to ask who they were," she confessed.

"I had a feeling they didn't want Ernie's findings to go any farther." She paused by her fax machine and powered it on. It gave a series of beeps and whirrs and started spitting out paper.

Luther watched her, curious to see why her fax machine was needed.

"I faxed myself a copy of Ernie's notebook. It's been in the memory all this time."

"Good thinking," he said, pleased by her cleverness but not really too surprised.

"The copy that I used to fax it went into the paper shredder," Hannah added, patting that appliance. "When Valentino's people searched my office, all they would have found was the shredded copy."

"Time to go," said Westy, sounding edgy.

Luther glanced his way. With his eyes, Westy indicated for Luther to look up. He did, scanning the ceiling until he saw what Westy saw: the eye of a camera nestled inconspicuously in the ceiling tile overhead. "All set, Hannah?" Luther asked. The camera in the ceiling didn't bother him as much as it bothered Westy. So what if Newman was watching them? It was obvious he had Hannah's best interests at heart, offering his own bodyguards to give her added protection. With four pairs of eyes watching over her, and with the Individual in Valentino's custody, Hannah was probably safer than she'd ever be again.

Chapter Thirteen

Hannah had given up her bedroom so Luther could rest. That was several hours ago, when she'd escorted a pale-faced Luther up the stairs of her town house, ordering him to sleep.

A strange feeling came over her as she checked on him at suppertime, bearing his dinner on a tray. She found him fast asleep, sprawled diagonally across her bed, so he wouldn't jam his toes against her footboard. The old wood flooring in her Alexandria town home creaked beneath her feet as she rounded the bed to look down at him.

He'd slept from early afternoon until twilight. The evening sun cast a burnished glow on the window shade, gilding the violet comforter. In contrast to the pale purple sheets, Luther struck her as starkly masculine, making her heart beat erratically. She wasn't used to seeing a man in her bed.

She was glad to note that the lines of pain were gone from the corners of his mouth. He hadn't looked too good when she helped him get settled, unbuttoning his shirt and pulling his T-shirt over his head. But now, with several hours of sleep behind him and hundreds of milligrams of Tylenol in his system, he appeared to be pain-free.

The sun glow highlighted the strength of his cheekbones. She stood there, spellbound by his latent male beauty, cognizant of a fullness of feeling in her chest. If her hands weren't occupied holding the tray, she'd be tempted to stroke the soft sable strands of his hair.

Luther was incredible, in so many ways, taking a bullet for righteousness' sake, uncomplaining to the point of collapse. She respected and admired him. But that wasn't the reason she felt pleased to have him sprawled half naked in her bed. It didn't account for her possessive urge to keep him there.

It was time to face facts: she was drawn to Luther, emotionally and physically, whether she wanted to be or not. She hadn't planned on having feelings for a man until her career was under way and she could choose her assignments. Long-distance relationships were doomed. But pretending she didn't feel anything was an act of cowardice. She was going to face these feelings head-on, the way she faced everything. There had to be a way to handle them.

But was Luther as drawn to her as she was to him? She wasn't sure. He'd just ditched his last girlfriend—*fiancée.* How could he even know what he was feeling?

Turning away to place the tray upon her bureau, she caught sight of her shadowed reflection in the mirror. She wasn't beautiful—not in the way that the sultry brunette, Veronica, was beautiful. She had flaming red hair and freckles. She was tall and strong. But at least she was wearing her own clothes again.

She tugged the tight-fitting, coral top over the edge of her hip-hugging jeans. She'd always prided herself on her flair for fashion. It came as a relief to look trendy again.

"Wow, you look different."

Luther's sleepy observation had her turning with a start, nearly upsetting the glass of ice water perched on the corner of the tray. "Oh, you're awake."

He was very awake. In his purple surroundings, his alert gaze looked more indigo than blue as he took leisurely stock of her. "Is this the real you?" he inquired with a half smile.

Hannah's stomach tightened with apprehension. "What do you think?" She held her hands out to her sides.

"You look young," he admitted, which caused her heart to drop. "And sexy," he added, causing it to leap up again.

"I, uh, brought you some dinner," she said, turning toward the tray. "I hope you like it. It's just SpaghettiOs with canned vegetables. I'm not much of a cook. Besides, all the food in my refrigerator went bad. Do you want to eat now? How's your back?"

She realized she was talking faster than he could answer, and she shut her mouth with a snap.

"I'll eat now," he said, struggling to sit up. "My back feels better."

She longed to help, but that entailed touching him, which she didn't trust herself to do. It was hard enough not to stare. Her gaze slid helplessly to the elastic band of his boxers as her sensory memory reminded her of how incredibly he'd filled her hand.

She passed him the tray, ice rattling in the glass, betraying her unsteady nerves.

Their fingers brushed as Luther took it from her. "Thanks," he said.

"No problem. Can I get you anything else?"

"No, this is great." He picked up his fork and stirred the noodles.

"I'll come back when you're done, then," she said, finding it awkward to just stand there, watching him.

"You mind if I help myself to your bathroom?" he inquired. "I'd like to take a shower."

"Sure, no problem. But what about the bandage?" He wore a big gauze bandage on his back.

He forked down a bite. "It's coming off."

"Are you sure that's smart?"

"I've been shot before," he told her, reaching for the water. "The wound heals faster when it's dry."

He'd been shot before? Suddenly his job seemed unnecessarily dangerous. "Just don't reinjure yourself. There are extra towels over the toilet." *Would you like some help?*

"I'll need you to put ointment on my back afterward."

She hadn't made that offer out loud, had she?

"Okay." She gripped the doorknob to keep a hold on reality. Luther was looking at her differently. There was heat in his gaze that hadn't been there earlier, except once before when she'd . . . "I'll be back in half an hour or so."

"Bye." He watched her leave, looking lonely on her queen-sized bed.

With anticipation winging through her, Hannah closed the door. She paused at the top of the landing. If Luther was actually flirting with her—which she was fairly certain he was—was she going to take their friendship to the next level?

She'd be crazy not to. He was every woman's fantasy, and she was no exception. Turning down the chance to be with him, even if it led to nothing, was wasteful. Life was short. You had to take pleasures as they came.

With her mind made up, she descended the steps on knees that jittered.

Westy glanced up from the newspaper he was scowling over. If Luther had looked out of place in Hannah's bed, Westy looked downright incongruous on her floral love seat, surrounded by tea tables with lace doilies, a collection of Depression glass, and ceramic figurines.

Seeing her flushed face, a knowing little smile kicked up the corner of his mouth. "How's Sleeping Beauty?" he drawled.

"He looks better," she said matter-of-factly, crossing the room to get a dust rag from the kitchen.

Her town home had been searched by the FBI, who'd made minimal effort to set things back to rights. They couldn't have found anything to aid their investigation, but they'd certainly left a trail of destruction behind them.

Three weeks of absence hadn't helped any, either. A fine layer of dust coated her antique furniture and family heirlooms. Her potted herbs in the kitchen had wilted and died. And as she'd told Luther, half the goods in her refrigerator needed to be discarded.

Westy spoke from behind the newspaper. "Westmoreland denies the FBI's allegations," he related. "He's got a slew of people coming forward to defend him—senators, ambassadors, CEOs."

Hannah carried the damp rag to the dining-room buffet. "Well, of course he's going to deny that he's the Individual," she said, wiping the dusty surface. "What does the FBI expect, a confession?"

Westy grunted. "He wants to take a polygraph."

Hannah hesitated, then resumed her work. "I hope they don't let him go if he passes it. I've heard of guilty people passing lie detector tests."

Westy said nothing to that.

Hannah suffered a moment's misgiving. Surely Valentino had been thorough before making his arrest, but what if he'd arrested the wrong man? Then the Individual was still at large and Hannah's well-being was as much threatened now as it had been before.

The unpleasant thought prompted her to cross to the bay window to peer outside. The Winnebago parked across the street was a reassuring sign. Not only did she have two SEALs safeguarding her, but her own bodyguards, Galworth and Stone, two stalwart men whom Westy referred to collectively as "the gallstones," were keeping watch on her front door.

Luther wiped a circle of steam off the bathroom mirror and took a good hard look at himself. Did he know what he was doing? Or was he caving in to his sexual appetite and abandoning his common sense?

It felt right. Once he'd gotten over his unsettling attraction to her, he'd felt amazingly comfortable with Hannah, like he'd known her all his life. So long as she was willing, what was the crime? he asked his reflection.

And she *was* willing. She might have fallen asleep on him a couple of times and treated him as a comrade at arms, but her eyes had betrayed sexual awareness for some time now, as did the pink stain in her cheeks, particularly evident now without the heavy makeup of her disguise.

And despite the fact that she looked a lot younger in her own clothes, she was a grown woman—twenty-six years old. A woman that age was capable of enjoying sex without investing it with emotional overtones.

That was more his tendency, he admitted with a grimace.

But not if he refused to engage his emotions. Wanting Hannah in any way beyond the physical realm was impractical. She was going back to the CIA when this was over, and not to a safe little desk job either. Her work as a case officer would put her in the company of dangerous and unpredictable people, requiring her to use her tremendous charm to win their trust in order to glean information. He knew she was up to it, but he didn't want to think about what might happen if she, for once, let her guard down.

He couldn't ask her to change her plans for him. On the other hand, he wasn't above enjoying her while he had the chance. So long as he kept things physical.

Sleeping in her bed had cinched it. He'd lain there, surrounded by Hannah's scent, seduced by the intimate atmosphere of her tastefully decorated bedroom: the ornate headboard, the collection of white and purple candles, half melted on a silver tray beside her bed; amethyst crystals dangling in her window to catch the sun. He'd studied the pictures of Hannah with her family, each lovingly placed in an artful frame, and he'd felt close to her.

Then he'd pictured her in bed with him, limbs entwined, and he'd known that the experience would be worth the loss that came later. He needed to be with her that way. He'd regret it if he didn't.

He dried his hair with the towel and fished several condoms from the pocket of his shaving kit. Grabbing the tube of antibiotic Nurse Rex had foisted on him when he left Pax River, he returned to the bedroom, naked. Imagining Hannah's expression when she found him in his birthday suit made him smile.

Ignoring Westy's knowing look, Hannah excused herself to fetch Luther's tray. She arrived at her door with butterflies in her stomach and her palms sweating.

"Come in," Luther called at her light knock.

She found him lounging against a pile of pillows, with the sheet up just over his hips. One arm was crooked over his head in a posture of supreme male confidence. The pose was tempered by the expectant, half-worried look on his face. The bedside lamp illumined the room with a soft golden glow that made his naked chest look airbrushed.

Hannah swallowed hard. "Did you, uh, did you take your bandage off?" she asked, heart thumping wildly.

He flexed his shoulder. "Yes. My back's still tight, but it's not hurting the way it was this morning. I have the ointment that the nurse gave me." He showed her the tube in his hand.

She shut the door, locking it surreptitiously. As she

approached the bed, she realized he was naked under the sheet. She could see the taut, smooth skin of his hip, and the vision made her head spin. *This is really happening,* she thought with an urge to pinch herself.

He handed her the tube. "You want to sit?" he asked, patting the space beside him.

"Sure." She eased onto the small space, her thigh brushing his. He'd helped himself to her magnolia-scented body wash, she realized. Somehow it came off smelling manly on him.

She admired the breadth of his powerful back, all sinew and muscle. Her gaze settled on the puckered wound near his shoulder blade, and she drew a quick breath. "Oh, God!"

"Is it that bad?"

It wasn't, not even with so many stitches bristling out of the pink gash. "It's just . . . I didn't realize how close to your heart it was. You could have been killed, Luther!" The realization shook her.

"I'm not that easy to kill," he said with a smile in his voice. He put a hand on her thigh, presumably to keep her from slipping off the mattress. His palm felt hot, even through the fabric of her jeans.

With unsteady fingers, Hannah squeezed ointment onto her index finger. She applied it to the inflamed area, careful not to irritate the stitches. "Am I hurting you?" she asked, aware of a certain tenderness creeping over her.

He could have been killed, despite his reassurance to the contrary. Life was like that. It could end in a moment, without warning. What if he'd died that night in Sabena?

She'd have lost faith in righteousness—faith that was already at an all-time low.

Without intending to, Hannah found her arms around him.

He accepted her sudden embrace, locking her arms in place with his. "You okay?" he asked. "Hannah?"

"Yes," she said, struggling to get a grip on herself. "I didn't realize what a close call you had, that's all."

He pulled her closer with his good arm. Hannah was highly aware that the only thing between her and his naked body was the thin cotton sheet. "I'm right here," he said solemnly. "We've both chosen careers that are dangerous. That's just part of making a difference."

Hannah nodded. The fullness in her chest made it too hard to speak. They were one and the same, she and Luther. She felt close to him already. His gaze dropped to her mouth. And with that scant warning, he kissed her.

She knew his lips were soft and warm, but she couldn't have predicted that they were also skillful, mobile, persuasive, and utterly single-minded.

She acquiesced to his unspoken demand and parted her lips with a whimper.

Hannah forgot to breathe. They kissed, on and on, each foray an experience unto itself. She found her fingers in his hair, gliding over his impossibly broad shoulders, the muscles of his upper arms. She felt her senses overloading. There was simply too much of him to take in at once.

"Need to get these clothes off," he muttered. His fingers grasped the hem of her shirt, lifting it over her breasts. He hesitated, blinking down at her plain cotton bra. "What happened?" he asked.

She knew immediately what he meant. "Those bras itched like crazy. Honestly, I prefer cotton."

Her admission made him burst out laughing. "Now that I believe," he said, reaching for the latch in front.

"Are you disappointed?"

"Are you kidding?" He peeled the cups back one at a time to feast his eyes on her. Lowering his head, he cupped each breast and brought it to his mouth.

Hannah gasped at the lash of his tongue, the hot suction of his lips.

She struggled to unbutton her jeans. Luther aided in the endeavor, tugging them down her legs. As she kicked them off, leaving her in her pink cotton briefs, wishing she'd suffered with the lace panties just one more day.

"You look sexy," he reassured her.

"Yeah, right."

"Honestly," he said, using her earlier word. As if to prove it, he ran a finger along the waistband, tickling the sensitive skin between her pelvic bones. Pleasure mingled with anticipation as he outlined a leg hole all the way to the inside of her leg. Hannah tried not to laugh. "That tickles!" she gasped.

He flung back the sheet, and she reached for him with two hands, thrilled to be reunited with this part of him, pleased to have proof that he desired her.

"We have a problem," he admitted gruffly.

She froze at the admission. "What?"

"I can't use my right arm. That makes it harder for me to be on top."

She gave him a slow smile. "Oh, that's not a problem," she reassured him. She pushed him gently on his back, coming up on her knees to bend over him.

His hands slid through the waves of her hair as he swore softly, enduring her reverence with a groan.

"Hannah." He pulled her up, ignoring her throaty protest. "You're going to embarrass me," he confessed. "Seriously. It's been a while."

She was glad to hear it, almost as glad as she was to feel his hands sweeping over her, his callused palms skimming over her breasts, her waist, her hips. She swung a leg over and straddled him.

His eyes glowed with desire. "I've dreamed about this."

"Really." She was glad not to be the only one.

Luther pulled her down for a searing kiss. His touch grew more intent, more urgent. Behind her sinking eyelids, Hannah's world tipped off its axis.

She'd never felt anything more blissful, more dreamy than Luther touching her. She grew heated to the point of sweating. He eased a finger inside her, and then another. Hannah bit her lower lip to keep Westy from hearing her cries.

The sound of foil tearing brought her back to reality. She opened her eyes to see that Luther had thought this through. He covered himself quickly, casting her an apologetic glance.

He cupped her jaw with one hand, drawing her down for another kiss. At the same time, he guided himself with excruciating deliberation.

He entered, withdrew, pushed deeper.

Hannah felt herself unraveling. How long had it been? Years now. But Luther's unhurried possession gave her unaccustomed body time to relax, to accept him, until she was finally taking all of him. "Oh, my God," she breathed.

Against her lips, she felt him smile.

"What's so funny?" she demanded.

"Nothing. You are something else, Hannah Geary."

Was that a good thing?

With a growl, he rolled over, taking her with him. He drove into her, shifting the mood from one of leisurely anticipation to sudden urgency.

"I thought you couldn't be on top," she said, wrapping her legs enthusiastically around him.

"I am feeling no pain," he reassured her.

Neither was she. In her world, where men were her colleagues and competitors, there had been no allowance for intimacy. She'd forgotten how lovely sex could be. She wouldn't regret this, she vowed, opening her eyes to look up at him, to brand this moment in her mind.

As their gazes met, a feeling ambushed her. *This is where I belong.*

Her eyes widened at the startling thought. Luther looked stunned, as if struck by the same insight. She tried to shake it off, but it clung to her tenaciously, prompting a response that boiled up like a geyser, from the inside out. As it shot her toward a blinding climax, Luther gave a muffled shout, driving into her one last time. They came together, scalded by the ferocity of their passion.

At last the heat subsided, leaving in its wake a bottomless warmth that she was loath to relinquish.

All too soon, Luther shifted his weight. Avoiding her gaze, he dropped a kiss on her lips and withdrew, rolling off the bed.

She admired his formidable physique as he strode naked to the bathroom. He shut the door partway between them. She heard him flush the toilet. Water ran in the sink. A long, long silence ensued.

Hannah waited, savoring the aftershocks of pleasure, refusing to think. At last, he appeared at the doorway to regard her at a distance, his expression for once enigmatic. Neither one of them said a word.

What was there to say? Hannah thought. Panic and belated regret furrowed into her.

"That was nice," said Luther, breaking the awkward silence.

Nice? Nice wasn't the word that came to her mind. Incredible, maybe. Frightening, perhaps, but not nice.

He jabbed his fingers through his hair. "Do you think we should have talked first?"

"About what?" She tried to play it cool. Maybe he couldn't see the pulse pounding at the base of her throat.

He frowned at her. "Nothing, just . . . you know, the usual." He approached the bed tentatively, his gaze darkening as it slid over her nakedness. He sat on the bed and tried to kiss her.

Hannah pulled back. "The usual?" she repeated. "Sorry, I don't do this often enough to know what that is." With her feelings in turmoil, she seized upon anger as the emotion to display.

He sighed, clearly regretting that he'd brought up talk in the first place. "I like you a lot, Hannah," he said gently. "You're a terrific friend, an incredible lover, but I don't see how we could be something more than that."

Right, and she hadn't either until just a few minutes ago when she was hit with that completely random thought: *This is where I belong.* Obviously he hadn't suffered the same insight. "Of course not," she muttered.

"I don't see, given your plans with the CIA and my job, how anything permanent could last," he pointed out, with tension in his face.

"It would be hard," she conceded, finding it difficult speak.

"I don't want to hurt your feelings," he added, giving her a searching look.

That was the wrong thing to say. Hurt took precedence over her emotions, putting victorious pressure on her chest. "You haven't," she lied. "Excuse me." She slipped past him to get off the bed.

With a troubled look, he watched her go into the bathroom and shut the door.

Hannah cranked on the water in the shower. That would give him the message that she wasn't coming out for an instant replay. Under the water's hot spray, she could shed a few tears and it wouldn't count as crying.

A part of her wondered at her reaction. She'd thought she was perfectly capable of sleeping with Luther while remaining emotionally aloof. She wasn't the romantic type. She'd had her eyes wide open when she opted for intimacy.

Perhaps she should have kept them shut. Then they wouldn't have shared that look that, for some reason, had made her feel like she was his.

Forget it, she told herself. *It was nothing. And just to be on the safe side, don't sleep with him again.*

Tarrying as long as possible, she went back into the room, girded in a towel. To her relief, Luther was gone. The sky behind her shades was dark. Hannah dressed in a mint-green nightshirt, which wasn't as soft as

Westy's Harley-Davidson T-shirt, but at least it covered her.

Heading down the stairs, she found the SEALs watching football on TV. "I think I'll call it a night, guys," she announced with forced brightness.

Luther sent her a long, solemn look. In his eyes, she could see both regret and concern. "Go ahead and sleep in your bed, Hannah. I got plenty of rest today."

"No," she said quickly. "I'll be in the guest room. You shouldn't stay up all night."

The disappointment on his face assured her that her message was clear. They wouldn't be sleeping together. No more sex until she figured out how to detangle her emotions from the act itself.

Westy looked back and forth between them, his little smirk notably absent.

"Hannah," Luther called as she turned back up the stairs. She looked back, heart clutching traitorously.

"Sleep well," he called.

"I will," she lied. "Good night, Westy."

"'Night."

Despite Luther's wishes for a good night's sleep, Hannah tossed and turned on the daybed in the guest room. At one in the morning, she heard Luther return to the adjoining bedroom. He groaned in pain as he eased onto the mattress. She wondered if he'd torn something when he'd flipped her over, driving himself deeply inside of her.

The memory of that experience brought on a rush of

renewed desire. She wanted to relive the pleasure again . . . and again. She sighed, turned over, and tried to sleep.

At three in the morning, she surrendered to her hunger pains and crept down the stairs to find a snack, moving as quietly as possible, so as not to disturb Westy who was sprawled upon a sleeping bag in the living room.

The streetlight outside was her only illumination, shining brightly through the sheer curtain at her bay window. Bypassing the two front rooms, Hannah crept down the hall to the kitchen.

She opened a cupboard, feeling for a box of gingersnaps. The cookies went best with milk, but that had been poured down the disposal.

Crunch. She bit into the stale cookie as quietly as possible.

The light came on suddenly, and she whirled with surprise, half expecting a stranger to be stalking her. It was only Westy, standing there with his long hair in disarray, his chest naked, and his gun clutched casually in his left hand. Hannah couldn't help but wonder why his broad, powerful torso didn't affect her the way Luther's did.

"You going to eat all of those?" he asked, gaze dropping to the box.

She handed it to him. He helped himself to a handful and gave it back. They stood there, munching gingersnaps in silence.

"You're good for him, you know," Westy said, finally.

"What?"

"Little John. You're good for him."

"You don't know what you're talking about," she said with that same feeling of confusion storming her.

Westy just looked at her, his blue eyes unbearably direct. "Some things can't be planned ahead of time. You take them as they come. Maybe you both need to learn that."

She took exception to his advice. "Yeah, well some plans are too sacred to be messed with," she countered. "For three years I've been holed up in a little cubicle analyzing foreign military reports. I've dreamed of nothing but getting the hell out of there, out of this country, to do something that actually matters."

"Sounds to me like you're running. Or maybe chasing someone."

Her jaw dropped as she stared at him. "What the hell do you know?" she said sharply.

Her temper didn't seem to faze him. "Just think about it," he said easily.

She didn't want to think about it. She stalked past him, shoving the half-eaten box at him as she headed for the stairs.

Who was Westy to tell her what her motives were? What was it with men, anyway? For three years she'd been placating Uncle Caleb, who didn't want her doing anything dangerous. Then there was Kevin, who'd starve to death if she didn't remind him to eat. Now Westy had the gall to insinuate that her motives for returning to the CIA were flawed somehow.

What did he know about her motives?

Another thought occurred to her as she flung herself down on the daybed. Maybe Luther'd asked Westy to talk her out of her plans. Maybe he wanted Hannah to stick around, to be part of his life.

Not likely, she thought, ignoring the little flutter in her

chest. She was her father's daughter, every inch of the way. If she meant to leave her mark on this world as her father had, she'd better get to it. No man, no matter how appealing, no matter how heroic, handsome, sensitive rich—God, the list could go on forever—was going to make her plot a different course than the one she'd chosen.

Chapter Fourteen

"What about a desk?" Hannah asked, peering past the dining-room table and upended chairs. Her basement was chock full of household goods from her grandmother's estate. Grandma Estelle had sickened and died shortly after the crash that killed her daughter and son-in-law. The furniture from two estates didn't fit into Hannah's diminutive town home. It sat gathering dust and mildew in her basement. At five o'clock in the morning, she'd gotten the great idea that she would give it to Luther as repayment for the money he'd spent on her.

"You don't have to do this, you know," he said, looking over the furniture with a hand jammed into the pocket of his jeans.

"I want to pay you back for all the clothes you bought me—"

"Clothes you'll never wear," he interrupted.

"That's beside the point," she insisted. "Plus I need to get rid of this stuff," she added.

"What about Kevin? Isn't he going to want any?"

"Kevin's already picked through it. He doesn't like antiques."

"Well, at least let me pay you," Luther insisted.

Hannah looked up sharply. Rays of sunlight shot through the high windows of her basement, lighting the troubled blue depths of Luther's eyes. "That won't be necessary," she said, her tone frosty.

He pulled his hand out of his pocket and rubbed his neck. "Okay, Hannah," he relented. "I'll take the desk, the dining-room set, the dresser, and the nightstand. And anything you want to get rid of."

"Thank you," she said. "You can start with that hat rack, and don't you dare use your right hand. We'll get Galworth and Stone to help. I'll line up a rental truck."

It took until midafternoon to empty Hannah's basement. Luther, fanning himself at the wheel of the U-Haul, glanced at his watch. It was fifteen hundred hours, hot as sin, and the U-Haul had no air-conditioning. Westy planned to take the lead in his Nissan. The Winnebago would follow at the rear. They should be back at the beach by nightfall.

Hannah, who'd just locked up her town house with her extra key, looked from the Nissan to the U-Haul, as if deciding who to ride with. To Luther's consternation, she marched past both vehicles and knocked on the door of the GallStones' Winnebago.

Oh, no, no. Valentino had warned him to stay vigilant, which meant he needed to insist that Hannah ride with either him or Westy. But did he really want to do that? She'd been in such a stormy mood all morning, he couldn't predict the outcome with any certainty, except that he'd probably come out looking like a fool. The gallstones were trained bodyguards. They ought to be able to keep her safe on the three-and-a-half-hour ride home.

With a sigh, he signaled the go-ahead to Westy, who was watching with consternation through his rearview mirror. With a shake of his head, Westy pulled out into the narrow street, afternoon sunshine glinting off his cobalt sports car.

Luther could understand Hannah being mad **at** him. They should have talked before they'd done what they'd done, even though she agreed that there was no future for them. But why was she mad at Westy?

He'd overheard them in the kitchen last night, talking briefly. He trusted Westy not to trespass into his territory, but the chief must have stepped over the line somehow. Hannah had spoken to him shortly and then stomped up the stairs. Now she was avoiding both SEALs.

Feeling vaguely sorry for himself, Luther tailed the Nissan toward the George Washington Memorial Parkway, driving with the windows down to cool himself. The Winnebago stayed right behind him. Christ, it was a good thing the Individual *was* in Valentino's custody. They couldn't be any more conspicuous than they were at the moment, driving in a freaking convoy to Virginia Beach.

It was dusk by the time the U-Haul had been fully unloaded. Hannah's furniture filled Luther's previously empty house. He stood in the living room, taking in the effect with mixed feelings.

The overstuffed sofa Veronica had disdained to take

with her went amazingly well with the braided rug Hannah had rolled out in front of it. An end table with a brass lamp on it flanked one end. A rocking chair sat across from the sofa, with a mahogany coffee table in between. An old-fashioned clock chimed every fifteen minutes from its perch on his fireplace mantel. He wondered if it would keep him up at night.

How was he supposed to forget Hannah when her possessions had taken over his home? He might have thought she'd done it intentionally, only she'd avoided him all day, making a point, perhaps, to prove that she wasn't out to claim him.

"What's the plan, sir?" Westy asked from his seat on the living-room sofa. The sky in the window behind him had deepened to indigo. It was getting late. All of them were tired.

Hannah stepped out of the kitchen, where she was cleaning up the crumbs from their sandwiches. "I'm beat," she announced, flopping down on the couch, as far from Westy as she could get, her legs sprawled before her.

Luther's gaze slid up her impossibly long legs. She was wearing jeans that clung to her curves and a hot-pink tank top in deference to the Indian summer heat. Her short wavy hair was windblown, and she looked sexy as hell.

The realization that he owned only one bed wormed its way into his brain. Concerns for Hannah's safety grappled with the desperate need to have her to himself.

"I don't see any reason for you to stay, Chief, if you don't want to. Newman's watchdogs are out front if anything comes up. We'll see you at the Trial Services Building tomorrow at zero eight hundred."

Westy glanced at his watch and rolled to his feet.

"I need to fetch Jesse from the sitter's," he said decisively. "See y'all in the morning, unless you'd rather come with me, ma'am?" he asked Hannah, flicking Luther an inscrutable look.

It was obvious Hannah was caught off guard by the offer. Through narrowed eyes, she looked from Westy to Luther and back again, as if determining which was the worse of two evils. "No, thank you," she said remotely. "I'm too tired to move."

Westy nodded. He sent Luther a quick salute and disappeared. The door closed quietly behind him.

"Did I miss something between you and him?" Luther asked, prompted by jealousy.

"I doubt it," she said in that same strange tone.

"Why are you mad at him?" he persisted.

"I don't know, you tell me."

"If I knew, I wouldn't be asking," he retorted, impatient with batting words around.

She switched topics on him abruptly. "How's your shoulder?"

"It's throbbing," he admitted.

"I'm sorry. Maybe this wasn't the best time to move my furniture."

"I'm fine. And thank you. Everything fits in really well."

She glanced at the chestnut table and chairs filling his dining area. "It does, doesn't it?" she said, sounding a little bemused.

Seeing the dark circles under her eyes, he forgot his frustration with her. "Would you like to shower?" he asked. It was obvious she hadn't slept at all last night. Neither had he. He'd relived their lovemaking second by second, whetting his appetite for more. Pride alone had kept him in the bed when he was oh so tempted to cruise down the hall and beg her to do it all again.

"You first," Hannah said. "The hot water will help your shoulder." She keeled over, kicking off her shoes as she sprawled along the length of the sofa.

The curve of Hannah's waist was almost his undoing. He turned away without a word and shut himself in his blue-tiled bathroom.

Twenty minutes later, he ventured into the living room wearing pajama pants. Hannah was sound asleep in the same position he'd left her. In the lamp's soft glow, her face looked young and untroubled. He went to fetch a blanket and pillow from his linen closet.

On second thought, he grabbed two blankets and two pillows. He didn't want to leave her by the curtainless window, and with his shoulder out of commission, he couldn't carry her to the bedroom. So, the only option was to lie down next to her, on the floor.

He dropped his linens to drape a blanket over Hannah, stuffing the pillow under her head. With a moan, she pulled it close, hugging it the way she'd once hugged him.

He nudged the coffee table off to one side and spread his own blanket over the rug. Switching off the light, he lay down and sought a comfortable position. There wasn't one. His shoulder protested mightily. But he'd put up with worse, lying in traction for six months, not to mention all those wretched weeks in SEAL training. He closed his eyes and willed himself to fall asleep.

Deep into the night, Luther sensed movement. Someone was standing over him. He couldn't immediately remember where he was, only that he was lying on the ground. He responded immediately and instinctively. Sweeping a leg out, he knocked whoever it was off their feet.

Hannah went down hard. The sweep had come so unexpectedly, she wasn't able to do anything more than put her hands down to break her fall. She landed on her tailbone, between Luther's legs. He threw one leg over her midsection, pinning her to the braided rug. "It's just me," she managed to gasp.

He released her immediately, groaning as they both sat up to take stock of each other. The waxing moon cast just enough light to throw Luther's form into silhouette. "Are you okay?" He ran his hands over her, the way he had on the RIB the night he'd whisked her out of Cuba. The pleasure of his touch made her forget her sore backside.

"Fine," she said. "I was on my way to the bathroom." She'd actually awakened from a disturbing dream in which someone was chasing her. Getting up to shake it off, she'd nearly stepped on Luther, not expecting him to sacrifice his comfort that way. She'd lingered over him, concerned and touched.

"You shouldn't sneak up on me," he said. His voice, gruff with sleep, was especially appealing.

"No kidding."

His hands lingered.

Hannah swallowed hard. She reached deep inside for the strength to move away. "Go sleep in your bed, Luther. It's not good for your shoulder to sleep on the floor."

"I can't leave you by the window," he countered, a note of frustration in his voice.

She glanced at the large pane, which offered a view of a moonlit yard and the roof of the neighbor's house. An uneasy chill cooled her bare shoulders as she recalled her dream. "I'll sleep in your bed with you, Luther," she offered, "but only to sleep."

"That's fine," he said.

She snatched up her pillow and blanket and watched him come painstakingly to his feet. How long, she wondered, would she be able to resist him? Whether she was good for him or not, she ached for the fulfillment she'd found in his arms. She'd never shared anything like that with any man. Most likely, she never would.

With his linens in his arms, Luther led the way down the abbreviated hall to one of the rancher's three bedrooms, still devoid of furniture.

Hannah stopped at the bathroom. Flipping on the light, she pulled a toothbrush from her overnight kit and blinked in the mirror. *What do you want?* she asked herself.

Her reflection gave no answer.

A minute later, she felt her way to the bedroom. She'd seen the room at dusk, stark with four bare walls and a king-sized bed. Luther's clothes had been piled in neat stacks in his closet. Thanks to her grandmother, he now enjoyed a solid oak dresser and a matching bed stand, impossible to see for the shade at his window. Hannah shuffled forward.

"I'm on the far side," Luther said, having taken the side nearest to the window. "I'd have left on a light for you but I don't have one."

"That's okay." He'd pulled the comforter and sheet down. Hannah shimmied out of her jeans and slipped into the cool cocoon, taking care to keep well away from him.

Still, there wasn't a spot on her body that didn't tingle with awareness.

"Good night," Luther murmured.

"Night." She lay still for a long, long time. Just knowing Luther's powerful maleness was right beside her made her nipples stiffen and her crotch grow damp.

"Tell me about your godfather."

The unexpected request made her frown. Obviously Luther's thoughts weren't as single-minded as hers were. "Why?" she asked.

"He seems like a really nice guy."

"He is," she agreed, recalling the months after her parents' death when Uncle Caleb had been the rock beneath her. "I owe him a lot."

"I guess you've always known him?"

"He and my father were best friends. He loved my mother, too, which is probably the reason that he never married."

"Oh, really?"

"He was devastated when their plane went down. We all were."

Luther turned his head in her direction. She could sense his compassion. "Why did he talk you out of staying in the CIA?" he asked gently.

Hannah swallowed down the lump rising in her throat. "Like I said, he was devastated when my parents died— I mean, truly devastated. He was so sure that if I went overseas, I'd be killed on my first assignment. He told me Kevin needed me to stay close by, and he begged me to take a desk job. Problem was, in order to get a desk job in the CIA, I would have had to wait six months for my request to be processed. Or I could work right away for

Uncle Caleb, who made an opening for me. So I promised him three years, no more no less, and I took the job."

"I'll have to thank him one day," Luther said.

"For what?"

"If he hadn't talked you into sticking around, Jaguar would probably be headed to jail. And I never would have met you."

If meeting her was that special to him, Hannah thought with a tug of sorrow, why had he made a point of saying they were incompatible?

"What are you looking for, Luther?" She went out on a limb to ask. Maybe there was some way to satisfy both their needs.

He drew a deep, thoughtful breath. "Commitment and a family," he said decisively. "I want a woman who can hold the fort down when I'm gone. I want security for my children. I want to give them the kind of choices I had when I was growing up."

Hannah's heart sank. She'd spent the last three years counting down the days until her promise to Uncle Caleb was fulfilled. To take her mind off her tedious desk job, she'd fantasized about the adventures awaiting her when she'd be free at last to travel, to apply her talents toward information-gathering, to follow in her father's footsteps.

Not once had she considered falling in love, getting married, having children. Never! It was the dead-last thing she wanted for herself. So, why the regret squeezing her heart? She wasn't going to change her plans, not for Luther. Not for anyone.

Silence stretched between them, ponderous and deep.

"It's pretty damn ironic, don't you think?" Luther added on a bitter note.

"What is?" Her voice sounded strangled.

"That we're so much alike in some ways and so different in others."

His words made her eyes sting. She had to swallow in order to speak. "Yeah," she agreed, trying to sound casual. She forced herself to turn away from him, toward the wall. More than anything, she wanted to roll into his arms and weep.

Why had fate done this to her—brought the perfect man into her life when she wasn't ready for him? At first, being with him had just felt comfortable, like a broken-in shoe. But then she realized he was also intelligent, loyal, and focused. She loved the way she felt around him. She didn't want to let him go.

But she would have to, because Luther's dreams and hers were bearing them off into different directions. They would never be at this same point again.

A hot tear slipped from the corner of Hannah's eye and dropped to the pillow. She didn't want to admit that this was love. That would make it even harder to leave when the time came. But she did know this—she was way more invested in Luther than she ought to be.

Rafael Valentino inserted the electronic key into the lock of an upscale apartment in Vienna. It released with a quiet click.

Everything about Rafe's apartment was quiet. Like a tomb, he thought, willing away the vision of the family vault in St. Raymond's Cemetery.

It wasn't right to think of them as dead. He should remember, instead, the noise that awaited him whenever he came home from a long night's beat in the NYPD. His wife Teresa would be herding the children from the bath to their beds, using threats to ensure their cooperation. She was the loudest of all of them, he recalled, his lips twitching in a sad smile.

He let the door to his apartment fall shut. It closed on a soft hiss of air that ended on a muted snick. *Quiet again.*

He kept the lights off, unwilling to chase away the ghosts that frolicked around him, hiding behind his legs to avoid their ranting mother. He could still distinguish their voices, even after three years. The baby, Emanuel, had a giggle so infectious that no one could hear it without laughing also. Serena, who was four, could hit notes that shattered glass. She was a lot like her mother. Tito, who took after his father, was thirteen. His voice had been just about to change into that of a man when . . .

Rafe snapped on the lights to keep his thoughts from returning to the day he'd found them all dead—even the baby. Shot in the head.

What had he expected, that he could lock up the two most powerful men in the Mafia, and not pay a price? A price so awful that he woke up every morning wondering why he bothered to get out of bed.

The lights flooding his furnished living room chased the ghosts of his family away. Rafe's stomach rumbled, reminding him that he'd skipped lunch—again. He stepped into the galley-style kitchen and opened the stainless-steel refrigerator. He had a choice of leftovers—Chinese takeout or stale pizza. He reached for a bottle of Heineken, twisted the top off, and deliberated.

Rafe never rushed a decision. It was that patient trait that made him good at what he did. He watched. He waited.

And right now he was watching the Individual. Soon, very soon, the Individual would be convinced enough of Westmoreland's conviction that he would make his move. And Rafe would be there to catch him when he did.

He and Westmoreland would share the honors, this time. Of course, Westmoreland was not the Individual. The director of the CIA had risked damage to his professional reputation in the expectation that his popularity would rise once the true culprit was arrested and his sacrifice became known to the public. Rafe would have to buy Westmoreland a Christmas present.

He lifted the bottle to his lips and took a thoughtful swig. That was when he felt it: a light draft running across the knuckles of his upheld hand.

Rafe put the bottle down. He turned toward the lights and extinguished them, plunging the apartment back in darkness. From beneath his silk-lined jacket, he pulled out the Magnum that was holstered to his chest.

He scanned the darkened corners as he crept down the hallway toward the only room with a balcony. His years as a street cop kept his heart beating steadily.

It occurred to him as he approached the door at the end of the hall that the Individual might have also set a trap for *him*.

The door stood slightly ajar. Rafe sidled up to it. With the tip of his Magnum he widened the crack. Light from the parking lot showed that the door to the balcony had been left ajar. He was not alone.

He stepped back quickly but not fast enough.

A weapon exploded.

Rafe saw the flare in the muzzle, felt a bullet strike him in the chest, throwing him back into the hall. At the same time, something gouged his throat, striking sharp and deep.

He lay on his back, stunned by the realization that he'd been shot in the chest, though he couldn't feel a wound. The gash in his throat was a bigger worry. Blood gushed warmly out of it, staining the collar of his shirt. It was also pouring down his throat. He swallowed fast, keeping it from filling up his lungs.

But he wasn't dead yet. He could still think; could still raise his gun with his right hand and take aim.

He did so, firing at the enormous shadow that was moving toward him. *Bang!* The Magnum kicked against his palm, sending his attacker scuttling in the opposite direction, running now toward the balcony.

Rafe fired again and struck his mark. The man roared and fell. But then he staggered up, unsteady on his feet. With a hand clutched to his chest, the man fired at Rafe and missed. He lurched through the exit. In the next instant came a strangled scream followed by a thud and then the wailing of a car alarm.

Diavolo! The man had just fallen. He could not have survived a four-story drop to the parking lot.

There went the Individual's hit man—probably Misalov Obradovitch—straight to the devil, with no chance at a plea bargain, no opportunity for the FBI to work him over.

Rafe spat blood onto the Berber carpeting and crawled toward the phone on his nightstand.

"Nine-one-one, do you have an emergency?"

He couldn't speak. His vocal cords had been severed with shrapnel of some kind.

"Sir, I can hear you on the other end. Tap the phone once if this is an emergency."

Rafe tapped the receiver against the leg of the night-stand.

"We're sending an ambulance to your location. I have you at 3900 Inglenook Drive, Apartment 4C. Is that correct?"

He tapped the receiver again, gagging on the river of blood that coursed his throat. His fingers closed over the Saint Michael medallion Teresa had given him when he was still a rookie. He found it twisted and broken.

Like everything else he'd ever valued. A gurgle of denial escaped him.

"Are you able to breathe?" asked the woman on the other end of the line.

What had happened to his medallion? But then he realized. Instead of hitting his heart, the bullet had struck the platinum disk, sending a piece of it straight into his throat.

It had to be a sign, a sign from Teresa that this wasn't his time to die.

He left the receiver on the floor and struggled to his feet, leaning over. The blood reversed direction, pouring out his mouth. His housekeeper would never forgive him for this.

But he had bigger worries than Margerie's scolding tongue. A doctor was going to want to put him in the hospital when he could least afford to leave his work. The Individual was bound to take advantage of that and make his move. Rafe had better not miss it.

Chapter Fifteen

Jaguar's defense lawyer examined the evidence strewn on her desk. Commander Curew looked more harried than ever, Luther noted, with the bun at the nape of her neck unraveling and the point of her collar curled. She worried the inside of her lip as she flipped through the pictures Luther had printed off the CD, comparing the photographed serial numbers with the numbers highlighted on the list of missing weapons he'd copied off his Palm Pilot.

"They match," she said with some amazement.

"Yes they do."

"I need to inform the NCIS right away." She reached for the phone.

"No, ma'am," Luther said, making her hesitate. "I have orders from the FBI to wait on this." With Hannah tapping an impatient toe and Westy guarding the closed door, Luther explained that they needed Special Agent Valentino's all-clear before involving the Naval Criminal Investigation Service.

"Lovitt has been working for Westmoreland all along," the commander marveled, putting the receiver down.

"He's been storing these weapons in Sabena," Luther added. "His brother-in-law's the sheriff, and the sheriff's brother owns the warehouse."

Hope flared in the commander's eyes. "Where'd you find that information?"

"On the Internet. I'm sure it's in the public records. All you have to do is query the magistrate's office in Sabena," Luther reassured her. "Do you think we can make our case now?"

She fingered the documents on her desk. "Captain Garret has a reputation for shooting down the admission of evidence. We'll have to make sure that the authenticity of each claim can be verified. These pictures could be hoaxes but if Lovitt's ties to Sabena can be proven . . . There's just one problem."

"What's that, ma'am?" Luther prompted.

"None of this information actually addresses my client's charges. Three sailors died on board the USS *Nor'easter.* Clearly one of them was killed in self-defense, but the argument that the other two jumped overboard doesn't begin to hold water, regardless of your corroboration."

"It does if they were working for Lovitt," Luther insisted. "Those men were former Special Forces, ma'am— mercenaries. If the Individual loaned them out to Lovitt, then they had orders not to be caught and questioned."

"I understand that, Lieutenant, and I honestly believe it. But according to their paperwork, Daniels, Smith, and Keyes were all legitimate Navy personnel." The JAG rubbed her forehead with agitated fingers. "God, I wish this process weren't so rushed!"

Luther glanced sideways and met Hannah's astute

gaze. He could tell what she was thinking: that Jaguar's future rested in the hands of this frazzled lieutenant commander.

"Just do your best, ma'am," Luther offered. "If there's anything we can do to help, say the word."

"You've done plenty," admitted the lawyer, stacking the evidence in orderly piles and sending them a forced smile. Her gaze lingered on Hannah as if marveling at her transformation. "I'll see you tomorrow morning before the trial starts," she told them. "Be here at seven in the morning."

"Yes, ma'am," Luther said, saluting her.

The woman was so overwrought she forgot to salute back.

The trio stepped from her office, making their way to the exit. At the checkout point, Luther retrieved his cell phone, which wasn't permitted past security. Powering it on, he noted that he had a message.

While Westy held the door for them, Luther listened to the missed call. On the front steps of the building, he came to an abrupt stop. He was conscious of the sun's warmth on his shoulders, the scent of mown grass mingling with the aroma of sausage biscuits coming from the Burger King on base. But he couldn't get his mind to accept what he'd just heard.

"What's the matter?" Hannah asked, turning to look at him.

Westy's gaze was just as perceptive. "Sir?" he said, stepping closer.

"Valentino was attacked in his apartment," Luther relayed. "He's in critical condition at Inova Fairfax Hospital."

"No shit," Westy breathed.

"Guess who went after him?" Luther added, shaking off his stunned surprise.

"Obradovitch," Westy guessed, on a growl.

"Bingo. Valentino crippled him with a return shot, and Obradovitch fell to his death trying to fast-rope off the balcony."

"Son of a bitch," Westy cursed.

Hannah said nothing. She looked dazed, unresponsive.

Luther looked to Westy for his interpretation. "What the hell's going on, Chief?"

Westy shook his head. "Maybe Westmoreland wanted Valentino off his back."

"Maybe." But the explanation didn't satisfy Luther. He turned to Hannah. "Are you all right?"

She nodded, wrapping her arms about her shoulders. Despite his better judgment, he put an arm around her. She accepted his comfort, melting against him without protest.

It felt good to hold her again, Luther thought. Shading his eyes against the sun, he sought out the Winnebago in the parking lot. Thank God for Newman's bodyguards. He didn't want to say it out loud and shake up Hannah's equilibrium any more than he already had, but he had the dampening suspicion that the Individual wasn't done causing mischief.

Sebastian tugged on the door of Leila's dance studio, disconcerted to find it unlocked. He stepped inside, setting off the electronic bell that chimed a refrain from *The Nutcracker.* Leila looked up from the cash register. She was counting money.

Counting money. With the door unlocked.

He stood there disbelieving, aware that his usual self-control was crumbling beneath an avalanche of anger, panic, and desperation. "The door is open," he pointed out as she paused to look at him inquiringly.

"Yes, I was expecting you." She had, in fact, called him this afternoon with news that she'd found Jason Miller's letter.

"What if it wasn't me?" he said, stepping in and letting the door fall shut behind him. He locked it.

Her questioning look turned to one of wariness as he stalked toward her, silent, his alarm and anger mounting, bubbling inside of him like lava.

"What do you mean?" she asked as he rounded the counter wordlessly. "What are you doing?"

"What," he said, not once breaking eye contact, "if I was a very desperate man, the same who'd robbed the shop two doors down from yours the other night?" With that brief warning, he snatched the money out of her hand, stuffing it back into the register.

Leila flinched away, looking at him as if he'd lost his mind.

Perhaps he had.

"What," he continued, pursuing her, "if I was not content with stealing your money." He raked a hungry gaze over her body, even more unsettled to find her wearing a form-fitting white top, a short pleated skirt, and tights. He trapped her against the wall, locking her in place with an arm on either side of her.

"Stop it," she said, on a fearful note.

Her fear was like a slap in the face. "Leila," he said,

stricken by the realization that, for a moment, she was actually afraid of him.

Frustration drained out of him. He lowered his head to her shoulder, suddenly repentant.

She stood stiffly beneath him, not understanding.

At last, he looked up. "Forgive me," he said. He brushed the pad of his thumb across her elegant cheekbone. "Please," he added more gently, "please lock your door when you count your money. Invest in an alarm system, one that notifies the authorities the minute your security is breached. I don't know what I would do if something were to happen to you."

He didn't know whether she would appreciate the advice, but it had to be a better tactic than scaring her.

She searched his face with her dark, exotic eyes. "Do you worry about me that way?" she asked him. The answer seemed important to her.

He gave her an incredulous look. "Of course."

"Because I might be carrying your baby," she guessed.

"No." He captured her face between his hands. The words "I love you" burned a path to his tongue. He held them in check, afraid to send her running. "Even if there is never a baby, I would worry." He kissed her tenderly, with all the reverence that roiled in him, wishing at the same time that he could find her ex-husband, who'd clearly never cherished her, and cripple him for life.

Leila swayed against Sebastian, weakened by his soul-sucking kiss. What was happening? One moment she'd been counting her money, congratulating herself on inviting Sebastian over to the shop instead of to her home, where she'd found the letter. Here at the studio—where there was no bed—she'd be less tempted to rip his clothes off.

Yet here she was, clinging to his broad shoulders, rubbing her tongue enticingly against him, her legs turning to rubber beneath her.

He broke away, giving her a thoughtful look. "Let's dance," he said.

"What?"

"Yes, I've wanted to dance with you again, since the night we met. Let's dance here." He gestured toward the studio with its large polished floor.

He was a fabulous dancer, she recalled, fluid and flawless. She was just as eager to relive the magic as he. "All right," she agreed.

He pulled her into the studio with him, not bothering to turn on the lights. The open space was illumined only by the setting sun, shining through the front door and finding its way through the front room to the studio. Amber sunlight fingered the polished floor.

"Music," Leila said, turning toward the small room that housed her collection of CDs and sound equipment. Quickening with anticipation, she selected a CD of Brazilian samba music and wondered if Sebastian knew the steps. If not, she'd teach him.

As the first exotic drumbeats came over the sound system, she approached him.

Sebastian held his hands out. She took them, waiting to see what he would do. With a drumbeat setting the tempo, he began to move. His steps were easy and elegant, but they weren't right for a samba.

"Like this," she told him, showing him how to move one step at a time, rolling on the balls of the feet. "Mirror my movements," she said. He did, stepping back as she moved forward. Within minutes, he had mastered the dance.

"You have a gift," she said without exaggeration.

"It is only that you instruct well," he countered, his syntax more Spanish than English.

Something within her eased, making her limbs less tense, freer to give outward expression to the quick, joyful music. He was doing it again, she realized, making her like him in a way that went beyond mere physical attraction.

They moved across the shadowed floor, stepping in and out of the patch of sunlight by the door. As with the last time she'd been alone with him, she was caught up in the pleasure of his company.

Suddenly the music changed, shifting from a quick samba to a sultry rumba. Without hesitation, Sebastian pulled her into his arms, so that her breasts were pressed to his chest, her hips flush with his. They moved with sensuous leisure, their thighs brushing with each step. The dance reminded Leila of the night they'd met and how their dancing had been a prelude to lovemaking.

Sebastian seemed to be thinking along the same lines. When her back came up lightly against the rails in one corner of the room, she realized he'd maneuvered her there for a reason. She lacked the resolve to chastise him. Instead, she met his kiss eagerly, relishing his lean hardness as he pressed himself against her.

For a long, long while, he was content to kiss her, drawing little moans of pleasure from her, rousing her passion. He brushed her nipples into aching peaks. He smoothed his hands over her backside, molding her against him.

Without warning, he sank to his knees. Leila's heart fluttered as he ducked beneath her skirt, kissing her thighs through her leotards. His tongue was hot and seeking. As it laved the most sensitive part of her, Leila clung to the bars on either side of her, shocked by his scandalous behavior but too overcome by pleasure to make him stop.

He tugged the waistband of her leotards over her hips. His tongue speared her again, this time with no barrier in the way.

Leila's knees gave out. She clung to the bars, sinking lower, delirious with need and want commingled.

He stood at last, working quickly to free himself from the confines of his uniform. That feat accomplished, he lifted her off her feet.

Leila locked her legs around him, urging him with frantic words. He kissed her breasts through her blouse as he claimed her with one stroke.

Inflamed by his singlemindedness, Leila shuddered around him, climaxing embarrassingly early. "Oh, I love you!" she cried, filling her starved lungs as her orgasm subsided. Immediately she realized what she'd said, and she froze, looking at him.

Sebastian's eyes blazed with triumph. He seized her hips, pulling her down on him as he drove inside her, groaning against her throat as he followed her into bliss.

Leila came rudely to her senses. She should not have said that! Raw fear caused her to wriggle free of Sebastian's embrace. She fled, leotard trailing from one ankle as she ran for the bathroom in the front of the building and shut the door.

"Leila!"

She locked it before he had a chance to pursue her. His reactions were slowed by the need to refasten his trousers. The doorknob jiggled, but the lock held.

Leila stared at her reflection, pale beneath the halogen light. What had she done? Her heart beat so erratically she could see the pulse point fluttering on her slender neck.

"Leila," Sebastian repeated, his mouth by the crack in the door. "What's wrong, *querida*? Talk to me."

She twisted the water on, needing to drown out his endearments, needing more time to determine how she was going to survive loving a SEAL. She didn't want to do this—no. It required strength that was beyond her capabilities. She couldn't love a man who waltzed into danger on a regular basis.

The thought made her queasy. She bent over, splashing water on her flushed cheeks. Feeling moisture between her thighs, she seized a handful of paper towels and wiped herself. At some point—she didn't know when—tears started streaming from her eyes.

"Leila," Sebastian crooned outside the door, "it's a simple matter for me to unlock the door. I am respecting your need for privacy, but I'm concerned."

"I'm fine," she lied, half wishing he would unlock it. She felt strangely light-headed, like she just might faint. He must have heard the tears in her voice, must have guessed she was lying, for the lock released with a click, and there he was, looking at her.

"You are not fine," he determined. He stepped inside and took her in his arms. "Come. You need to sit down."

He urged her into one of the chairs in the waiting area right outside the studio doors. Leila sank weakly onto the cushion. Sebastian snapped on the lamp beside it and crouched down, his gaze searching. "Is it such a terrible thing to love me?" he asked perceptively.

"Yes," she said, wiping a stubborn tear from her cheek. "Why?"

She drew a shuddering breath. "Because I can't be with a man who will leave me."

"I will never leave you," he said with burning sincerity.

"Of course you will," she replied, gesturing with frustration. "Every time your pager beeps, you'll be running off in the middle of the night. I'm not like Helen, Sebastian. I'm not strong enough to stand the thought of you in danger."

Understanding cleared his furrowed brow. His expression softened, then reflected humor as he chuckled out loud. "Ah, *querida,* all this anxiety is for nothing."

"What do you mean, nothing?" she demanded, angry that he should laugh at her.

"I'm retiring from the Navy in sixty days. The paperwork is done. My future is yours, if you still want me," he added with appealing modesty.

"You're retiring?" she repeated, stunned. "But you said that the Navy was your life, that you couldn't imagine doing anything else."

"That was when I met you. You have caused my dreams to change," he said simply.

Those words summoned a fresh flood of tears.

"Now I want a different life," Sebastian continued. "I want to finish my car so that you don't shudder every time you look at it. I want to make a home for our baby."

Stunned disbelief gave way to melting gratitude. Leila regarded him in amazement. In one simple sentence, he had banished all her fears.

"Better now?" he inquired.

There were challenges still to be faced, of course. Raising a baby, if there was one, to be healthy and happy was no small task. They would have to compromise on issues of faith. Deciding where to live—his place or hers? Both too small.

But with Sebastian at her side, those challenges were adventures to be anticipated. No hurdle was too high when they climbed it together.

"Much better," she confessed, loving him so much her heart felt near to bursting.

Chapter Sixteen

Hannah had to admit that Commander Lovitt cut a fine figure in his dress-white uniform. The short, silver strands of his hair reflected the sunlight streaming through the courtroom's four tall windows. The colorful ribbons pinned to his uniform vied for space over his left front pocket. He answered the prosecutor's questions with remarkable credibility and not a second's hesitation.

Captain Bart Garret had coached him well.

Hannah sat in the second row immediately behind Jaguar's family—his pretty blond wife and his teenaged daughter. Wedged between Luther and Westy, her legroom was almost nonexistent. SEALs sat shoulder to shoulder on the defendant's side of the courtroom, making seating tight.

Representation on the prosecution side, on the other hand, was limited to mainly senior Navy personnel—Lovitt's colleagues—newspaper journalists, and the prosecuting attorney's unremarkable wife, who apparently followed her husband to work.

As Lovitt's lies began to mount, Hannah stirred, her

backside sore from sitting on the hard bench for two hours while the prosecution strengthened its case. Its first witness had been a young SEAL, PO3 Rodriguez, who testified that he'd escorted Jaguar on board the USS *Nor'easter* on the morning of August the nineteenth. Jaguar had grown increasingly disoriented. He'd seized Rodriguez's gun and shot the commander in the forearm. Then he'd shot Rodriguez in the chest, narrowly missing his heart. Rodriguez had been released from the hospital only days ago.

Commander Lovitt had taken Rodriguez's place on the witness stand and was telling a similar tale. At one point, his gaze collided with Hannah's. He'd looked quickly away, stuttering as he seemed to lose his train of thought.

"Plagued in what way?" Garret was asking. With his hawkish features and long, long legs, he reminded Hannah of a stork.

"Plagued with paranoia," Lovitt elaborated. "We've all heard of veterans who go off the deep end. The farther we went out to sea the more Lieutenant Renault lost touch with reality. I assured him that I was turning the boat around. PO3 Rodriguez was getting very nervous and fingering his weapon. That was when the lieutenant jumped him. I tried to pull him off, and the weapon discharged. It cracked the glass in the pilothouse. Lieutenant Renault snatched the weapon out of Rodriguez's hand and shot me. Right here in the forearm."

"Commander, kindly show the courtroom the wound you sustained when Lieutenant Renualt fired upon you."

Lovitt uncuffed his sleeve and rolled it back to reveal a healing scar.

Garret thanked him, sending a disdainful look at the

defendant's table, where Jaguar sat ramrod straight with his chin held high. To Hannah he looked anything but crazed.

"You may continue, Commander," the lawyer exhorted.

"Well, I lost consciousness briefly. When I came to, the pilothouse was empty except for Rodriguez who was lying in a puddle of blood. I was sure he was dead. I could hear gunfire up above me and coming from the back of the boat. I could also hear a helicopter circling. I thought, thank God, the MPs are here. They'll subdue Renault before he kills anyone else.

"But it wasn't the MPs," Lovitt added, shaking his head gravely. "Renault had summoned his platoon members, somehow. I don't know what kind of story he told them, but they'd fast-roped from the helo and were firing on the duty personnel."

"How many sailors were aboard the PC that day, Commander?"

"Just three. It was a Sunday."

"Did the sailors provoke the SEALs to shoot at them?"

"Of course not. They never had a chance, poor bastards. The SEALs would have mowed them down. But it was Renault who took my weapon, a .45-caliber pistol, and picked them off from behind."

"You saw this happen?"

"Yes. First I radioed for assistance. Then I left the pilothouse in search of another weapon. That was when I caught sight of him on the deck above me. He fired on two of the sailors who were taking cover below. He shot their legs out from under them," he added, his voice cracking in horror. "They were writhing in agony, incapable of defending themselves, when he hauled them to the deck rail and pitched them overboard to drown. God, it was terrible!"

From the corner of her eye, Hannah saw Luther tip his head to one side and then the other, betraying tension in his neck. Lovitt had missed his calling for the silver screen.

"When you saw the accused throw the men overboard, what was your response, Commander?"

"I made my way to the machine gun mounted on the forecastle. It was the only weapon left to me."

"Then you weren't using it to fire on the circling helo?"

"Good God, no. The Osprey is a multimillion-dollar helicopter. I wouldn't dream of shooting at it."

"Tell us how it came to be destroyed, Commander."

"Lieutenant Renault came after me. I threatened to shoot the Osprey if he jumped me, but he did anyway. My fingers flexed on the trigger, and the chain gun spewed a half-dozen rounds. Some of them struck the tail rotor and the pilot lost control. The bird dropped into the ocean."

"What did the accused do then?"

"He put me in a choke hold. He was trying to kill me," Commander Lovitt added with convincing drama. "There is no doubt in my mind."

Westy muttered a string of curses that sent Hannah's eyebrows toward her hairline.

Garret turned his attention to the judge, the glum-looking Admiral Pease, whose poker face betrayed no response to Lovitt's story. "Your Honor, I am finished questioning this witness," Garret announced. "At this time I relinquish him to the defense."

Finally! It was Commander Curew's turn to take the floor. As the defense lawyer approached the bench, Hannah noted with dismay the creases in the woman's uniform.

"Commander," the young lawyer began, her wavering voice betraying intimidation, "you say that you initially intended to have Lieutenant Renault back on your team. Please enlighten the court as to your reasons."

Lovitt glanced at Jaguar, his expression regretful. "Before his captivity, Renault was once a promising young officer. I thought he deserved a second chance."

"Before?" Commander Curew jumped on the word. "Is it not true that as a prisoner in the People's Democratic Republic of Korea, my client retrieved valuable intelligence which will be used to fight the war on terror?"

Lovitt's shoulders twitched. "That is true," he conceded.

"And were you not commending Lieutenant Renault for his bravery the day that you lured him out onto the PC?"

"Lured?" He took offense to her word choice.

"With the promise of return to active duty," she explained.

"He was more than eager to accompany me aboard the vessel," Lovitt protested.

"And yet, within moments of boarding, you claim that he expressed unwarranted fears and misgivings? You claim that Rodriguez, feeling nervous, fingered his weapon. Is it possible, Commander, that Lieutenant Renault had good reason for feeling threatened?"

"No, no. Rodriguez kept his weapon pointed at the

floor. It was Jaguar who snatched it out of his hands. He shot me for no reason!"

"In regards to the .45-caliber pistol that you carry out at sea, had you withdrawn the weapon at this point?"

"No. I was stunned. I couldn't believe I'd been shot by one of my own men."

"And then you fainted."

"Yes."

"In that case, you never actually saw Lieutenant Renault fire on PO3 Rodriguez."

Lovitt blinked. "Well, that's correct, but no one else could have done it."

"And when you regained consciousness," she continued, ignoring him, "Rodriguez was bleeding and the lieutenant had left the pilothouse. It was then that you heard gunfire."

"Yes."

"Coming from the rear of the boat."

"Correct."

"Why would the SEALs shoot at unarmed sailors, Commander?"

Lovitt searched for an answer and shook his head.

"Was it possible that the sailors on board had weapons and were firing back? After all, PO3 Keyes was shot while attempting to fire an antitank gun into the heart of the patrol craft."

Lovitt seemed unprepared to answer the question. "Well, certainly there are weapons in the armory aboard the boat," he allowed. "The sailors may have armed themselves to protect me, but I never saw their weapons." He slanted a nervous glance toward the prosecuting attorney.

"If there are weapons aboard the PC, Commander, why didn't you arm yourself with one of them?"

"I couldn't have moved toward the aft portion of the boat without being seen," he argued.

"I see. So you thought to protect yourself by threatening to shoot the V-22 Osprey helicopter but you had no real intention of firing at it."

"Objection," Captain Garret sang out. "Your Honor, the defense is making my client repeat the same testimony that he has already given. Where is her argument?"

Admiral Pease sent a disapproving frown at the defense counsel. "Commander, if you have an argument, kindly get to the heart of it."

Commander Curew drew herself up with indignation. "Very well. Allow me to offer an alternative interpretation of the events occurring on board the USS *Nor'easter* on August the nineteenth." In a surprisingly clear narrative, she presented the version that the SEALs would shortly attest to, suggesting that Lovitt had secrets to hide and, hence, a motive for killing Jaguar, which he had attempted to do the year before in North Korea.

Throughout her narrative, Lovitt remained impassive, but Hannah imagined she could see tiny beads of sweat forming on his brow.

As Commander Curew concluded her argument, Captain Garret came to his feet. "Your Honor," he opined, his tone dripping with scorn, "the defense makes a mockery of your courtroom with her fantastical interpretation."

Admiral Pease frowned down at Commander Curew. "You are leveling some heavy allegations, Commander," he observed. "It is my hope that you are not wasting this court's time by leading us on a wild and wasteful goose chase."

"Your Honor, I will prove to this court that my statements are valid and that my client has been wrongfully accused."

"Hmmph," said the admiral, clearly unconvinced.

The faces of the jury also reflected skepticism.

Just wait, Hannah thought. With all the evidence they had stacked against him, and a little bit of luck, Commander Curew was bound to make good on her promise. Jaguar would walk away a free man, and Lovitt would spend the next decade or so behind bars.

But by four in the afternoon, the direction of the trial was still uncertain. As Commander Curew had predicted, Captain Garret hindered her argument repeatedly, calling into question the validity of every scrap of evidence undermining Lovitt's integrity. While the burden of proof was supposed to fall upon the prosecution, it didn't seem that way to Hannah.

With little progress made, the trial was called into recess until the following morning.

Though they'd been sitting still for the better part of the day, the SEALs were slow to file out of the benches. Luther looked around at his companions' long faces. "Let's go to Rascal Jack's," he suggested. "We need to let off steam."

"What's that, a bar?" Hannah asked, rubbing her sore backside.

"It's a pool hall," Westy answered, watching Garret's wife as she waited for her husband to finish conferring with his assistant.

"Do you play pool?" she asked Luther.

"Westy does."

She looked back at Westy, whose gaze hadn't wavered.

"You've been staring at that woman all day," she told him.

"She's good," he said, stepping to one side so she could sidle by him.

Hannah took another look. Mrs. Garret wore no makeup, a beige dress, and tucked her mousy brown hair behind her ears. "Good at what?" she wondered out loud.

"Being invisible," he replied, his blue eyes bright with curiosity. "Makes me wonder why."

Hannah snorted. "Isn't it obvious? She doesn't want to be here. Her husband's an ass, and she's miserable."

Westy cut her a startled look.

"Come on," Hannah urged. "She's not your problem. I'll challenge you to a game of pool."

"Just so you know, Westy's going to win," Luther divulged, shepherding them toward the exit.

"Well, thank you for the vote of confidence," Hannah retorted, "but you've never seen me play."

When he'd made his suggestion that the SEALs head over to Rascal Jack's, Luther hadn't counted on Hannah being the center of attention. Not that he could blame the SEALs, old and young alike, for gathering around her stool.

She wore a butter-yellow pantsuit that made her look stylish and savvy. She bantered with the men, demonstrating an ability to hold her own while SEALs pressed closer, drawn to her like moths to flame.

Swilling a club soda with lime, Luther found himself

craving a tumbler of scotch—something with enough punch to take the edge off his agitation. So what if twenty guys were drooling over Hannah? They'd talked about this. His plans and hers didn't jive. They were incompatible. He had no claim on her.

Bear, who occupied the stool to his left, gave Luther a knowing look. "Man, you are so hot for her, I can see steam comin' out of your ears."

"I don't know what you're talking about," Luther growled.

Bear chuckled. "In that case, maybe I'll take a shot at her myself."

He edged off his stool to join the other men.

Luther squeezed his lime into his Perrier and sent a seed flying.

A shuffle of feet had him glancing to his right. Westy had come to Hannah's rescue. He was leading her toward a pool table, one hand on the small of her back. Luther swiveled on his stool to watch them.

SEALs gathered around the table with Bear and Vinny at opposite ends. The chief gestured for Hannah to break.

She did, hitting the clustered balls with such force that she sank three of them, claiming solids.

On her second turn, she nailed another one.

Luther stopped watching the table and started watching Hannah. As she stalked around the end of the table, the material of her pantsuit clung to her sleekly muscled thighs. She considered the various shots available to her, her bright hair bouncing and shifting. He remembered how soft it felt, sliding through his fingers.

Hannah settled for a shot that required her to lean *way* over the table. Twenty pairs of eyes admired her curves.

Luther felt his blood pressure rise. Hannah brought the stick back, and *pow*! she hammered the cue ball, sending yet another solid into the corner pocket.

Bear and Vinny hooted with appreciation. At his end of the table, Bear fluttered a five-dollar bill in the air and pointed to Hannah. Vinny nodded. The bet was on.

And Westy hadn't even had a turn yet.

Hannah eyed the field. Indicating the side pocket, she leaned down and banked the red solid off the far right wall, straight into the center hole.

"Ho, ho, ho!" Bear exclaimed. There was only one solid left, a green one nestled against the short end of the table on Teddy's side.

Hannah studied it from all angles as she orbited the table. *Come on, baby,* Luther thought, cheering for her silently.

She looked up abruptly, meeting his gaze through the crowd. *Don't call me that,* Luther imagined her saying. He smiled faintly, and she looked away, frowning as she brought her focus back to the game.

The crowd grew hushed, considerate of the concentration required to keep her lead. The music in the jukebox throbbed in the background.

You can do it, Luther thought as Hannah gave the world's most difficult shot her very best effort.

She almost succeeded. The ball fell just shy of the pocket, leaving Westy the opening he needed to secure his reputation.

Vinny pulled a five-dollar bill from his wallet, licked it, and plastered it to his forehead. Luther groaned, recalling that Vinny was—what?—nineteen years old?

As Westy moved around the table sinking one ball after

the next, Luther watched Hannah's expression. Given her wry smile, she had to sense that Westy was going to beat her. It didn't seem to bother her. Her equanimity, along with everything else about her, impressed him.

I want to keep her.

The thought came out of nowhere. Luther put his glass down before he dropped it.

No, no. It'd barely been a month since he dumped Veronica. He'd sworn to himself that he'd never ever date another woman who didn't share his vision of family and fidelity. Compatibility was everything.

But I want Hannah. I can compromise.

It wasn't in his nature to be flexible. All his life, he'd envisioned marriage to a sweet and sexy and domestic female. They'd have three kids, two boys and a girl.

Hannah was sweet and sexy, but she wasn't the least bit domestic. She wanted to work overseas, for God's sake. She had plans of her own.

But maybe they could work around that. He went overseas himself, all the time. If they could see each other several times a year . . . There had to be a way to make it work. There wasn't another woman like Hannah. He'd be a fool to let her go!

He came abruptly to his feet and walked to the table just as Westy sank the eight ball. The crowd parted for him like the Red Sea for Moses. Westy glanced up from his winning stroke and caught sight of him. He grinned with approval as he laid his stick down.

Luther stepped over to Hannah. "Can we talk?" he asked quietly, his heart beating with mixed fear and hope.

"Sure," she said, looking puzzled. She thrust her pool stick at Bear. "Where?" She looked around.

Rascal Jack's was packed with SEALs and regulars trickling in. There wasn't a private corner anywhere. The music was too loud.

"Let's go outside," Luther suggested. The late September sky had mellowed to a color not unlike the juice they'd sipped by the pool in Guantanamo. Newman's bodyguards were in the parking lot. How dangerous could it be to get some fresh air with two dozen SEALs within calling distance?

The cool air came as a welcome contrast to the bar's smoky interior. Luther hunted for a place to sit. His legs were feeling shaky, like they did right before high-altitude, low-open parachute jumps. What if Hannah turned him down?

But the curb was filthy, littered with trash, spilled beer, urine, and God knew what else. Rascal Jack's shared a parking lot with a tattoo parlor and a dry-cleaning shop. It wasn't the most romantic spot to ask Hannah to start a relationship with him.

The scrubby pine trees at the back of the buildings offered privacy, but he preferred to keep close to Newman's bodyguards.

Luther honed in on the tailgate of his truck. Leading Hannah over to it, he wiped the dust off the bed liner so they could sit without sullying their dry-clean-only outfits.

Hannah eased onto the tailgate and waited. Uncertain where to start, Luther stared straight ahead, past the chain-link fence that separated them from Oceana Naval Air Base's landing field. A cargo plane, a C-5 Galaxy, the size of a whale, lumbered up the runway in preparation for takeoff, its engines flaring. With the crimson sunset beyond it, the view was almost picturesque. And if that damn plane could get off the ground, Luther thought, then so could his relationship with Hannah.

The engines roared, giving him added time to organize his thoughts. The nose of the Galaxy went up. For the longest time, it seemed to hover just above the ground before climbing ponderously into the sky. Hannah waited.

"You know how you asked me what I want the other night?" Luther began, glancing at her quickly.

Her wide eyes struck him as especially green. "Yes," she said.

"My plans aren't set in stone, you know."

She searched his face, needing clarification.

Luther gave up beating around the bush. "I think you're amazing, Hannah," he admitted. "I want to have a shot with you. If I have to change my expectations, then I will. I just don't want to let you go when this is over."

She looked stunned, completely bowled over.

"Guess I took you by surprise," he added, because the silence was killing him.

She drew a deep breath, then huffed it out again. "Oh, Luther." She was about to say something more when her gaze shifted past him, toward the tattoo parlor. "What the . . . *Get down!*" She threw herself at him, tackling him into the bed of the truck.

In the same instant a *hiss* and a *thunk* made Luther realize that a bullet had just punctured his vehicle inches away from where he lay now, on his back with Hannah on top of him. He pulled her head down, wriggling toward the side of the bed, hoping it would shield them. "Where'd that come from?" he asked.

"Shooter on the roof," she said in a thin voice.

Damn it, where were Newman's bodyguards? Luther snatched the cell phone off his webbed belt.

Thunk. A second bullet embedded itself in the truck bed, just inches from Luther's thigh. "Shit!" he whispered, twisting his body, so that Hannah was on the inside, protected.

That was when he saw the blood.

On her head, just above her temple running into her hairline. The color of her hair failed to camouflage the scarlet stain, oozing into her roots. His look of horror had her reaching up with her fingertips. "The bullet just grazed me," she said, but her face looked pale.

Luther ignored his shock long enough to peek over the edge of the truck bed. He caught sight of the shooter, standing up on the roof of the tattoo parlor, trying to improve her chances of hitting them. If his eyes weren't playing tricks on him, it was Tanya Obradovitch.

He'd been right, damn it. The Individual was back in action.

Luther made a call that went straight through to Galworth and Stone, who were probably playing gin rummy in their Winnebago, damn them.

"Yes, sir," Stone answered cheerfully.

With a few choice words thrown in, Luther summarized their situation. Not twenty seconds later, a shot was fired from the Winnebago, then another. Luther braved a second peek. Tanya Obradovitch was retreating.

Galworth and Stone burst from the Winnebago in the same instant that Navy SEALs peered out of Rascal

Jack's, summoned by the sound of gunfire. Luther caught sight of Westy, who hurried toward him.

"What's going on, sir?" He glanced at Hannah and paled. "What the fuck?"

"The Obradovitch woman was on the roof there, taking shots at us. Go get her," Luther ordered.

"Take her inside, sir. I'll cover you." Westy stalked to his car. He threw open the back, pulling out his pistol and submachine gun. He tossed the latter at Vinny who came up behind him.

Luther gathered Hannah into his arms. "I can walk," she said. He ignored her, taking care not to jostle her as he carried her into the building, nodding at those who held the doors.

He could hear Westy breaking volunteers into teams of two and sending them in different directions. Tanya Obradovitch would be apprehended shortly.

The jukebox still blared. Luther laid Hannah on the pool table's velveteen surface. The few remaining patrons gathered curiously around. "Call an ambulance," Luther told one of them as he swept the few remaining balls aside. "How do you feel, baby?"

She pretended to glare at him, her face pallid with shock. "I told you never to call me that," she said.

Her head wound was his first priority. He drew away to unbutton his dress shirt, fingers shaking so badly that it took him longer than usual. Casting his dress shirt aside, he stripped off his T-shirt, folding it into a long bandage. As he wrapped it gently about her head, he considered how she came to be shot. She'd seen the shooter first, launching herself at Luther to keep him from being struck.

"You covered me!" he raged, tying off the ends of the bandage.

Hannah hissed with discomfort.

"Christ, Hannah, you could have been killed!"

She grimaced. "No. You were the one she was aiming at, Luther," she said rather desperately. "I saw the light from her laser sight designator sitting right on your chest."

Shaken, he could only stare at her. "That makes no sense."

"Somebody wants to hurt me," she interpreted. Her teeth chattered.

Luther looked up. He pointed at a sober-looking sailor. "You, find some clean towels or a blanket if they have one."

The man disappeared.

"Hannah, listen," Luther urged, leaning over her, fingertips lightly touching her face. "They're going to catch the shooter," he promised. "And when they do, she's going to explain why the Individual is doing this. And then you'll be safe."

She clasped his hands with fingers that felt icy cold. Luther's chest and eyes were pressured with emotion. He turned Hannah's palm toward his lips and kissed it. If he weren't so worried for her, he'd march outside right now, arm himself, and hunt down the Obradovitch bitch himself.

"I'll be all right," Hannah whispered, as if sensing his inner torment.

But then her eyes rolled in their sockets and her lids drifted shut.

"Hannah!" he said, terrified that she would slip into a

coma and never emerge. He knew enough about head wounds to know that it was best for the injured party to stay awake. "Hannah!" But she failed to rouse at the sound of her name, and he didn't dare shake her, risking further injury.

He wheeled away, dragging his hands through his hair. "Where is that ambulance?" he shouted.

"It's on the way," someone said. "The cops are here."

"Here are some towels." The young sailor approached with an armful of drying towels. He helped Luther cover Hannah up. They propped up her feet to counteract her shock.

But nothing could ease Luther's shock. As he stared down at Hannah's limp body, goose bumps raced over his naked torso. He'd been in situations where teammates had been shot, injured, even killed. But this was different, because this was Hannah.

It was like his future—this whole new life he'd started to envision with her—hung by a thread.

Chapter Seventeen

Even with her eyes closed, Hannah was cognizant of the sun streaming through the hospital window. She awakened to it by degrees, turning her head slowly so as not to exacerbate the pounding at her temple. The bandage secured so tightly over her brow seemed to make it worse. Over the thudding in her ears, she could hear the hospital workers hustling about, tending their patients. It had to be mid-morning or so, which meant that Jaguar's trial was well into its second day.

That thought brought her eyes fully open. The first thing she noticed was that the chair that Luther had pulled up alongside her bed was back in the corner of the sterile chamber, empty. He'd remained with her from the moment she'd been roused by paramedics to the wee hours of morning when she'd finally been let to sleep. Luther's steadying presence had made the unpleasant ordeal nearly tolerable. A technician had taken X-rays. Then a doctor stared into her eyes and asked questions, while nurses poured stinging solution into the gash in her scalp. The police had hovered on the other side of the door, impatient to speak with her. Thank God for Luther who'd not only fielded their questions but enlisted their services in keeping watch on her door throughout the night.

When Hannah was finally left to sleep, Luther had remained with her, flouting the rules of visitation. No one seemed inclined to toss him out. He'd pulled the armchair up by the bed and stayed there. Drifting off to sleep, Hannah had reconsidered the words he'd shared so earnestly before the shooting began. He'd said she was amazing; that he wanted to keep her in his life. She'd sensed, as he sat by her bed like a patient guardian angel, that he was waiting for her answer.

Now he was at the trial, presumably defending Jaguar's innocence. Supporting his teammate was exactly what he ought to be doing, not investing his time in a woman who had bigger plans than settling down and having his babies. The loneliness that rose up in her took her breath away.

On the heels of loneliness came trepidation. Was she even safe with Luther gone? But then she remembered that the police, along with Galworth and Stone, were guarding her door. More than that, Tanya Obradovitch had been apprehended, according to the call Luther'd received on his cell phone while she was still in triage.

Hannah threw back the covers, pressured by her bladder to get out of bed. She found that her head hurt far less when she was sitting up. With relief, she put her feet to the floor. She could hear Newman's bodyguards in the hallway, chuckling over something the policeman had said.

The police would want to speak with her this morning. Not wanting to greet them in a hospital gown, she hunted for her clothes and found her yellow suit hanging in the narrow locker beside her bed. She took it into the rest-room. Following a brisk shower, she put her clothes back on, amazed to find that her suit hadn't suffered any irreparable damage.

Jittery from her exertions, Hannah emerged from the bathroom and drew up short. There was a man in her room. He turned at her entrance, his face lined with worry. "Hannah, my girl!"

"Uncle Caleb. What are you doing here?"

Taking in her bandage, he shook his head with self-recrimination. "I should never have let those SEALs run off with you, not even with my bodyguards keeping watch. They're fired," he added, capturing her face lightly in his hands, his eyes cloudy with concern.

"How did you hear?"

"My men reported in. Oh, Hannah. I'm so sorry."

"It's not your fault, Uncle Caleb," she reassured him, touched that he'd abandoned his busy schedule to visit her. "We let our guard down, thinking it was safer with Bill Westmoreland in custody."

Newman dropped his hands to his side. "I'm sure you've realized this, but it's definitely not," he said grimly.

"What do you mean?"

"I need you to come with me, Hannah," he exhorted, as persuasive as he'd been three years ago when he begged her to leave the CIA. "I'm afraid you're not safe here."

His certainty reawakened her uneasiness. "But they caught the woman who was shooting at us."

"That doesn't mean anything. Mercenaries are a dime a dozen," Newman argued. "Westmoreland only has to crook his fingers and another will come forward to take that woman's place."

Hannah's scalp tingled. "But what does Westmoreland have against me?" she asked, unable to fathom the man's antagonism.

Newman seemed to deliberate. "All right, I'll tell you," he decided. "I've done a little probing, Hannah. The FBI has kept it secret for years, but your father's plane went down for a reason. Its engine had been tampered with."

The meaning of his message filtered slowly through her mind. Her father's plane had been debilitated?

"Westmoreland knew he was second in line to becoming the DCI," Newman continued gravely. "He had a motive for wanting Alfred's plane to crash. You are your father's daughter. It makes sense that he would want you out of the way, if only to keep you from haunting him."

Every extremity in Hannah's body turned cold. The accident that had brought her to her knees hadn't been an accident, after all! Her father had been killed so that Westmoreland's ambitions could be fulfilled. "Why didn't you tell me this before?" she whispered, reeling with shock.

Uncle Caleb steadied her. "I wanted to protect you," he replied, his eyes wet with emotion. "Now you see why I never wanted you to join the Agency?"

She nodded numbly. She would have been working for the very man who murdered her parents. She searched her godfather's handsome face. "How long have you known?"

"I've always suspected," he replied. "The FBI's suspicions were revealed only recently, after Westmoreland was arrested. Hannah, I need you to come with me," he urged again. "Come with me now. I'll fly you to an island in the Yucatán. You can stay there for as long as it takes for this matter to blow over. You won't need to bring anything with you. I'll buy you whatever you require."

She clutched him, indecisive. Leave now? Without knowing the outcome of Jaguar's trial? Without telling Luther good-bye?

Looking into Uncle Caleb's gaze, she saw fear—fear that she would join her parents in death if she didn't act. Some deep-seated part of her also was afraid, not so much of dying but of disappointing Luther by putting herself before his selfless compromise. He was willing to make concessions, but she wasn't. She'd waited too long for her freedom to turn around and cash it in.

"Okay," she decided, trembling with mixed relief and dismay at her cowardice. "I'll go with you."

Seated on the witness stand, every muscle in Luther's body from his neck to his toes was taut with frustration. Not only was he torn by the need to leave Hannah at the hospital, especially with the memory of Valentino's warning echoing in his mind, but the defense counsel's arguments were getting them nowhere.

Luther had fully expected the photos taken at the warehouse to send the trial in a positive direction. Not five minutes into his testimony, Commander Curew's questioning was cut short by the prosecutor's objections.

"Your Honor," Captain Garret called on a scathing note as he shot to his feet, "kindly remind the defense who is on trial here. This line of questioning in no way pertains to the accused and the charges that he faces."

"Objection sustained," Admiral Pease agreed. "Counselor, you have veered off course once again," he scolded with tedious impatience.

"But, Your Honor, these pictures offer proof that Commander Lovitt's dealings are less than honorable and that he therefore has a motive for—"

"Enough!" railed the admiral. "Unless and until Commander Lovitt is formally charged, I will not tolerate your insinuations or your slander. Now keep to the matter of your client's charges and stop wasting the court's time!"

Commander Curew sent Luther an overwrought and apologetic look. "You are dismissed, Lieutenant," she addressed him, "thank you." As she hung her head in defeat, it was alarmingly clear that she had given up.

Luther withdrew from the witness stand on leaden feet. His gaze slid to Commander Lovitt who, in contrast to his confident demeanor yesterday, sat slouching in the third row behind the prosecutor's table, looking ill at ease. Lovitt was clearly realizing that his crimes were dogging him; that he could not avoid being bitten by them for much longer. Seeing him so discomfited eased Luther's concerns.

Once the NCIS intervened and Lovitt was arrested, Jaguar could make an appeal that would likely counter the rulings of this trial. But, for the time being, Jaguar would have to endure the stain of guilt. The defense lawyer was losing her case.

"I have concluded my arguments, Your Honor," she mumbled, casting a regretful look at Jaguar, who returned it with stoic understanding.

Just then, one of the doors of the courtroom burst open. "Excuse me, Admiral!" Luther recognized Commander

Curew's paralegal, a young enlisted female. "I have an urgent parcel for the defense."

Admiral Pease scowled but waved the woman in.

Commander Curew took the FedEx envelope from her paralegal. Ripping it open, she studied its contents with hands that trembled. Every man and woman in the courtroom held a collective breath.

"Well?" Admiral Pease prompted. "Are you finished or not, Counselor?"

"Your Honor," Commander Curew replied in a voice pitched with excitement and discovery, "I move that the charges against my client be dismissed!"

Admiral Pease all but rolled his eyes. "On what grounds, Commander?" he demanded to know.

"The Navy has no corpus delicti," Commander Curew replied, waving the documents in her hand.

Admiral Pease sent her a patronizing glare. "The two missing sailors have been declared dead, Counselor," he retorted tediously.

"Yes, Your Honor," Curew agreed, approaching the bench. "The two sailors whom my client supposedly tossed off the USS *Nor'easter* on August the nineteenth are MIA and presumed dead." She thrust the documents in her hands out for him to take. "However, Petty Officers Daniels, Smith, and Keyes have been dead for more than ten years! These are their death certificates."

Admiral Pease snatched up the paperwork that Curew thrust at him triumphantly. He perused the documents with a beetled brow.

"Objection, Admiral!" Captain Garret cried. "The defense had already concluded her arguments before presenting this material. It is inadmissible!"

"Overruled," Admiral Pease shot back, sending an impatient glare at the prosecutor. "You know as well as I that you can't try a man for a crime that hasn't happened."

"Then I question the authenticity of the documents at hand," Garret added, storming up to the bench to take them from the judge.

"Each death certificate is marked with an official seal belonging to the county of health from which it was issued," Commander Curew said, quick to defend her findings.

Captain Garret looked over the certificates with meticulous care. He carried them to the prosecutor's table to compare them with his notes. Finally, with a flush of humiliation staining his hollowed cheeks, he turned a glare upon Commander Lovitt, who sat with his shoulders hunched to his ears.

Garret stalked to the front of the courtroom, his polished shoes loud on the hardwood floor. He thrust the documents back at the judge. "Your Honor," he said with distaste, "as these death certificates appear to be authentic, the accused is clearly not guilty of the murders of Daniels, Keyes, and Smith; however there is still the charge concerning the destruction of naval property—"

"Commander Lovitt fired the chain gun, Captain," Admiral Pease retorted. "Do you honestly believe that with a two-hundred-and-seventy-degree field of fire, he would have hit the *Osprey* if he didn't mean to shoot it?" He snatched up his gavel and brought it down with a resounding smack. "The case of United States Navy versus Lieutenant Renault has been dismissed on the basis of insufficient evidence!" he called over the excited murmurs of the spectators. "Guards!" he added, waving forward the security officers who'd brought Jaguar into court. "Take Commander Lovitt into custody."

"Hoo-yahs!" rose up from the rows of Navy SEALs. In one accord, they spilled from the benches to swarm Commander Curew, who backed away in flustered modesty. Luther threw an arm around Westy's shoulders, squeezing him in triumph. They'd done it, by God! Jaguar was a free man.

Westy felt tense within his embrace. "Excuse me, sir," he said, stepping over Luther's legs. Luther watched as the chief made his way to the rear exit in the wake of the prosecutor's retreating wife. Oh, lord, he was actually following the woman.

A cheer at the front of the room reclaimed Luther's attention. A horde of young SEALs had hoisted Commander Curew onto their shoulders and were parading her around, deaf to her threats of an impending lawsuit.

Sebastian appeared out of nowhere to pump Luther's hand. "We did it, sir. Let's go talk to Jaguar."

Jaguar was clinging to his deliriously happy family. As Luther and Sebastian stepped close, he broke away to accept their felicitations, looking a decade younger with the burden of his charges lifted. SEALs lined up behind them to do likewise.

Still grappling with the victory that had come upon them so suddenly, Luther turned full circle. Why was he feeling uneasy rather than victorious? Vinny thumped him on the back. Teddy wiped his streaming eyes. "I have to go," Luther said, heading for the door.

Two men in navy windbreakers blocked his path as he stepped into the hall. Luther noted the FBI logo on the front of their jackets. He assumed they were in the area to collect Tanya Obradovitch and decided to drop by for a statement, but then he recognized the youth standing behind them from the photos in Hannah's bedroom.

"Lieutenant Lindstrom?" queried the shorter of the agents.

"Yes."

"Agent Crawford," he introduced himself. "This is Special Agent Hearn and Kevin Geary."

Luther shook hands all around, finding Kevin's hands as big as his own.

"We got word of the incident last night," Agent Crawford added, peering past him into the courtroom. "We're here to take Miss Geary off your hands."

Luther took immediate offense. But why get defensive when Hannah's safety was the main issue?

"Where is she?" Kevin added, looking worried.

Luther cringed inwardly. "She's at the municipal hospital," he admitted. "She was grazed by a bullet yesterday."

Agent Crawford glared at him. "You didn't mention that yesterday when you called Valentino's office."

"Hannah didn't want her brother worrying."

"The boss isn't going to like this," Crawford rapped. "Let's go." He jerked his head toward the exit, indicating that Luther should lead the way. "How far is the hospital from here?"

"It's right outside the gate. What's going on?" Premonition made the hair on Luther's nape rise. He glanced behind him, but Westy wasn't back in the courtroom, yet.

"Hurry," Agent Crawford urged, prodding him toward the door.

Luther headed for the parking lot without Westy,

uneasiness roiling in him. "I want to know what's going on," he demanded.

But the agents ignored him. "We'll follow you," Crawford said. "Kevin, you ride with the lieutenant and fill him in."

Kevin jumped into Luther's passenger seat, and Luther drove them swiftly toward the hospital. "What's going on?" he asked.

Kevin's eyes were the same startling green as his sister's. "Westmoreland isn't the Individual," he said softly.

Not the Individual? It took a split second for Luther to grasp that the Individual was still at large. "Who is then?" he asked, accelerating abruptly.

Kevin looked out the window, clearly still in shock. "It's our uncle Caleb."

Five minutes later, Luther pulled into the hospital parking lot with his tires squealing and a cold sweat under his dress uniform. He caught sight of Galworth and Stone walking toward their Winnebago, and pointed his truck straight at them, one hand on the horn.

"Where is Hannah?" he demanded through his truck window.

The bodyguards shared a look. "The boss came and got her," Stone revealed. "He fired us," he added, sending Luther an accusing glare.

"Took her where?" Luther asked. His throat ached with the desire to shout at them.

Stone shrugged apathetically. "I don't know. He said he flew into Oceana. I guess he's flying out of there, too."

Biting back a curse, Luther floored it, flinging Kevin against his seat as he drove them back in the direction they'd just come from. God, he'd probably driven right past Hannah and not even realized it.

"We have to stop them," Kevin said in a tight voice. His freckles stood out starkly on his pale face.

"We will," Luther reassured him, though there was no telling how much of a lead Newman had on them. He sent a glare through the mirror at the FBI agents tailing him. "Why the hell didn't Valentino warn me who the Individual really was?" he muttered, not expecting an answer.

"He didn't tell me either," Kevin admitted. "He wanted Uncle Caleb to let his guard down so he could catch him. I guess if either Hannah or I knew, we'd have acted differently and Uncle Caleb would have pulled the plug."

"I could have kept the truth from her," Luther insisted. "Valentino should have told me." But then Valentino's warning resounded in his head and Luther slapped his forehead. "Damn it, he did warn me. I just didn't get it. What does he want with her?" he demanded grimly.

Kevin shook his head. "We don't know. Agent Crawford told me just this morning that he sabotaged my father's plane."

What? Luther darted Kevin an incredulous look. Newman had killed Hannah's parents? Jesus Christ, this did not look good. "We are going to stop him," he promised, hating the eviscerated look on Kevin's face. He couldn't have said who he was reassuring more—Kevin or himself.

But as he sped through a yellow light, turning left at the intersection that took them toward Oceana, he realized a twin-engine turboprop plane was roaring over the treetops practically on top of them. Kevin's words confirmed his worst fears.

"No we're not," said the young man, putting his hands over his face. "That's Uncle Caleb's plane."

As director of the DIA, Caleb Newman had two airplanes at his disposal: a Cessna Citation jet, like the one that had killed her parents, and a Beach King-Air twin-engine turboprop like this one, a plane easier to land in unlikely places, such as a tiny airstrip on the Yucatán Peninsula.

With the sensation of having left her stomach behind, Hannah watched the airstrip at Oceana drop away beneath them. The last time she'd flown, with Luther beside her, she'd been nervous. In this smaller plane, with her head throbbing and her emotions in turmoil, she thought she might throw up.

It wasn't just her fear of flying that was making her ill. Something was wrong, but what? Was it the news that her parents had been murdered? She wiped her clammy palms on her pant legs. Oh, God, with her heart so heavy, she couldn't even think!

Newman patted her forearm as she clutched the arm of her chair. "Nervous, sweetheart?"

"I'm okay," she lied.

"You will be," he promised. "Just picture a sandy beach and a clear blue sky. Soon you'll be lounging by the ocean, safe from danger."

The reference to the ocean reminded Hannah of Cuba. If she never heard another wave roll onto the beach, she'd be fine with that. But it'd be rude to point that out; after all, Uncle Caleb was only trying to help her. "I can't hide forever," she pointed out.

He regarded her profile with a worried gaze. "Well, of course not, dear. But you'll stay there awhile, I hope. At least until this business with Westmoreland is resolved."

"Once Westmoreland is out of office," she reasoned, determined not to be talked out of her plans a second time, "it'll be safe for me to rejoin the CIA."

He sighed sadly. "What can the CIA offer you that I can't?" he inquired. "We have an overseas division. If you're that eager for travel, I'll reassign you."

"Right," she said, trying to contain her sarcasm. "And you'll also make sure that my assignments are the safest, least critical assignments possible. That's not what I want, Uncle Caleb. I want to make a difference."

"You can leave that to me," he said simply, turning his gaze forward.

And just like that, the conversation was over, and she hadn't convinced him of anything.

"I *am* going back," she insisted, aware that she sounded childish.

"You're stubborn," he said, his lips thinning. "Just like your mother."

The odd remark made her hesitate. "What's my mother got to do with this?" she demanded.

"I told her not to get on that plane. And look what happened to her," he said, his tone unusually rough.

Hannah frowned. "Why would you have told her not to? You couldn't have known anything would happen." Or could he have?

He gave her a quick, inscrutable look. "In your father's

line of work, dear heart, you never know who your enemies are."

A terrible suspicion trickled through her consciousness. Bill Westmoreland wasn't the only one with a motive for crippling her father's plane. If Rebecca Geary hadn't followed her husband to his inauguration, she'd have become a widow, and Uncle Caleb would have had her to himself.

What a terrible thing for her to think—her beloved Uncle Caleb killing his best friend intentionally? He'd never do that.

"Mr. Newman, sir." It was the pilot, summoning Uncle Caleb to the cockpit.

Hannah assessed her godfather as he released his seat belt and approached the cockpit door. All her life, he'd shown her love and tenderness, yet suddenly there seemed to be something wrong about the way he sought to control her.

The words of the pilot drove her suspicions deeper still. "Sir, we have orders from Norfolk Departure telling us to return to Oceana Air Field," the pilot imparted with urgency.

They were being told to turn around. Why?

"Stay on course," her godfather insisted. "Get us out of their airspace as fast as possible."

The hard note in his voice had Hannah reaching for her seat belt. Who was Uncle Caleb running from and why? She stood up, inching toward the front of the plane to eavesdrop.

"Norfolk Departure," relayed the pilot, "this is King Air NDI 02A. I am having trouble receiving you. Please say again."

"Putting you through to Oceana Tower Control," said a male voice followed by a hiss of static and a high-pitched squeal. "This is Agent Crawford, FBI. Am I speaking to the DIA-owned transport?"

"Roger," muttered the pilot.

Hannah drew a startled breath. FBI? Why would the FBI want Uncle Caleb to turn around, unless . . . unless . . .

Her mind stumbled over the obvious. What if Uncle Caleb was the Individual? What if he'd shipped her off to Cuba with the crazed misconception that he was protecting her? Wasn't he doing the same thing now, whisking her off to the Yucatán so she wouldn't get any more involved in this matter than she already was?

Who did he think he was, some kind of benevolent, all-powerful puppet master?

The truth dawned with terrible clarity. Of course he did. Uncle Caleb was the Individual. He wasn't just trying to control her life; he wanted the whole world dancing at his fingertips.

Chapter Eighteen

Newman leaned forward and switched the radio to off. "Ignore them," he instructed the pilot.

No! Hannah thought. She couldn't afford to take a vacation while the SEALs fought to prove Jaguar's innocence and the FBI stood on its head to catch the Individual.

Without warning, she spun around the partition, driving her elbow hard into Uncle Caleb's ear. The force of the blow flung him against the door of the cockpit where he crumpled in a heap. *That's for Mom and Dad,* she thought, trembling at the depth of his betrayal.

"What the hell!" The pilot's hands wobbled on the control yoke as he gawked over his shoulder at her.

Hannah crouched over Newman's unconscious body, feeling in the inner pocket of his jacket. She found what she was looking for and snatched the nine millimeter free, swiveling on her toes to point it at the pilot. "Turn this plane around," she commanded, "back to Oceana."

She leaned forward and switched the radio back on.

The pilot put his right hand on the throttle levers but nothing happened. Hannah disengaged the gun's safety and leveled the pistol at his head. "Are you going to fly this plane, or would you like me to fly it?"

She was bluffing, of course, but he had no way to

know that. To her relief, he pulled the plane into a banking turn.

"King Air, do you copy?" It was the FBI agent on the radio.

Hannah snatched up the handset on the throttle console. "This is Hannah Geary," she said, hearing the tremor in her voice. "Caleb Newman is down. The pilot is turning around under duress."

An audible cheer went up on the other end. Hannah thought she heard Luther's distinct baritone. "Is . . . is Lieutenant Lindstrom there?" she stammered, heart high in her chest.

There was a pause on the other end. "Hannah."

It was Luther. Tears stung her eyes and prickled her nose.

"Are you okay?"

She choked on the words that wanted to come pouring out of her—how more than anything she wanted to be safe in his arms. "Uncle Caleb killed my parents." Saying the words out loud made her stagger back against the cockpit door.

"I know, baby," Luther crooned. "As soon as you get back, the FBI will arrest him."

"We should have realized," she lamented, forbearing to scold him for calling her baby. She peered anxiously over the nose of the plane for any sign of Oceana's airstrip. Thanks to her experience examining satellite photos she picked out the pencil-thin line that came into view in the distance.

"Hey, guess what? Jaguar's case was dismissed," Luther said, relaxing her with his conversational tone.

"What?"

"Yes, surprise, surprise. Those sailors on board weren't Daniels, Keyes, and Smith. Turns out those three were already dead, killed back in the Gulf War."

"Oh, wow." She wondered whether it was Lovitt or Uncle Caleb who'd resurrected the records of common sailors, giving them to renegade commandoes.

With a start, she realized Newman was stirring. He pushed himself to a sitting position and shook his head groggily. Hannah dropped the radio to turn the weapon on him. "Stay right there!" she shouted. "Don't move."

Seeing her distracted, the pilot swung his right arm back and seized her wrist. The weapon discharged. Newman screamed as a bullet ripped into his groin. He fell back, writhing. The pilot, belted into his seat, tried to drag Hannah toward him. He groped for the weapon, twisting her arm to take it from her.

With her free hand, Hannah seized his full head of hair and slammed it against the cockpit wall. Hard. He did more than just release her. He slumped into a dead faint. The plane started into a dive.

Oh, dear God, when was she going to realize her own strength? Hannah spared a glance at her godfather. He was curled into a fetal position, moaning. She tried to rouse the pilot. "Wake up!" she shouted. She eyed the windscreen, horrified to note the angle of the plane. They were definitely descending.

The pilot didn't stir. *Oh, no. Oh, God. This couldn't be happening.* She snatched up the handset. "Luther?"

He responded to the panic on her voice. "What is it?"

"I'm in big trouble here," she admitted. "Newman's been shot and the pilot is unconscious. The plane's going down," she added. "We're going to crash!"

"No, you're not." He said it with so much certainty that she eyed her situation one more time. Oh, yes, they were. The plane was headed straight for the ground.

How ironic that she'd dreamed this scenario over and over again—except that in her dreams her parents were with her. "I'm going to die," she said, resigning herself to the inevitable.

"No," said Luther stubbornly. "I won't let you. Listen to me, Hannah. Put your hands on the throttle levers, the ones with the black handles—"

"Hold on a sec," she interrupted. First she needed to get the pilot out of her way. She unbuckled the belt that strapped him in, put her arms around his girth, and lowered him to the floor next to Newman. Then she jumped into his seat and snatched up the handset.

"Tell me what to do," she begged.

"Find the throttles with the black handles," he repeated, "and pull them all the way back. Then pull back on the control yoke."

"It's not going to work," she told him. It never worked in her dream.

"Do it, baby. We have you on radar. You're not that far off course. If you can bring the nose up twenty degrees I can talk you in."

Yeah, right. Happy endings only happened in the movies, not that she had much choice.

As she pulled back the black handles, the engine noise diminished. Next, she pulled the control yoke, fighting the increasing pressure. To her amazement, the tops of the trees disappeared from view, but then she was looking at pure blue sky as she soared straight up. A moan of terror escaped her.

"Not too much," Luther cautioned. "Ease back down until the nose reaches the horizon and add some power back in."

She pushed the yoke forward until the horizon came into view and timidly added power.

"How fast are you going, Hannah?"

"I don't know." Even to her own ears, she sounded terrified.

"Look at the airspeed indicator. It's right in the middle of the instrument panel, clearly marked."

Hannah searched frantically and finally found it. "One hundred ten," she said.

"More throttle!"

Responding to his urgency, she jammed the throttles forward. The plane lunged, and the propeller noise became a scream.

"Easy, baby. Keep the handles about two-thirds of the way forward."

Hannah reduced power. She was having a hard time holding the plane level. Each increase or decrease of power made the nose rise and fall, and the pressure of the yoke was tremendous. "I can't hold it!" she cried, especially not while holding the mike, and she wasn't going to let go of that.

"Are you buckled in?"

"No." The plane was all over the sky, rising and falling like a roller coaster. How was she supposed to buckle herself in, hold the mike, and keep the controls steady all at the same time? "I can't let go!"

"Hannah, listen," Luther urged. "Do you see a sort of a wheel sticking halfway out of the center console, close to the throttles?"

"Yes."

"Which way is the plane trying to go, up or down?"

"Uh . . . down."

"Okay. Roll the wheel toward you until you feel the pressure on the yoke ease off to nothing."

Hannah obeyed, and to her huge relief, the nose rose gently. The control yoke was blessedly pressure-free.

"That's better," she breathed, freeing a hand to buckle herself into the pilot's seat. She clung to the mike.

"Now, find the rudders on the floor," Luther instructed, "and push the left one until I tell you to stop. You're a little right of course."

She did as he said, and the nose of the plane started skidding through the air. *Oh, my God.*

"Now, release the pedal and have a look. Do you see the airstrip ahead of you?"

She'd kept one eye on it all this time. "I see it."

"Tap the right rudder with your toe and line yourself up exactly. Make small movements. You have plenty of time."

She heard him muffle the radio and issue orders to have the airstrip cleared; to have emergency vehicles standing by. Her heart clutched with dread at the thought of approaching the ground.

"I'm scared, Luther," she confessed.

"I'm scared, too, baby. But if anyone can do this, it's you. It's a piece of cake in a turboprop, trust me. I'm going to talk you right through it. Okay?"

She blew out a breath. "Okay."

"That's my girl. Now that you've sped up, I need you to slow down. Pull back on the throttle handles until they're about halfway back. As you slow down, the nose will drop. Roll the wheel back until it comes up level again."

As tense as a trapdoor, she followed his instructions. Like he'd said, the nose began to drop. She rolled the trim wheel back and the nose returned to the horizon. The white needle on the airspeed indicator began to drop. "It's dropped below a hundred fifty," she told him. "How am I going to hold this mike and land the plane at the same time?"

"You can put the mike down and still hear me," he reassured her. "Look down low to the left of the throttles. Do you see a handle with a top that's shaped like a wheel?"

It was practically under her hand. "Yes."

"That's the landing gear. Push it all the way down, then nudge the throttles forward just a bit."

"Right now?"

"Yes, now."

She did, and a mechanical sound followed. She sensed the plane slowing down, and she responded by nudging the throttles back up.

"What's the airspeed now?"

"One hundred."

"That's a little slow." He tried to mask the tension in his tone, but she heard it all the same. "Add a little more power and roll the trim forward just a touch."

She obeyed him, and the sound of the engines increased. The airspeed indicator began a slow climb up. She was conscious of the jacket of her yellow suit sticking to her back.

Having fun yet, Hannah? she asked herself.

Surely her father had done this very thing while trying

to land his floundering plane in a bit of open field. Only he'd hit the trees instead. *Oh, God, don't think of that!*

"I'm back to one twenty," she volunteered.

"Perfect," Luther said, his voice steadier. "Now look along the top of the instrument panel. See the three green lights lit up?"

"Yes."

"That means the gear's down. Look on the face of the instrument panel near your right knee. Do you see another smaller handle shaped like the rear edge of a wing?"

"Yes."

"That's for the wing flaps. Pull it down to the first notch in the slot."

She did, and the plane began to slow again. The nose rose slightly.

"How's the airspeed?" Luther asked.

"Down to one hundred ten again."

"Hold it right there. If it tries to go slower, roll the trim forward to make the nose go down. If it tries to go faster, trim up. Remember this," he added. "It's important: You are going to control the speed by moving the nose up or down. You're going to control your altitude with the throttles. Got it?"

Speed nose. Altitude throttles. "Got it."

"If you pull off power the nose will drop, and the plane will start to speed up. You have to counter that by raising the nose and holding speed at a hundred ten."

God, there was so much to think about at once! "I'm going to put the mike down now," she told him, needing to free her hands.

"Go ahead."

"Luther?" she added, thinking this might just be her last chance to communicate with him.

"Yes, Hannah?"

She hesitated. What could she say that would convey how much she'd loved every moment spent with him? "I've had fun," she said, disappointed that her words fell short.

He choked out a laugh. "Baby, your idea of fun is killing me."

"I know. I'm sorry." She put the handset down, determined to put him out of his misery.

She checked the airspeed indicator, the trim wheel, and the throttles, taking great care to keep the plane at an even speed and level.

Luther's voice came a moment later. "Okay, Hannah, push that wing-shaped handle down one more notch. Trim the nose so your speed stays at one hundred. Fortunately, the wind won't be a factor."

Hannah pushed the handle down again, and the plane reacted by raising its nose. The airspeed indicator started down, and she hesitated, thinking first, before rolling the trim wheel forward to increase her speed.

Looking out the windscreen, she cringed to see how close the ground was getting. At least she was centered on the runway. She tasted salt on her upper lip.

"Time to pull the flap handle to the last slot," Luther instructed. "You're going to slow down to ninety. Remember, control your speed with the trim and your distance from the ground with the throttle. Do it all very gently."

With her heart in her throat, Hannah pulled the flap handle back.

The plane reacted as it had before, slowing down and

raising its nose. Rolling the trim forward, she tried to make the speed settle on ninety. Looking up, she saw that she was much too close to the ground, and the runway was still some distance away. Panicked, she shoved both throttles forward.

The engines roared and the nose rose abruptly. *Oh, God, she was losing control!*

Luther's voice was a balm in her ears. "Gently, Hannah," he reminded her. "It doesn't take a lot of throttle to keep you up there."

She pulled the throttles back and the nose dropped again. She let it fall. Miraculously, the airspeed indicator settled on ninety. The ground came closer. She made a slight correction with her feet.

Suddenly the nearest end of the runway seemed to be approaching at blinding speed.

"You're doing great, baby," came Luther's voice, calm and fully focused. "You have a huge, long runway in front of you. Just let the plane settle in. When you get about twenty feet up, pull the throttles back, then as you sink toward the runway, pull back on the control yoke gently. Use the rudders to go straight. You can do it, Hannah. I love you."

Concrete was flashing underneath her now, and she seemed to be going so fast that there was no way she could survive contact with it.

"Throttles back," Luther instructed as the ground rushed up under her. The engine noise died away.

"Control yoke—gently!"

She pulled back on the yoke and then back some more. The pressure was tremendous, but she didn't dare let go to use the trim tab. The runway disappeared under the nose of the plane, and then there was the screech of rubber on cement, and she bounced in her seat.

One foot almost slipped off the rudder, but with a supreme effort of will, she kept the plane from veering off the runway.

"Good girl!" There was huge relief as well as jubilation in Luther's voice. "The brakes are on the top of the rudder pedals. Push them gently. Make sure that you keep going straight!"

Hannah depressed the brakes, and the plane began to slow. The end of the runway came into view, but it wasn't close enough to frighten her. She pumped the brakes until the plane slowed. At last it stopped.

Hannah let out a long, shuddering breath. Tears of relief flooded her eyes. She put her hands over her face. Oh, merciful God, it was over. And she was still alive.

For a long moment, she savored the sensation of being utterly motionless, while howls and cheers poured out of the radio.

Suddenly the plane began to move again. She jammed her feet back on the brakes and grabbed the mike. "Help! How do I keep it stopped?"

Her question prompted uproarious laughter from the control tower which made her furious.

Luther's voice, choked with emotion, came to her ears. "Sorry, baby. We're a little hysterical up here. Look on the far right side of the throttle console for two mixture controls. Pull them all the way back."

She did, and the whine of the turboprop descended a musical scale.

With badly shaking fingers, she followed his final instructions to turn off the ignition. The instruments jumped and the lights on the panel dimmed. Hannah swallowed convulsively. With her adrenaline receding she was suddenly aware that her head was pounding and she felt more than a little nauseated.

She had fully expected to die. It had seemed inevitable, given her recurring nightmare. But with Luther metaphorically holding her hand, she'd managed to land the plane and give her dream a different ending. She couldn't have done it without him.

It suddenly occurred to her that Luther had slipped a rather profound confession into his last directions.

I love you, he'd said.

She closed her eyes, letting the warmth of that message steady her heart. *Oh, Luther, I love you, too.*

She didn't have the strength to hide from that truth. Nor was she above basking in it while she could.

She was only human. And more than anything in the world she needed to feel Luther's arms around her, to know that she was safe and sheltered in his care.

Freeing herself from the seat, she headed for the exit, stepping distastefully over the drooling pilot and Uncle Caleb, who was curled up in a puddle of blood. Seeing him still conscious, she paused long enough to bend over him.

"You never loved my mother," she accused, her voice shaking. "Love isn't about owning someone. It's about putting their happiness first."

With that, she released the airtight lock on the exit, pushing it open and off to one side.

Without any consideration for her quaking legs, she leaped to the tarmac, several feet below her. Her knees buckled and she pitched forward, scraping her hands and knees so badly that she couldn't get up.

"Ow! Okay, that hurt." She rolled onto her backside and inspected her bleeding palms. Her head felt as if it had been split with an ax. Instead of getting up, she waited in the shade of the wing as emergency vehicles bore down on her with sirens screaming.

"Comfortable?" Luther asked, stroking a hand up and down Hannah's bare arm. She sat in her nightshirt on Luther's big green couch, basking in the heat of a fire. While Luther occupied the length of the couch, Hannah lay between his legs, her head resting on his chest, soaking up the blaze with her eyes closed.

"Comfy," she purred. She didn't want to think beyond this moment, beyond her gratefulness to be alive and, for the time being, happy.

"Are you still sore?"

"Very." There wasn't a muscle in her body that didn't ache, but if she held perfectly still, she felt fine.

"What are you thinking about?" he pressed.

Hannah sighed. Putting off their discussion any longer was pointless. She could sense Luther's agitation, his growing need for an answer. He'd told her today that he loved her, and that had come on the heels of his admission yesterday that he didn't want to let her go. He shouldn't have to wait.

But the day's fantastical events had prevented her from giving him an answer yet. The paramedics had swarmed her on the tarmac, arriving just before Luther and Kevin who'd run clear from the tower control building. Both of them had been gasping for breath, with tears in their eyes. They'd taken turns hugging Hannah while the paramedics tended to Newman and the pilot, who were rushed from the scene, escorted by an FBI agent.

Hannah had been whisked to the terminal building where the second FBI agent, Crawford, fielded the questions coming from the military police. She'd sipped the orange juice thrust into her hand and tried to calm her shaking and shuddering. Guessing her quandary, Luther had pulled her onto his lap, at which point Kevin's jaw had gone visibly slack. Bit by bit, Luther's warmth had invaded Hannah's shocked muscles, so that her shuddering subsided.

Now, with the heat of the fire upon her and some serious painkillers coursing her system, she felt so lethargic, she wasn't sure she could move. But the moment had come to push Luther gently away from her, even though every selfish bone in her body wanted nothing more than to take what he'd offered her and run with it. But like she'd told Uncle Caleb, loving Luther meant wanting his happiness. And he wouldn't be happy trying to make it work with her.

She straightened away from him, wincing at the pain it caused her. "Okay," she relented, "it's time to talk." She tucked a stray hair behind her ear.

His look of earnest concern was almost her undoing. God, it would be easy to take what he offered. But then he would be the one to suffer, and she couldn't stand the thought of that. "I heard what you said to me as I was landing the plane," she admitted quietly.

The look in his eyes was almost fearful. "And?" he prompted, searching her face.

"And I love you, too." She stroked his strong jaw, heart aching like a giant tumor in her chest.

For a second, his face took on an incandescent glow, but then the glow faded and his eyes became watchful. "Why do I sense a 'but' coming?" he inquired.

Hannah sighed. "Isn't it obvious, Luther? I can't ask you to sacrifice your dreams for me. You want a wife who'll 'hold the fort down' while you're off chasing terrorists," she quoted. "I'm not that kind of person. I'm barely even house trained!"

Her attempt at humor drew a wan smile from him, but his dark blue gaze remained serious. "I realize that," he argued. "I told you, I'm willing to make some concessions."

"That's not a concession, Luther. That's a sacrifice. You want kids, too, remember? I'm not the maternal type—not yet anyway. I haven't even thought about having kids. All my thoughts for the last three years have been about the work I want to do. I want to travel; meet people I've never known before; master their language; make contacts; do something that'll save hundreds if not thousands of American lives. I want my life to mean something!"

"Do you think I can't appreciate that?" he countered with quiet force. "I had those same thoughts myself, sitting in a car wreck waiting for emergency workers to get me out."

She winced at the anger underlying his reply. "Okay, so you understand where I'm coming from," she allowed. "But that doesn't mean you'll be happy with me. You said yourself that our careers would make it impossible. I don't want to settle down right now and have a family. Can you honestly tell me that you're willing to postpone your plans for me?"

He looked at her then as if she were a stranger. Hannah suffered the certainty that her argument had finally struck home. And just like that, she'd locked herself out of his heart forever.

"I wouldn't mind postponing them awhile," he insisted, but his words now lacked conviction.

She shook her head. "I wouldn't want you to do that, Luther. Not for me. Not for anyone."

A long, painful silence descended between them. Hannah could feel her heart thumping heavily in her chest as if weighted by iron chains.

This is where you insist that I'm worth it, she thought, trying to send that message kinetically. *If you really loved me, Luther, you'd wait for me until my restless feet bring me home.*

But Luther didn't say anything. He turned his gaze toward the crackling fire, and though his arms remained every bit as tender, she felt him withdrawing from her emotionally, mentally.

Sorrow broke over Hannah, sorrow too high, too wide and deep to breach. She put her head onto Luther's chest and let the tears come. What did she expect? That if she pointed out their differences he'd commit himself anyway?

The need to cry put such pressure on her chest that Hannah gave into it. Luther laid his cheek on the top of her head and held her tighter. "Let it out, Hannah," he encouraged on a raw note, his fingers tangling gently in her hair. "I've got you for now, baby."

For now. Those words brought on a fresh wave of grief.

Hannah wept until she fell asleep, exhausted, cradled in the temporary refuge of Luther's arms.

Luther didn't sleep. The fire had dwindled to a gasping ember when he carried Hannah to his bed. He settled her under the sheets, then climbed in next to her. His room felt cold in contrast to the fire-warmed living room. But Hannah's limp body was warm. Her nightdress had ridden up to her waist, and her thighs were silky-smooth against him as he gathered her close. He lay there thinking.

With just a few logical words, Hannah had doused his newborn dreams in common sense. Of course, he'd realized that keeping Hannah would entail sacrificing his well-laid plans, but when she talked about postponing a family, he found himself thinking of Veronica, who'd wanted a family right away. If he and Ronnie hadn't worked out, what made him think he could make a long-distance relationship with Hannah work? Her dreams entailed lengthy overseas assignments, networking, and intrigue. She would barely have time for him.

It didn't matter that he loved Hannah so much more than he'd ever loved Veronica. That didn't change facts. Their timelines didn't jive. They had different dreams. How would they ever make a marriage last?

Toward the darkest hours of night, Luther gave up questioning the injustice of their situation. There was nothing left for him to do but enjoy the precious minutes left to them.

He slid a hand under Hannah's nightshirt and touched her gently. To his gratification, she stirred, reaching behind to caress him in return. He shucked off his pajamas and put her questing hand on his aching flesh.

Hannah made a sound of sleepy appreciation. She wriggled her backside closer and he brushed her panties over her hips, removing the last barrier between them. He took his time, touching her leisurely, memorizing every beautiful feature of her. She moaned. "I can't move," she protested.

"Just lie still," he encouraged. He wanted this to be a gift, one that she'd remember.

Her skin grew warm and faintly damp as he devoted himself to pleasuring her. Though he ached to find his own relief, he held back, content to draw the tiniest gasp, to breathe the scent of her excitement, to make the hidden muscles inside of her contract.

When he finally entered her, she was slick and burning from the inside out. He moved as gently as he could. Not until several blissful moments passed did he realize he'd forgotten to wear a condom. He started to pull out.

"No," she protested, locking him in to place.

"I forgot protection," he growled.

"Don't leave me now." It was a heartfelt plea, one that he capitulated to all too willingly. She wanted nothing between them; nor did he. He could feel her silkiness all around him, feel her contracting as her climax gathered.

He set his jaw, determined to draw this moment out forever. He didn't want to let Hannah go. She was his. He was hers. Why did life have to get in the way?

"Oh." She moaned long and low, her body writhing in a sensual dance against his. "I love you, Luther," she confessed, lost in her release.

That did it. His pleasure erupted, spilling over him

with heat and power. Luther commanded himself to withdraw, to compromise his pleasure for the sake of Hannah's dreams.

It took every ounce of his willpower. He ejaculated on her thigh, his forehead resting on her shoulder, hands clutching her to him.

The feeling of incompletion that ripped through him brought tears to his eyes. "I'll get a washcloth," he said, rolling out of bed.

When he came back, Hannah was nearly asleep again.

"I hope I didn't hurt you," he said, referring to the injuries she'd sustained in the last two days.

She turned and eyed him in the shadows. Sorrow hovered between them like a specter. "I hope I didn't hurt you, either," she whispered perceptively.

He threw the washcloth aside and took her in his arms again, taking comfort in her presence, as he always had.

Chapter Nineteen

Sebastian had never seen the ballroom at the Shifting Sands Club as filled to capacity as it was tonight. Every member of SEAL Team Twelve had come to honor him at his retirement party.

The tables stood decked in snowy linens, chinaware, and shimmering crystal. Elaborate bouquets of white mums and red roses vied for space on the tabletops, as meals of roast beef and Cornish game hen were laid before each guest. With Christmas just three weeks away, the festive scene was enhanced by the enormous decorated tree occupying the far corner.

Because of the tree, the tables were crammed together to make space for the dance floor, already awash with lights reflecting off the mirrored ball. The tasteful background music was a misleading indication of the pounding beats that were bound to come later. Already, the long lines at the open bar earlier had caused the volume to swell. The guests were having a good time.

Sebastian sat at the head table, which had been set upon a dais as if this were a medieval feast. Gazing at the familiar faces to his left and right, he found that the lump in his throat made it difficult to consume his dinner. He laid his fork down and sipped his ice water. He promised himself he would not allow his famous composure to slip tonight. He would not cry.

Leila, who was seated next to him in a heart-stopping scarlet dress that glowed beneath the crystal chandeliers, gave him a searching, sidelong look.

"Are you all right, Sebastian?" she asked, laying her own fork down.

"Of course," he said, summoning a smile for her. But then he looked past her at Jaguar who was whispering something into Helen's ear and Luther who was cutting his roast beef into squares, and his chest felt full and tight. He was going to disgrace himself.

Leila removed the napkin from her lap. "Would you come to the restroom with me?" she asked him unexpectedly.

He looked at her more closely. "Are you not feeling well?"

"I'm fine," she said with a reassuring smile. "I'm not sure where the restroom is, though."

"All right." He pushed his chair back and escorted her out into the hall, ignoring curious glances.

Once in the privacy of the hallway, Leila turned to face him, her fingers settling lightly on the arms of his black dress uniform. "I can't ask you to do this," she told him, her eyes wide with regret.

He shook his head. "Do what?"

"To retire for me. Oh, Sebastian, you look so sad!"

He put his hands over hers, loving her intensely for her concern. "Of course I am sad, *querida*. These men have

been my family for many, many years. I will miss them."
He cleared his throat, trying to remove the stubborn lump
lodged there.

"How can I make this easier for you?" she asked, lacing her fingers through his.

"You have already," he reassured her with a kiss.

She darted him a mysterious look. "Perhaps this will
help." She withdrew her hands to fish an object from the
sequined purse dangling at her shoulder. "I've been carrying it around for a few days now, waiting for just the right
moment . . ." With trepidation in her eyes, she handed
him a plastic square.

"What is this?" he asked, not recognizing the device.

"Look inside the circle. What do you see?"

"A plus sign," he said. His gaze rose slowly up to hers.
He felt the blood slip from his face. "Is this what I think
it is?"

"Would you like a family of your own, Sebastian?" she
countered tremulously.

He put a hand to his forehead, feeling suddenly light-
headed. "We are going to have a baby?"

Her eyes took on a brilliant sheen. "Is that what you
want?" she asked uncertainly.

There was nothing forced in the smile he gave her now.
"*Querida,* you have made me the happiest man on earth!"
he swore, grinning.

"Are you sure?"

"Am I sure! Come with me."

Suddenly, instead of comforting him in a private place,
Leila found herself being dragged into the ballroom. Every
couple in the room took note of their entrance while pretending politely not to stare. Sebastian marched her straight

over to the DJ. He leaned forward, whispering something into that man's ear.

The DJ handed Sebastian a microphone. "May I have your attention," Sebastian said, his voice especially lilting over the sound system.

Dozens of heads swiveled in their direction. "I know you are just finishing your meals and the cake has not been cut, but I have something to say."

The room fell respectfully quiet. Close to panic-stricken, Leila sought out Helen's gaze at the high table. Her friend wore a small, expectant smile. Leila's heart began to beat unnaturally fast. Surely Sebastian was only going to thank his guests for coming. Perhaps he might even break the happy news that he would soon be a father.

She swallowed against her suddenly parched throat. How would that look to others, when they weren't even engaged?

"Some of you have known me for ten years or more," Sebastian began. "We have been to the ends of the earth, where the ocean drops away into darkness." A moment of profound silence followed those words. "Experiences like those create a bond that time and space cannot erase. So there is no good-bye. Instead, I ask your blessing on this new life that I intend to lead."

Leila's ears began to ring. She was aware of Sebastian reaching into his back pocket. He fished out a velvet pouch, loosed the string that held it shut, and pulled out a diamond solitaire. It winked at Leila beneath the turning mirrored ball.

Sebastian sank to one knee. Leila's own legs wobbled. A low murmur of approval spread through the audience. Taking both her hands, Sebastian looked up at her, his expression more intent, more certain than she had ever seen it. "Leila, it would be my greatest pleasure if you would consent to be my bride and the mother of my children. Will you marry me?"

She was conscious of the quiet that descended over the room as spectators waited for her answer. She waited for a tiny panicked voice within her to cry no!

But the purity in Sebastian's coffee-colored eyes kept the fearful voice silent.

"I will," she whispered, trembling from head to toe.

The smile he gave her was as brilliant as the Christmas tree behind him. He stood and tipped the mike toward her lips. "Tell everyone," he exhorted.

She cast a self-conscious look at the audience. "Yes," she said simply.

The room broke out in "Hoo-yah, Master Chief!"

The ring slipped silkily up Leila's ring finger, a perfect fit. Music blared suddenly from the speakers at her back.

"Care to dance?" Sebastian asked, one eyebrow winging over the other.

She thought, with hysterical relief, that at least he didn't look sad anymore. She went willingly into his arms, thinking, *This is where my life begins.*

Seated at the end of the high table, Luther watched Sebastian and Leila float with effortless ease about the dance floor. They looked perfect together, both of them dark and slender, intensely bound up in each other. He had the distinct impression they were in a world of their own.

With the feeling that he'd been knifed in the chest, Luther reached for his tumbler of scotch. He took a small sip. As the burning liquid curled down his throat, he set the tumbler down.

Drinking wasn't going to ease the heartache that kept him constant company. He had to believe that time would help eventually, but it hadn't yet. Over two months had passed since Hannah left Virginia Beach with her brother and Agent Crawford. He'd welcomed the dangerous missions that had cropped up since. The only thing that took the edge off his constant heartache was unmitigated fear.

Jesus, how long was he going to feel like this? "Excuse me," he muttered to Teddy and his date. Ignoring their obvious concern, he pushed his chair from the table and stepped off the dais, heading for the exit that led to the balcony.

A bitter wind hit him squarely in the face as he stalked to the cement railing and gazed out over the inhospitable ocean. It was here that he and his squad members had first discussed Jaguar's charges and what they could do to help him. It was here that Master Chief had told him that Hannah Geary was alive, that the FBI needed help to retrieve her. He'd had no idea how thoroughly she would invade his existence.

Cold, salty air pinched Luther's cheeks. He welcomed the discomfort.

Hannah. The surf seemed to say her name as it crashed onto shore on the other side of the dunes. *Hannah. Hannah. Hannah.*

Why was it, if they were so incompatible, that he could close his eyes and feel her inside of him? The thought pushed tears into his eyes that the wind quickly dried.

The sound of approaching footsteps had him turning around alertly. With dismay, he recognized Veronica's silhouette. She'd come to Master Chief's retirement party as Ensign Peter's date.

"Hey," she said, sounding different with the waves crashing in the background. "I saw you step out. I wanted to tell you something."

"What's that?" What had ever drawn him to Veronica in the first place? he wondered. Her dark eyes and stubborn chin gave her an inscrutable look, so different from Hannah's clarity.

"I'm sorry for telling Eddie about that Hannah woman you were with. I didn't realize how much he had to hide."

Eddie? It took him a second to realize she was talking about Commander Lovitt, who'd skulked around Westy's house intending to shoot Hannah before she could jeopardized his reputation. "You should be sorry," he retorted, unforgiving. It occurred to him that Veronica had slept with Lovitt, too. She was probably more disgusted with herself than anything else, but he still wanted to wring her pretty little neck for nearly getting Hannah killed. He shoved his hands in his pockets to keep him from doing just that.

Veronica shivered but she held her ground, apparently determined to speak to him despite his hostility. "I also wanted you to know that . . . you're a really good guy, Luther. I'm sorry that I didn't treat you right."

Surprise kept him mute for a minute. Well, well. He didn't feel like a good guy right now. He felt angry and hurt and dangerously unpredictable.

"I want you to have this back," she added, holding out a shiny object.

He realized it was the ring he'd given her, a ring that had cost him five grand. "Keep it," he said, not wanting to put his hands on it. It meant nothing to him, less than nothing. If she forced it on him now, he'd fling it into the ocean.

"Are you sure?" she asked.

"Yes." He was positive. At this rate, he wasn't ever going to get married. He'd never love another woman the way he loved Hannah.

"All right." With a frown of perplexity, Veronica turned around and walked away from him.

Luther watched her go. He wished he could walk away from himself so easily. Instead he was stuck with this god-awful feeling that he'd let the best thing in life get away from him.

Chapter Twenty

Alexandria, Virginia
1 January ~ 1:53 P.M.

On this first day of the New Year the weather was typical for northern Virginia—just above freezing and inhospitably humid, so that the cold went straight to the bone.

Why, Hannah wondered, had she chosen to jog along the Potomac River, where a chill blew off the water? Her lungs ached, her nose was running, and despite the light sweat she'd worked up under her running suit, her extremities were turning numb.

With the end of the city block in sight, she slowed to a brisk walk and steadied her breathing. She had to be punishing herself. Not a single other soul was cruising the historic area today. They were probably sleeping off their hangovers, still curled up in bed with their lovers.

The thought sent a pang of envy through her heart. *Oh, Luther,* she sighed.

And this is just the beginning, taunted a voice inside her head. She'd received word of her first assignment shortly after Christmas. She was headed to Greece for two years with a cover job as a secretary in the American embassy. It was a fantasy assignment if ever there was one—Greece! Who didn't want to go to sunny Greece, the birthplace of human civilization?

She reminded herself how lucky she was. Most rookie case officers got the gritty jobs like Kyrgyzstan or Nigeria. Someone in the agency—probably Westmoreland himself—was looking out for her.

So why the reluctance weighting her down? She stepped off sidewalk and crossed a cobblestone street, vapor trailing out of her mouth. The warm climate of the Mediterranean would be a welcome change.

Only, she didn't want to go.

She told herself that she was worried for her brother. Kevin had finished his dissertation and graduated with honors, but now he worked such long hours in the Johns Hopkins laboratory that he needed regular reminders to go home and sleep.

Only it wasn't Kevin's welfare that kept her from wanting to leave. If she'd be honest with herself, she'd admit it was the dreams: dreams of herself and Luther. There wasn't a night that she didn't dream that she'd agreed to stay with him, and she was back in his arms—safe and utterly content. Sometimes there were children with them, little boys with dark hair and deep blue eyes.

She'd mentioned the dreams to her counselor. Dr. Andre Guhl had lost his entire family in a car wreck while he'd been driving. He'd helped her cope with her parents' deaths and with Uncle Caleb's betrayal. But when she mentioned her dreams of Luther, he'd just looked at her. "Are you sure you want to leave the country?" he'd finally asked.

"Of course. It's what I've always dreamed of."

"Until lately," he pointed out. "Why not forge your own path instead of following your father's?"

The suggestion had made her think of something Westy said. *Sounds to me like you're running. Or maybe chasing someone.*

She'd been chasing her father's memory all this time, as if it would bring him back. "Just think about it," her counselor had urged.

Hannah blew warm air on her stinging fingers. She came to a dead stop at the corner of Second Street and North Royal. She'd done nothing lately *but* think about it. This morning, on the first day of the new year, she was making up her mind.

She wasn't going to Greece. She wasn't going anywhere but back into Luther's arms, where she belonged.

She started running again. Relief made her feet sprout wings. She sprinted down Royal Street, thoughts racing ahead of her. The first thing she needed to do was to contact Luther. But what if he'd moved on already, in search of his ideal mate? No, he couldn't have. Their bond wasn't so easily broken.

Hannah flew along the brick-lined sidewalk. Rounding the corner of Bellvue, she blinked in disbelief. There was Luther shutting the door of his truck, starting to pull away. "Luther!" She shouted his name but he didn't hear. He pulled out into the street.

Hannah gave chase, flailing her arms.

To her relief, he caught sight of her and backed up. She reached his driver's side door just as he stepped out. The instinct to throw herself into his arms battled with dignity and the awkwardness that came from time apart.

He looked good. He wore a navy blue, button-down

dress shirt under a black, wool coat and black jeans. His hair was slightly longer, his cheeks wind-chapped as if he'd spent a lot of time outdoors. He'd obviously forgotten to shave that morning, and an appealing five o'clock shadow darkened his chin.

"I almost missed you," he commented as the silence stretched between them.

"I was out running. You want to come in?"

He dropped his truck keys into the pocket of his coat. "Sure."

She led the way to the front step, pausing to fish her hidden key out from under the flower pot. Her fingers shook as she released the lock. "The house is a mess," she apologized, stepping in. "Sorry. I was planning to clean it today before Kevin came over."

"He's on his way?" He looked around.

"No, tonight. Free food. It's the only thing that'll lure him away from his work. Have a seat," she offered, taking off her sweat jacket. She wore an FBI T-shirt underneath. "Can I get you something to drink?"

His gaze was fixed on her T-shirt.

"Valentino gave it to me for Christmas," she said, tugging at it self-consciously.

"He gave me one, too," Luther admitted, with a twitch of his lips.

"Mine came with a job offer," Hannah blurted. Yeah, and now that she thought about it, she'd worn the damn thing a half-dozen times without realizing why she was so attached to it.

Luther looked at her sharply.

"I'm going to take him up on it." The certainty that flooded her made her feel especially good.

She'd rendered him completely speechless.

"So what do you think?" she asked, breathlessly.

"You're going to work for the FBI," he repeated.

"Yes," she said with a wondrous smile.

His expression darkened. "I thought you couldn't wait to go back to the Agency," he said on an accusing note.

"I couldn't. I did. I even got my first assignment. Greece," she added, watching his anger morph into puzzlement. "But now I don't want to go."

He ran a look up and down the length of her, as if trying to determine whether she was really Hannah Geary or her evil twin. "Do you want to sit down?" she asked again.

She moved into the living area and sat in a high-backed chair, forcing him to do the same. Obviously getting him a drink wasn't in the script. "I guess we have some catching up to do," she began.

"I guess so." He lowered himself onto her love seat. The antique legs creaked in protest.

"I've thought about you a lot," she said, watching his reaction.

"Me too," he said, his expression unreadable. "I read that Caleb Newman got twenty-five years. Made me wonder what you thought."

Hannah heaved a deep sigh. "I think he'd be better off in a psychological ward," she answered. "There's something totally creepy about thinking you have the right to control other people's destinies." She shook her head. "I still can't believe he killed my parents."

Luther sent her a compassionate grimace.

"So, how've you been?" she asked, hungering for news. "How's everyone—Westy and Jaguar?"

"Westy's in Malaysia," he replied, skipping over himself. "He's been gone since late October. I haven't heard a word from him. Jaguar's back on active duty. He's the new XO, now. Oh, and Master Chief got married right after his retirement. He's going crazy building an addition on his house because he and Leila are having twins. They're due in May."

"Twins!" she marveled.

"Sebastian has ultrasound pictures. All you can see are two little blobs."

A vaguely envious feeling touched her heart. "Master Chief must be happy."

"He's ecstatic."

"What about you?" Hannah prompted.

"Same old thing," he said shortly. "Lots of missions. Short. Cold. Brutal."

His terseness kept her quiet. She sensed there was more he wanted to say. But then he started to stand. "I guess I should be going."

"No!" She slid to the edge of her chair, prepared to tackle him, if need be. "Please, don't go yet."

He sat back down with a sigh. "I've tried to forget you," he blurted, "like you wanted me to." The muscles in his jaw jumped.

"I never wanted you to forget me," she protested, her throat suddenly tight.

"You know what I mean. Let you live your life. Not bother you."

"Oh, Luther, you could never bother me." That he could even think so brought tears to her eyes. She reached for a box of tissues and snatched one out. "Sorry," she apologized. "I've been doing this a lot lately. It's supposedly good for me."

Luther's look of astonishment was almost comical. "Maybe I should go. I don't want to upset you."

"No, please." She waved him down. "I know I've surprised you by changing my plans but, believe me, no one's more surprised than I am."

He stood up. Now she'd done it. He was leaving.

But he wasn't. "Come here," he said, holding his hands out to her.

She placed her hands in his, loving the tender strength in them as he pulled her to her feet. And then, to her very great relief, he wrapped his big, beautiful arms around her.

In the warm, safe haven of Luther's embrace, Hannah sighed. God, if she could stay right here for the rest of her life, she'd be a happy woman. Why hadn't she realized that before?

Fortunately he seemed in no hurry to let go. "This always seemed to help," he said. He smelled of sportsman's soap and ironing starch, a dearly familiar combination.

"I've missed you," she confessed, her tears dampening his shirt pocket.

Under her ear, his heart seemed to beat faster. "I've missed you too," he said roughly. "I've been pretty freaking miserable, actually," he added, "putting myself in danger over and over again. It finally occurred to me that I don't like my life without you in it."

She pulled back to regard his stormy eyes. "You shouldn't have let me go," she chastised him.

"What?" He frowned in protest. "You told me to let you go. You said I shouldn't postpone my life for you."

"That's what I thought," she admitted. "Is it too late to change my mind?"

He drew a breath. "Do you want to?"

She queried her heart one final time, hearing only certainty. Everything was different now, as if one domino had fallen, tipping over the next and the next, reordering her priorities. "I want to," she replied.

Hope illumined the depths of his deep, blue eyes. "Are you serious?"

"Yes. I want the whole package: a job with the FBI, you as my husband and a gaggle of kids, three of them at least."

She gave a shriek as Luther snatched her off her feet and planted a fervent kiss on her lips. Within seconds the kiss heated them both to a point of no return.

"Yes," said Luther, putting her back on her feet.

"Yes what?"

"You asked if I would marry you," he pointed out.

"I did?"

"I'm part of the package, right?"

She grinned with understanding. "You're the best part."

"So where's the ring?" he teased.

"Uh, I didn't get one yet."

"Better hurry. I'm out of patience."

"Who needs a ring?" she tossed back, pulling his head down for a deep, distracting kiss.

"We'd better go upstairs," Luther rasped several breathless moments later.

Hannah turned to lead the way. She wasn't sure who tripped whom, but Luther broke their fall. Pinning her to the steps, he kissed her with the same single-minded intensity that she remembered. Suddenly the bedroom seemed much too far away.

With frantic fingers they sought skin until both of them were more naked than dressed.

"Don't stop!" Hannah panted, threading her fingers through the soft strands of Luther's hair as he kissed the length of her body.

He chuckled at her command. "Let's go upstairs," he suggested again.

Hannah gazed up at the ceiling, eyes glazed, face flushed. "Okay," she agreed. Rolling over, she started to crawl up the steps on her knees.

She didn't get far. "Oh, Luther," she groaned as he pulled her back against him. "We'll never make it to the bedroom."

"You'll never forget the day you asked me to marry you either," he pointed out.

As if she ever would. It was the best day of her life. She would savor every second of it down to the rasp of his stubbled jaw as he nuzzled her neck.

Westy was right, she realized. Some things in life couldn't be planned. They were gifts to be accepted with grace and gratitude. She and Luther had both needed to learn that lesson.

More
Marliss Melton!

Please turn this page
for a preview of

TIME TO RUN

available in

February 2006

~

Sarah Garret stopped just short of pushing through the doors into the bright September sunshine. *Damn him!* She hit the glass with the heel of her hand, then looked at it in dismay, putting it quickly behind her back.

I'm acting like him now.

The thought filled her with disgust. God forbid she would ever strike her nine-year-old son in anger. What was Garret turning her into?

She took a steadying breath and slowly exhaled. It would all be over soon, she promised herself. She'd dotted nearly all the i's and crossed all the t's. God, but it had taken years to plot an escape route that couldn't be guessed or followed, and she still had doubts about the bus.

But unless she found another means of getting them to Texas, she'd have to take her chances with public transportation. Garret wouldn't know which direction she'd taken, she comforted herself. He didn't know a thing about her birth mother.

"Are you leaving already?"

The question was asked practically in her ear. With a stifled scream, Sarah whirled, one arm raised in a purely defensive gesture.

It was the Navy SEAL who'd spoken to her earlier. Putting her hand down, she struggled to recover.

"I'm sorry," they both said at the same time.

He actually reached out and steadied her. The hands on either of her shoulders were big and warm and had an immediate calming effect on her racing heart.

"I didn't hear you," she explained.

"My fault." With a squeeze, he released her, dropping his hands to his sides.

Just like the last two times she'd talked to him, she felt herself drawn to his intense blue eyes. There was something so kind about them, even in a face that was craggy from spending too much time in inclement weather. He was a SEAL, she knew, from the fact that he'd supported his fellow SEALs in that trial last year, only he didn't look like a SEAL. His hair was longer than hers. He had a full goatee, and—goodness—there were holes in his ears for earrings, more than one.

Nonetheless, a Trident pin, the SEAL insignia, was clipped above his left breast pocket. He boasted a daunting number of ribbons, far more than Garret had. The service stripes on his left arm indicated he was an enlisted man—not an officer like her husband.

According to unspoken Navy protocol, she wasn't even supposed to talk to this man—forget that Garret would blister her hide if he ever found out. But something in those blue, blue eyes made her trust him.

"Are you leaving?" he asked.

"No, I . . ." *I'm a prisoner.* "My husband can't get away. His work is keeping him busy."

"Ah," he said with an understanding grimace. "So you'll miss your class."

Dismay tugged at her as she thought of what the Arwanis would think.

"I can give you a ride," he offered unexpectedly. "I'm headed to Norfolk myself, right now."

She glanced up in surprise. He wasn't as tall as Garret—maybe six feet even, but his shoulders were twice as wide given the muscularity of his torso. His blatant masculinity struck her with sudden force. He wasn't . . . he couldn't be picking her up!

Of course not. What was she thinking? She wasn't even remotely pretty. Besides, SEALs were governed by a strict code of ethics, or so she'd heard. "Oh"—she waved a dismissive hand—"no, thank you. That's very nice of you, but . . ." *Garret would kill me.*

She could have sworn that she hadn't said those words out loud, but then the SEAL said, "Leave him a note on the bench saying you've found a ride."

She opened her mouth to decline his offer when a stubborn flame leaped up inside her. Why shouldn't she say yes, even if he was picking her up, which he wasn't. He was just being nice, something Garret had never been and couldn't begin to fathom.

"You know," she said, thinking out loud, "I think I will." She opened her big purse, looking for her pencil.

Before she could find it, the SEAL had produced a pen and a little notepad and was holding them out to her.

"Thank you," she said. Accepting both objects, she walked away.

It took all the courage she could muster to scribble a short explanatory note. Her fingers trembled so badly, it was scarcely legible. She left it on the bench where Garret would find it, then hurried to the exit, battling the urge to run.

Her heart beat fast and heavy. *Think of it as practice,*

she told herself. Pretty soon she'd be leaving forever, and then she'd find out just how gutsy she really was.

The prospect filled her with terror.

The sight of the SEAL waiting by the front doors calmed her nerves. She ought to be leery of hitching a ride with a perfect stranger, especially one with holes in his ears. But as she approached him, he cast her a warm smile and stretched out a hand. "I'm Chase, by the way," he said. "Chase McCaffrey."

His hand was rough with calluses but warm and sure. She knew the strangest urge to hold on to it and never let go. "I'm Sarah." Her voice sounded different, huskier. She was attracted to him, she realized, tugging her hand free. The truth surprised her. He wasn't her type at all.

He tipped his head toward the door. "Shall we?"

He held the door for her. It was a sunny afternoon—hot, actually, for late September. Sarah took a deep breath and savored the humid air, the scent of sun-warmed grass, hot pavement, and the aroma of charbroiled burgers from the Burger King on base. It smelled like freedom.

Only a dozen or so cars dotted the parking lot. They passed a number that she thought might be his. But then he stopped before an enormous motorcycle—all chrome rims and black leather—and she went suddenly light-headed. Good Lord, wasn't this a Harley-Davidson?

The SEAL handed her a helmet while at the same time giving her an apologetic look. "I hope you don't mind. I need a part for my car, which is why I'm headed to Norfolk."

Mind? This was crazy, insane. If Garret caught word of it, she was going to pay dearly for her recklessness. She stood there, paralyzed, clutching the helmet and staring at the motorcycle.

He waited patiently for her to make her decision. "I'll go slow," he cajoled, his eyes crinkling at the corners as if her shock amused him.

Okay. She was going to do this. She needed to build her confidence before the big day. With a rebel smile, she jammed on the helmet and found that it fit her perfectly— it was made for a woman.

So, her SEAL had a habit of picking up damsels in distress. She didn't know whether to be offended or flattered.

He mounted first, holding the bike upright between his long, muscular legs. Then he patted the space behind him, and she looped her purse strap over her head. Hiking up her dress in a manner that would have sent her mother into a dead faint, she mounted on board behind him.

"Scoot closer," he instructed. His voice was the sexiest thing she'd heard since James Dean. "And wrap your arms around me tight." He depressed an ignition button, and the bike throbbed to life beneath her. Backing up, he readied them for departure, and with a twist of his wrist, they were off.

As promised, he didn't go fast, but she squeezed her thighs around him, terrified she might fall off. After a few tense minutes, she relaxed. They were scarcely moving faster than the twenty-mile-an-hour speed limit. The wind billowed up her dress. Someone with sharp vision might catch a glimpse of her white cotton panties.

Amazingly, she didn't care. The breeze offered relief from the hot sun. As they broke away from the huddle of buildings and into the open, with green grass on either side of them, he picked up speed. No longer afraid, Sarah yielded to the sensation of flying through the air with nothing to cling to but the hard body of the man before her.

She wasn't sure what was more exhilarating: the wind's caress or the breadth of Chase's torso in the circle of her arms. Her breasts were flattened against his back. She wondered if he could feel her nipples, tight with excitement, pressed against him. She hadn't done anything remotely this exciting in a decade! He felt hot to the touch, yet she couldn't feel a trace of sweat under the linen uniform.

He swept them out of the gate and onto a double-lane highway, where he went faster still. Her exhilaration mounted. She'd delivered herself to temptation, and she was going to enjoy every minute of it, while she could.

A short while later, Chase veered off onto a narrow side street, one that was shaded with oak trees. This was not the way to Norfolk, she realized with an uneasy start. He took a wide turn and zipped into the driveway of a small white house. His feet came down on either side of the bike, and he cut the engine abruptly.

Sarah's heart skipped with trepidation. What had she gotten herself into?

"I need to change out of my uniform," he explained, taking off his helmet. "I hope you don't mind. It'll take just a second."

"Oh." The explanation made sense, but all the same, she needed to be cautious. What if he weren't such a nice man after all? What if he'd led her to his house in order to strip her clothes off and ravish her?

The thought sent a gush of liquid heat through her. She

was shocked by the telltale symptom of desire. Heavens, she was married. What was she doing entertaining such a feeling?

"Hop off," he invited easily. It was then that she detected a western drawl.

She did, aware that her knees felt like Jell-O. She struggled to get the helmet off her head, but her fingers wouldn't cooperate.

Chase reached out and released the catch.

"Thanks," she murmured, her voice ridiculously thin.

He just smiled. "Come meet Jesse."

She could hear a dog barking at the door. The moment Chase unlocked it, a huge black Lab came bounding out. Sarah tensed, having little experience with dogs.

"Jesse, sit," Chase commanded, and the dog immediately went down on his haunches, his tail swishing back and forth like a windshield wiper.

Reassured by the dog's obedience, Sarah stepped forward and stroked his broad head. The Lab regarded her with shiny brown eyes. In fact, he seemed to be grinning. Her fear evaporated. "Nice dog," she said, impressed.

"You don't have a dog," Chase guessed.

"No, I've always wanted one but . . ." She shrugged. But Garret couldn't abide animals, so that was that.

"You can wait out here if you'd like, or you can come in," Chase said. "It's cooler inside."

His civil offer put her imagination to shame. He wasn't even thinking about sex, she realized with chagrin. Curious to see how he lived, she said, "I'll come in."

He cast her a look of approval. "Great."

The little house boasted two stories, a front porch, and a huge, fenced yard in the rear for the dog. Trailing Chase into the cool interior, she found herself looking at a comfortable couch. Rustic furniture, so at odds with the Chippendale that Garret preferred, filled the diminutive living room. The colors were burgundy, green, and beige. She let her gaze drift over the walls and realized that either a woman had hung the pictures or Chase the SEAL had a flair for decorating.

A wildlife motif was reflected in the pictures of buffalo and deer, in the bearskin rug by the fireplace, and a wood sculpture on the country coffee table. It looked like something out of *Country Living*.

"Make yourself at home," Chase said, already working on the buttons of his dress uniform. Beneath his quick fingers, the shirt seemed to fly open. He wore a sleeveless white T-shirt underneath.

"Would you like something to drink?" he added, tugging the shirttails out of his slacks.

"No, thank you." Her eyes were shamelessly glued to him.

"You sure? Not even water?" As he shrugged out of his dress uniform, she saw with a wave of dizziness that he boasted a huge tattoo on his left arm. While his dress shirt had hidden it, the sleeveless T-shirt seemed to highlight the black-ink drawing of . . . she peered closer and made out four skulls rising from their graves. *Yikes.*

On an arm corded with muscle, the tattoo struck her as a savage work of art.

"Water would be great," she said, finding herself suddenly parched.

He disappeared toward the rear of the house. "You might be more comfortable in here," he called.

She trailed him into the adjoining room and found him pressing a glass to the ice dispenser on his fridge.

The kitchen had clearly been remodeled. It was a big, bright room with French windows in the eating area overlooking the backyard. Jesse jogged past her and slipped through a doggy door to enjoy the sunshine.

"Here you go." Chase's fingers brushed hers as he passed her the glass. "I'll be right back."

He gave her an intimate look, then turned and disappeared up a staircase tucked into the wall, taking the steps two at a time.

True to his word, he jogged down those stairs mere seconds later, dressed in jeans and a black T-shirt. The vision of him in casual attire was every bit as unsettling as the uniform. And she'd been right about the pierced ears. He wore two small silver hoops in his left ear and one in his right. He looked like a very, very bad boy.

Her mother had warned her about such men.

She was out of her mind to be with him.

"All set?" he asked.

She took a quick sip of her drink and put it down. "Yes." The sooner he delivered her to the Refugee Center, the less she'd have to worry that Garret would find out about this crazy little detour.

As Chase leaned over to leave a scoop of food in Jesse's bowl, Sarah found herself staring at his butt. She'd never ogled a man's backside in her life. Oh, but this one was too nice to overlook.

"Let's do it," he said, pulling his keys out of his pocket. He made a quick but thorough inventory of her figure, then looked straight into her eyes. The breath froze in

Sarah's lungs. This was it: *he was going to make the suggestion that they go upstairs.*

But then he was striding toward the front door. It shocked her to the core that she was disappointed.

Once outside, they redonned their helmets. Chase assumed dominion over the metal monster and waited for her to mount behind.

They shot off again, the wind cooling Sarah's overheated imagination. The ride from Virginia Beach to Norfolk would take a good twenty minutes. She committed herself to enjoying every second of it. She had a feeling she would regret it later. Despite her note to Garret explaining, very vaguely, that she'd been offered a lift to Norfolk, he had a gift for turning up the truth. And he wasn't going to like what he learned.

As they drove west, Chase kept their speed moderate, passing only a few cars that poked along. Sarah closed her eyes. Traveling on the highway was not as fun as zipping along less crowded roads. But with her eyes closed and her cheek pressed to Chase's broad back she could forget the danger and enjoy the moment.

His ponytail tickled her nose. She slitted her lids to study the color of his hair. The curls at his nape were shorter and darker than the burnished ponytail caught up with elastic. Any girl would envy such a thick head of mahogany hair. She did.

And he smelled good. She put her nose to the cotton weave of his T-shirt and inhaled a pleasant bouquet of laundry detergent and a cedarlike scent that made her think of the wood sculpture in his living room.

If only she could stop the march of time, then she would freeze this very moment, holding off the consequences forever. Odd that she would feel so giddy on the back of a Harley-Davidson going sixty miles an hour.

She ought to have done this when she was younger. Why hadn't she taken more risks, been a little reckless, *lived* a little before consigning her life to someone else?

She knew why, of course. She'd wanted to be the perfect daughter to her elderly parents. And to that end, she'd succeeded. Her marriage to Garret ten years ago had been a coup de grâce in her parents' eyes. They'd moved to a retirement community in Florida, content with their labors. Their daughter had married a lawyer. Their work was done.

A familiar bitterness encroached on Sarah's happiness, and she pushed it away, pretending that Garret didn't exist, that she was twenty-three again and she was free to do as she pleased.

Oh, the choices she would make!

The first of which would be to live for herself. Not for her parents. Not for anyone.

Holding Chase this close, she became aware of the heat between them. Under the cotton of his T-shirt, his muscles felt firm and dense. There wasn't an inch of extra fat on the waist her arms encircled.

Her thoughts strayed lower. She wondered if the hair at his groin would be dark brown or auburn like his beard. Gracious, she'd never even thought such things before! Yet, once imagined, she couldn't get the image of a naked Chase out of her head.

She wondered if he really looked like that!

Feeling her cheeks heat, she was grateful he couldn't see her expression. After all, he seemed to have no problems reading her mind.

Too soon, they entered the city limits of Norfolk, swooping off the ramp to merge into the busy traffic. Chase seemed to know exactly where the Refugee Center was located, heading down all the right roads, taking the shortest route to the waterfront building. He pulled up in front of the metal structure and turned the motorcycle off.

For a moment, he just sat there. She wondered if he was as disappointed as she was that their interlude was over. Reluctantly, she put one foot down and struggled off. She readjusted her dress, then worked at the helmet strap. Giving up, she stepped closer so Chase could help take it off.

As he freed the clasp, he stared straight into her eyes.

"Thank you for the ride," she said, feeling self-conscious but not uncomfortable. His gaze was so *direct*. She wondered what he was thinking. Had his kindness meant anything at all or was it just a decent gesture to a dull married woman?

He had no idea she would remember this ride forever, would replay it a hundred times in her head, creating different scenarios, wondering what if . . .

"Sarah," he said, cutting into her thoughts.

The dead seriousness of his tone made her eyes widen.

"What will Garret do if he finds out?"

It was a question she hadn't wanted to ask herself. Her stomach tightened unpleasantly. She forced a smile and shrugged, wanting to give the impression that Garret wouldn't mind. "He'll be fine with it," she lied, not that she planned to tell him any details.

"I don't think so," Chase countered. "Memorize my number." He told it to her twice, then made her repeat it. "I want you to call if you need anything."

Was he serious? His vivid blue gaze hadn't wavered.

"Sure," she said, trying to guess just what it was he wanted from her. His gaze was so astute. It was almost as if he'd guessed what her life was like. But how could he have? And why would he want to help?

"Call me this weekend," he repeated.

She nodded as if to say yes, but she knew she wouldn't. No matter how much she wanted to confide in him, she wouldn't let herself be led by pipe dreams. Men weren't creatures you could trust. She'd determined long ago to stand on her own two feet, to trust no one ever again. She didn't need a hero to save her. She was going to save herself and Kendal, too.

"Do you need a ride home from here?" he asked, severing eye contact to sweep the area.

"No, thank you. I'll take the bus. It goes right to my neighborhood."

"The city bus?" He turned an incredulous frown on her.

"Um . . . yes. I take it all the time."

He seemed stunned and angry at the same time, muttering something under his breath. "Be careful," he said, no doubt making reference to the unsavory characters who shared her mode of transportation.

When he looked at her again, there were emotions in his eyes she didn't understand. He stretched out a hand, and she blinked in surprise as he smoothed his thumb across her cheek. With his other hand, he gunned the motor, and then he was off, ponytail streaming in the wind, wide shoulders disappearing down the busy street.

Disoriented, Sarah stared after him. In the first few years of her matrimonial hell, she'd dreamed that a stranger would come along and whisk her from her private nightmare. That dream had long since withered and died. Yet there was something about this Navy SEAL that resurrected it. He didn't own a white steed, but the Harley came pretty close.

She shook her head at her imagination. A tattooed, pierced bad boy was the last distraction she needed in her life right now. She wasn't about to call him. In fact, the best thing she could do was to forget about Chase McCaffrey.

No matter how good his backside looked in a pair of Levi's.

About the Author

Daughter of a U.S. foreign officer, Marliss Melton enjoyed a unique childhood growing up overseas. As one of five children, she was encouraged to think creatively and wrote her first book at age thirteen. Following college, Marliss pursued her dream of publishing while teaching high school English and Spanish. A Golden Heart and RITA finalist, she writes both medieval romance and romantic suspense. Her husband, a warfare technology specialist, is her real-life hero. She juggles two teenage boys, three step-children, a baby girl, and an adjunct teaching position at the college of William and Mary.

THE EDITOR'S DIARY

Dear Reader,

When desire flares up, who can help but succumb? Whether it's a sexy ex or a roguish stranger, life is full of delicious surprises in our two Warner Forever titles this June.

Who would ever have thought that a smelly, featherless and flightless parrot could be so valuable? Dana Wiley in Lani Diane Rich's MAYBE BABY certainly never did. But when her mother is held by kidnappers who are demanding it for ransom, Dana has to get her hands on that bird. The only problem: Nick Maybe, the man she left at the altar six years ago, is the only person who knows where the parrot is. With kissable lips and unforgettable eyes, Nick hasn't changed a bit. And Dana can't deny he's stirring up that old black magic. But as the bird is worth a cool quarter million, they aren't the only ones on the hunt. With two thieves on their tail, Dana can't help but think: could Nick be her hero...again? *New York Times* bestselling author Jennifer Crusie calls Ms. Rich "a great voice," so grab a copy and find out why.

New York Times bestselling author Lisa Jackson raves that Marliss Melton's first book is "filled with romance, suspense and characters that will pull you in and never let you go." Well, hold on tight because her latest book, IN THE DARK, is even better. DIA Agent Hannah Geary was wrongfully thrown in a Cuban prison and left for dead. Now she wants revenge. Not just for herself, but for her partner who was killed too. All of the evidence points to a rogue SEAL commander. But to catch a bad SEAL, she needs a good one. Lt. Luther Lindstrom needs Hannah's help too, but he's used to calling the shots. And the last thing he needs in his life is a sexy, strong willed woman. But as the danger mounts and Hannah and Luther are steps away from one of the FBI's most wanted criminals, Luther's defenses break down as his desire for Hannah grows. But will it be too late for them both?

To find out more about Warner Forever, these titles and the authors, visit us at www.warnerforever.com.

With warmest wishes,

Karen Kosztolnyik

Karen Kosztolnyik, Senior Editor

P.S. Get ready for a cold shower-next month's titles couldn't be hotter! Sue-Ellen Welfonder weaves the sensual tale of a betrothed knight who's tempted by a stunning and mysterious stranger who cannot remember her identity in ONLY FOR A KNIGHT; and Toni Blake delivers IN YOUR WILDEST DREAM, the irresistibly erotic story of a woman who must infiltrate the world of high-priced escorts to find her sister-and the sexy bartender who helped her.

*Want to know more about romances at
Warner Books and Warner Forever?
Get the scoop online!*

WARNER'S ROMANCE HOMEPAGE

Visit us at www.warnerforever.com for all the
latest news, reviews, and chapter excerpts!

NEW AND UPCOMING TITLES

Each month we feature our new titles
and reader favorites.

CONTESTS AND GIVEAWAYS

We give away galleys, autographed copies,
and all kinds of fun stuff.

AUTHOR INFO

You'll find bios, articles, and links to personal
Web sites for all your favorite authors—and
so much more!

THE BUZZ

Sign up for our monthly romance newsletter,
and be the first to read all about it!